"HUNGRY, ZEUS?"

"Not for food," the half-breed god replied. "Instead of eating a deer, I shall become a bull." As Fitz mind-watched, the blond young man was slowly transformed into a wild ox, one of a giant breed that in some distant future humans would call aurochs. The young bull set out across the rolling plain, leaving his sister to her bloody feast.

. . . The man-bull sensed a flicker of motion and lifted his dripping muzzle from the stream, but before he could bellow his awful challenge he caught full sight of the creature on the rock above him, a stunningly beautiful human female. So much did the lissome form arouse the man within the bull that the hybrid mind let slip its control.

As for the girl, the cold trembling fear of the aurochs was swiftly lost in an all-consuming awe that left her unable to move as she witnessed the god's transformation from beast to tall and fair young man. It was not in Zeus's nature to resist such a temptation . . .

ROBERT ADAMS

MONSTERS AND MAGICIANS

STAIRWAY TO FOREVER

BOOK II

MONSTERS AND MAGICIANS

Copyright © 1989 by Robert Adams

A Baen Books Original

Baen Publishing Enterprises
260 Fifth Avenue
New York, N.Y. 10001

First printing, January 1989

ISBN: 0-671-69797-8

Cover art by K. W. Kelly

Printed in the United States of America

Distributed by
SIMON & SCHUSTER
1230 Avenue of the Americas
New York, N.Y. 10020

PROLOGUE

Yancey Mathews missed going back to the county farm to finish his sentence in enforced and unremittingly hard labor by the width of a cat's whisker . . . or so everyone readily informed him. This even after he had told the pure truth—leaving out only the part about having tried to shoot his neighbor, Mr. Fitzgilbert, and being so drunk that he had managed to miss with both barrels at a range of less than twenty yards.

But he *had* told the unvarnished truth; told just what had happened, as he recalled it. How he, minding his very own business while standing in the back yard of Mr. Fitzgilbert's next-door neighbor, Old Man Collingwood, had seen Fitzgilbert come out of his back door, suddenly leap completely over the twelve-foot chain link fence and the barbed-wire strands that topped it, lay hold to poor Yancey, and fling him up onto a tree limb a score of feet above the ground, whereupon he had lost consciousness.

Yancey had not come to until after sunup, brought back to a conscious state by the repeated shouts and threats and baseless insults of Collingwood, standing on the ground below. Stung to the quick by the old man's slanders of his two darling sons, Yancey had tried to quit the limb, only to lose his balance and find himself hanging beneath it by his belt, which somehow had been lapped around both his own skinny waist and the oak limb. It had taken a brace of sheriff's deputies and a stepladder to at last get him down.

He had told them all the true story, right from the beginning. The arresting deputies had laughed at him, then thrown him into the tank with the rest of the preceding night's collection of drunks. Upon arrival, Sheriff Vaughan had heard him out, then shaken his head and said, with a wolfish smile, "Yancey, I think you done vi'lated your parole, las' night. Didn' I warn you 'bout thet? 'Bout behavin' yourse'f and all, boy? Well, you'll be back on the farm lickety-split, this time. You oughta get there jest about in time for the plowin' and plantin', too."

Turning to his accompanying deputies and the turnkey, he had ordered, "Take Yancey out'n here and put him upstairs, heah. One you read him his rights and let him make any phone calls he wants to, too. Judge Hanratty, he's due in . . . lessee, Monday of nex' week; Yancey should oughta be over the shakes by then.

"I'll let Missus Pugh know 'bout this so she can go out and put Welfare back on pore Char'ty Mathews and them two hellions Yancey got on her. I'll call Mike Mills over to the Courthouse, too, and see 'bout gettin' another free lawyer, a P.D. for Yancey, you know damn well he could pay one no way . . . 'cept in empty beer cans."

The young lawyer the county finally turned up for him had heard him out, too, then just sat across the table from him for long minutes, staring at him and rolling a yellow pencil between the slender fingers of his butter-soft, hairless hands. At length the sallow-skinned lawyer had nodded his head of modishly-long black hair once, leafed through the papers contained in a manila file folder until he found what he sought, pulled out that sheet and used the yellow pencil to underline some things on it.

Returning his brown eyes to stare at Yancey, where he had sat cold sober, shaky, haggard and clad in ill-fitting jail clothing, he had asked, "How much had you had to drink that night, Mr. Mathews?"

As Yancey had begun to shake his head, the young man—almost a boy, Yancey thought—had warned in a cold voice that had snapped like a bullwhip, "And don't try to lie to me. If you do, I'll know and you can then just find yourself another attorney . . . if you can. You're not exactly any good attorney's dream of a client, you know.

"Now, how much did you have to drink that night? How many beers?"

"I . . . I don't remember all that good, Mistuh Klein," Yancey had half-whined, avoiding that icy, penetrating gaze as best he might. But that fearsome gaze had finally trapped his bloodshot eyes and he had felt compelled by cruel circumstance to add,

3

"Not much. Mebbe four . . . five . . ." The lawyer had said not a word, but his thin lips had become thinner and those terrible brown eyes had bored like a cold-steel star drill powered by a twelve-pound sledgehammer, and so Yancey was constrained to add, "Six-packs. Four, mebbe five six-packs . . . but they was all pony-cans, Mistuh Klein, little 'uns, all of 'em."

"*Holy shit!*" exclaimed David Klein, most feelingly, "Even if those *were* all pony-cans—which I do not believe for one minute, but never mind that, for now—that would be over a gallon and a half of beer. After drinking that much, a man as skinny and fleshless as you are, I don't see why you weren't comatose. I can't imagine how you were able to stagger a block or so over level ground, much less climb up into an oak tree, before you passed out."

Yancey had snuffled, then, whining dolefully, "You don' b'lieve me neethuh. An' I swear awn the Holy Bible, Mistuh Klein, suh, I done tole you the whole, gospul truth, 'bout whatall happuned thet night. Thet Fitzgilbert bastid, he flang me up in thet tree. I dint climb up, I couldn' of, I allus been pow'ful afeered of heights, is why. Jest you ast, ast enybodys' done done construcshun work with me. I'm scairt of high places."

By the time Yancey had finished he was sobbing, and tears were trickling down through his three days' worth of stubble.

To Sheriff Vaughan, David Klein had said, "My client swears to the truth of his story about this Fitzgilbert having thrown him up into that tree, after jumping over the fence and attacking him without any provocation whatsoever. Has anyone yet talked to Mr. Fitzgilbert about it?"

After pouring himself another mug of coffee from his office silex, the sheriff sat back down, sipped, then set aside the mug and sighed. "Mr. Klein, no, suh, nobody's talked to Mistuh Fitzgilbert, 'cause nobody can, not 'round here. Mistuh Fitzgilbert ain't even in the country, ain't been for weeks. He travels around a lot and, last I heered, he's in Africa, huntin' elephants or suthin."

"Well, then," probed Klein, doggedly, "could someone who might have resembled Fitzgilbert to my client in his somewhat intoxicated condition have jumped over that fence and . . ."

Vaughan had shaken his greying head vehemently. "Cous'luh, couldn't *nobody* of jest jumped ovuh thet fence, I tell you! Thet fence is a almost-new, twelve-foot cyclone fence with three strands of bob-wire at the top. It can be climbed—Yancey, he's climbed it afore and so has his two sons—and that's all . . . lest you can fly.

"B'sides of the fact thet Mistuh Fitzgilbert, he's 'bout your height, though with a bit of a heftier build, but no ways strong enough for to th'ow a ridge-runnuh size of Yancey twenty foot up into no tree, nor carry him up, neethuh.

"You are gonna represent Yancey, then?"

It was David Klein's turn to sigh. Nodding slowly, he said, "Yes, I told the poor man I would . . . and I will, for all that you've just blown the defenses I was putting together out of the water. You must like him, despite everything, to . . ."

Slamming a horny palm onto his desktop with such

5

force as to set all on it into motion, Vaughan burst out, "*Like him?* Mistuh Klein, I purely hate Yancey Mathews's pickled guts! He's made life a pure, unholy hell for that pore little gal he conned into marryin' up with him and he's set his boys such a bad example and let 'em both run so lawless and hog-wild for so damn long of their lives I don't think enything's goin' to ever straighten the two of 'em out, lest it's a bullet or a load of buckshot.

"Cold sober—which he ain't often, ain't never if he can help it—Yancey is mean as a snake, connivin', thievin' and I don' know whatall; drunk, he's a murder just awaitin' a time and place to happen at. I think . . . I *knows*, the bestest place, the onliest place cut out to his measure for him to be, to spend the rest his natcherl life at, is on the county farm, where he knows if he lets eny his white-trash meanness come out, he'll purely get the shit kicked out of him and thet damned quick-like, too.

"The reason I made sure Mistuh Mills sent for you is I don't want nobody to never be able to say or make it look like I got even a no-good hillbilly scumbag like of a Yancey Mathews to get railroaded by this county jest 'cause of he was a troublemaker and dint nobody like him. Heah?"

As it happened, on the very evening of the day Yancey first met Attorney David Klein, Public Defender, Circuit Judge Harold Hanratty put his big, seal-brown thoroughbred at one fence too many and wound up in surgery for his trouble. It was more than a month before an adequate substitute judge could make his way to that county and Klein made good use of the time, having Yancey thoroughly examined, physically, mentally and emotionally, by competent specialists.

All of these specialists were located in the city and, although Sheriff Vaughan hated the expenses of deputy-drivers and transport for the handcuffed, shackled prisoner, he gritted his teeth and bore it as best he could, solacing himself with pleasant reveries of rawboned Yancey Mathews, working his skinny butt off on the county farm, with nothing to drink except water, coffee, tea and orange juice for the next several years . . . at the least. Hopefully, poor little Charity Mathews would use the absence of her spouse and his knobby knuckles to recognize the error of staying his wife, divorce the miscreant and find herself a good, decent, sober, law-abiding, God-fearing man with a good job, like she deserved.

But the sheriff's daydreams were not to be, this time.

CHAPTER I

Once down from the last of the sand dunes and onto what he had come to call the Pony Plain, the man on the motorcycle gave the machine gas, moving as fast as he dared over the expanse of sandy soil grown with tough species of grass, weedy shrubs and stunted trees and running with herds of big-headed ponies and many another beast, some of them of exceedingly strange appearance.

Had it not been for the fact that the plain was not really level, cut here and there at odd intervals with deep gullies, he would have squeezed even more speed from his bike's powerful engine, for he had no slightest wish to encounter another of the fearsome monsters called Teeth-and-Legs, as he had on his last trip across in this direction. Yes, he had finally managed to kill the hairy thing before its huge, black-clawed, manlike hands and its fearsome array of orangish fangs had gotten close enough to rend his flesh, but it had proven itself more than fast enough to pace his bike across the broken terrain and had absorbed far and away too many of the .44-magnum slugs spat out by Fitz's carbine to suit the man.

He still bore the carbine and his revolver, but he also now carried an old but well-kept Holland and Holland double rifle, an elephant gun—its gaping bores bigger than more modern shotguns' bores and its two chambers containing custom-made cartridges that looked of a size more likely to be made for an automatic cannon than a hunting piece. Despite the best recoil pad that the gunsmith had been able to obtain and carefully fit to the butt of the rare, very expensive gun, despite its world-heavy but recoil-absorbing weight, Fitz had experienced from it an unremittingly brutal kick. However, the things that the thumb-thick lead-alloy slugs would do to even the weather-hardened wood of the ancient, partially wrecked dromon in the dunes back near the beach gave him a sense of near confidence in the rifle's ability to put down even a Teeth-and-Legs with one . . . or, at most, two shots.

Still, he had no slightest desire to have to test the capabilities of the massive weapon. If he could cross the plain to the wooded hills without encountering a Teeth-and-Legs, he would be pleased. With a hill or two between him and the plain, he knew that he could unload and case the double-barreled rifle; for some reason the monsters never came into the hills.

Recalling how the thing he had had to kill the last time had tried to ambush him, he paused on each available elevation to scan the terrain ahead, behind, and on either flank with his binoculars, and he travelled well clear of the thicker clumps of vegetation and the verges of the gullies, where possible.

In the times before he had become aware of the existence of the terrible Teeth-and-Legs, he had spent much time—both by day and by night—on the Pony Plain. He had ridden the bike, walked, and camped out on it, observing the singular varieties of wildlife, some very similar to the beasts he had either seen in the flesh or at least in pictures in the world in which he had grown to his present fifty-five years of age. But there were others which he had never seen or even imagined.

"This Teeth-and-Legs, now," he thought to himself, "not even my set of the *Encyclopedia Britannica* describes anything remotely resembling the things. The closest beast I can think of would be a baboon of some kind, but monstrously distorted and vastly oversized. The one I shot had a head as big as a fullgrown lion's, a body almost as big as a gorilla's, legs longer and thicker than mine ending in feet more like human feet—adapted to running, obviously, not to climbing—and arms that hung past its knees with hands like hams; it had a long muzzle like a huge dog or a bear and a full complement of orangish-whitish teeth with fangs that a Bengal tiger wouldn't have been ashamed to show. Oh, and a shortish tail, too, as I recall.

"God, but that thing was fast; it could have run down any antelope, no sweat, or outraced even a cheetah. From the look of the body it must have been as strong as the proverbial ox, too. Looking back, though, I should've realized that something out of the ordinary was going on that day when I set out and saw so very little of any of the other animals on my route across. They keep as much distance as possible between them and the Teeth-and-Legs, wisely.

"The ponies are odd in many ways, too. I don't know all that much about the various kinds of equines, but I'm still not sure that these are ponies at all. Yes, they're pony-height, big-headed for their size, thicker-legged than most horses, but their necks don't have real manes, just short bristles like a zebra or Pre . . . Prz . . . that weird-named wild horse some Russians found in Asia years ago after everyone thought it was extinct. Their coloring is way different, too—solid red-roan, most of them, with chocolate-brown neck bristles, tails and a broad stripe of it down the length of their spines. Some few of them look to have very faint stripes running around their lower legs, too.

"Danna says that she recalls reading somewhere, some time, an account by some naturalist or other of a small number of horses or ponies some place on one of the larger Caribbean islands that she thinks she recalls were colored like these . . . but she admits that she read it only once and long ago and can't be sure.

"But both of us are stumped as to just what these things I call rat-tailed ostriches could be. They're most about the size of an ostrich, they live and feed and move about in herds or flocks or whatever you call them like ostriches, they have legs and feet like an ostrich and they lay humongous eggs like ostriches, their heads and long necks look like ostriches', but there the similarities end. Now comes

12

the weird parts: they don't have any feathers where ostriches have feathers, rather hair—fine, thick, downy hair—and instead of wings, they have a pair of spindly arms and hands or paws or whatever with three long fingers and a shorter one that is semi-opposed, like my thumb, almost. And then there's their tails—a long, tapering, scaly tail—they can move them, but rather stiffly, and seem to use them mostly for balance.

"I've not seen any of the flying lizards close enough to get a good idea of the details of them; I don't even know if the various sizes and colors of them are sexual dimorphism, stages of growth of the same animals or different animals altogether.

"Then there's those weird birds with claws on their wing joints, that like to clamber in the thorn trees and eat the berries and any strange bugs they can catch. They have beaks like birds, but I think they have small teeth, too. But they at least do have feathers, not fur like the ostriches.

"Most of the smaller, furry animals, look fairly much like the small furry beasts anywhere else. But then there's the flying rabbits. The grown ones are about the size of a prairie jack-rabbit, though they look to have much thicker bodies at first glance, when you see them moving about on the ground. It's not until they get spooked and jump that you see that what you thought was a thick body is actually folds of furred skin that stretches from the forelegs to the hind legs and allows them to glide when extended, so that they can cover distances that would be incredible if not flatly impossible for rabbits back where I came from.

"There's also some kind of horned animal that I've

only seen from a distance with the binoculars—and that only once, so there must not be too many of them or they are just rare in this area, one or the other. They're as big as the ponies or bigger, look kind of antelopish and all have a pair of long, curving, pointed horns with raised ridges around the shafts of them. The herd I saw wasn't at all large, smaller than some of the pony herds, in fact; but if there's any prey animal out here that could take on a Teeth-and-Legs with a chance of winning, I'd put my money on those great big antelopes or whatever, with their size *and* their horns.

"Something lives in the bigger lake over to the east that's big enough to take paddling birds the size of a duck; I saw it happen, twice, when I was camped beside that lake once. It may be just a largish fish, like a muskellunge or a pike, but I don't know, I never saw anything but ripples and the birds being pulled underwater. Nonetheless—he chuckled aloud at the memory—I stopped swimming in that particular lake.

"I know damned good and well there're other predators—large and small—around out here. I've found several shed snakeskins and seen feline pawprints of a number of sizes on the muddy banks of the ponds and lakes; but the only snake I have actually seen was in process of being eaten by a small eagle perched atop a big thornbrush. Apparently, the raptors and the Teeth-and-Legs are the only real predators out here that hunt by day—them and the terrestrial lizards, none of which are all that big."

Atop another rise of ground, the man paused as usual and swept his immediate surroundings on all sides carefully with his eyes before using the big binoculars. Some mile ahead, a herd of ponies had converged along the nearer fringes of a reedy pond to drink and graze on the short, tender red-green grasses that grew there and in the hills beyond, but not out on the more arid plain.

Fitz recognized the herd stallion, a big one for his weedy breed—between fourteen and fifteen hands. The equine was missing part of his near-side ear, and the cheek below that eye bore three long furrows of scar tissue, quite dissimilar to his other battle scars. Fitz had often wondered at the origin of the facial scars in times past while roaming the plains among the herds. Now he thought he knew: the big stallion had at some time faced and fought a Teeth-and-Legs and survived the encounter. One tough pony!

Unslinging his two-quart waterbag, Fitz drank to the courageous pony stallion in the bottled mineral water which, its provenance not withstanding, still harbored an unpleasant, vaguely-chemical undertaste and aftertaste as compared to the fresh waters of this place. Disgusted, he upended both of the waterbags and poured the otherworldly liquid out onto the sandy soil at his feet; he could refill them shortly when he reached the pond ahead, with water, *real* water.

In the deep-cut, steep-sided gully that dropped away from the rise on which he sat his idling machine, lizards of a plethora of sizes and shapes and many different iridescent colors scuttled among the rounded pebbles of the seasonal stream bed seeking insects and worms. They and the scattering of small birds obviously set to the same mission all ignored him and his noisy transportation, not considering him a threat.

He had cased his binoculars and was just about to proceed when, with the speed of insanity, everything happened at once. With a wild blur of fluttering wings and squawks of alarm, all the birds in the dry stream bed took flight, the lizards abruptly flicked out of sight, and suddenly there was one of the huge, pithecoid Teeth-and-Legs standing on the dry, round pebbles, its fierce, feral gaze locked upon him and its orangy teeth and fangs displayed in an utterly unhumorous grin. With a howl, the thing raised its overlong arms and ran two steps, then leaped upward.

Sitting there, Fitz was appalled to see a pair of big, black-nailed hands appear on the verge of the cut; he gauged the depth of the gully at least twenty feet and not even something on the order of this outrageous predator should have been able to leap so high straight up . . . but it clearly had done just that. He could hear the feet clawing the clay wall for support and the debris of that frenetic clawing cascading down to rattle among the pebbles below.

Realizing that there was no time to unship either the double rifle or the carbine and knowing from the first encounter the fatal folly of trying to outrun one of the things on his bike, Fitz instead drew his big magnum revolver, levelling the long barrel just as the gigantic, toothy head came into sight above the rim of the cut. He rapid-fired, double-action, at the horrible head. On impact of the weighty slugs, the hairy skull above the beast's eyes dissolved into winking-white bone splinters, grey-pink globs of brain and a spray of bright-red blood, the remainder of the head tilting far, far back under the impacts of the bullets. His fifth and final shot missed as the dying creature's grip slackened and the body tumbled back down the side of the cut to sprawl among the pebbles and send little lizards streaking in every direction.

Although the visible body's only movements were twitching muscle-spasms, Fitz still felt the pressing need to reload. He was able to open the revolver and eject the brass all right, but found himself fumbling out a speed-loader, dropping it, and having to use the second one to recharge his handgun. Replacing the pistol loosely in its holster, he unslung the Holland and Holland, and it was as well he did.

Preceded by a roaring howl that echoed back from the walls of the cut, another of the Teeth-and-Legs, this one if anything larger than the dead one, issued from somewhere to bounce onto the blood-flecked pebbles, race along the bed to a lower stretch of bank and mount to the same level as the man, only some score of yards distant . . . and rapidly closing, teeth flashing and long fingers hooked for clawing.

Fitz stood up, one foot still on either side of the cycle, brought the rifle to his shoulder—some part of his roiling mind surprised at how the very heavy weapon seemed now almost weightless—sighted on the hair-covered chest of the nearing monster, and squeezed off the load in the right barrel.

Not really braced as he should have been before firing a piece with such brutal recoil, it was all that he could do to stay on his feet at all, so he did not witness the moment of impact of outsized bullet with oversized killer-beast. But when he looked down the barrels again it was to see the Teeth-and-Legs on its

17

back on the ground—though still thrashing, roaring and trying repeatedly to arise.

After briefly considering putting the left barrel's load into the downed creature, too, he decided that the rifle's butt had done him enough injury for one day, slung it, and instead drew his revolver, sending three of the 240-grain, soft-point .44 bullets into the beast's head. Not until he clearly heard the death-rattle did he reload and holster the revolver, reload the rifle, pick up the dropped speed-loader, then head for the distant hills at full throttle, lest more of the monsters should suddenly make an appearance.

As he neared the pond he swung well clear of the ponies, rounded a smallish body of water to the site of the bubbling spring that fed it, and refilled his two waterbags, after first rinsing them of the remaining residue of that other-worldly water. A glance into a blue sky flecked with wisps of lacy white clouds showed him that the sun was barely past its meridian and so, knowing that he had plenty of time to get back up to the cave where he had left his companions, he indulged himself in stripping and wading out to a deeper section of the icy-cold pond to swim and lave off the sweat. For he knew that the pony herd would give him adequate warning of the approach of Teeth-and-Legs or any other dangerous beasts.

When finally he waded out of the frigid, refreshing water to air-dry himself beneath the patchy shade of some palms and cycads, the ponies were still there on the other side of the pond, the young ones frisking about while their elders gorged on the short, tender grasses. Not intending to halt again until he had reached his destination, Fitz took advantage of the opportunity to eat a brace of tomato-and-lettuce sandwiches, washing them down with a cup of the cold, clear water from the spring.

Shortly he was setting his machine to the slope of the first hill, threading his way between the trees and thick shrubs up a gradual incline toward the point at which the incline abruptly became more preciptious. But luck was with him, for where the slope steepened and the underbrush thickened, he chanced across the path that he and the Norman knight, Sir Gautier, had hacked through it when they had manhandled the motorcycle down from the higher hills two or three days previously. Staying to this path made the ascent faster and much easier than had been his first climbing of the hill; it meant that he could ride, though in low gear, rather than push the bike while hacking a way through the dense brush with his machete.

Although he remembered, knew just what to expect at the top, he still felt surprise when the bushy, natural wooded and steep slope abruptly became level, grassy, parklike land with a vast assortment of hardwood and fruit trees growing in so uncrowded a manner as to appear unnatural. As before seen, both in ascent and descent, the expanse was virtually alive with birds and game of all descriptions.

On his last ascent he had seen two deer, spotted, adult deer, one of them bearing an impressive rack of palmate antlers. They were nowhere in sight this time, but a group of four smaller and unspotted cervines of some sort were visible, browsing some yards off to his left as he came up into the level ground and headed toward the hill that loomed beyond it. These deer—if that is what they truly were—were much smaller, the biggest no more, he estimated, than a bit over two feet at the withers and with antlers about the size and shape of wooden sling-shots. What he could see of them as they slowly moved around under the thick-boled trees showed bodies all of a solid reddish-brown color and rear legs looking to be a bit longer than forelegs.

The big persimmon tree was not, this time, being raided by an opossum and birds, but rather by six or eight big, tailless, dog-faced monkeys or apes of some sort—all a yellow-brown on the back and sides, shad-ing to a yellowish-white on the chest and belly. Fascinated, Fitz halted and idled the bike fairly close to the spreading tree, hoping to get a better look at these, the first primates—unless one considered the savage Teeth-and-Legs to be of that order—he had seen in this world.

One of the larger of the beasts ran out along a limb high above, until it began to sag under his weight—Fitz estimated that the big one weighed in the neigh-borhood of forty to forty-five pounds—keeping a secure grip on his elevated avenue with both his hands and hand-shaped feet. Halting, he looked down at the upward-looking man, showed a mouthful of good-sized teeth, then *barked*.

Fitz started at the completely unexpected noise. The ape had the exact sound and timbre and pitch of an Eskimo Spitz once owned by a friend of Fitz. He still was laughing at himself when the big beast cupped one hand behind him, defecated into it, brought the hand up long enough to regard and sniff at its contents, then hurled said contents down at the unwanted observer.

The foetid mess missed . . . barely, and Fitz decided to move on. Even over the noise of his engine, he could hear the raucous, triumphal barks of the most inhospitable apes in the persimmon tree.

Following the blazes he had hacked into treetrunks when he and Sir Gautier de Montjoie had crossed on the way back down to the Pony Plain, he once more passed close to the hollow full of blackberry bushes. Repeated shakings of the tops of these showed clearly that some thing or things fed within the depths of the prickly thicket, but he could not see it—possum, raccoons, that long-legged and skinny bear or whatever.

Remembering that the ascent of the knife-sharp ridge was far too steep for the engine of the loaded bike, he dismounted and pushed it to the narrow summit, being a bit amazed that the near exhaustion he recalled from the last time he had had to do it alone failed to this time materialize.

"Not bad for a man over a half-century old," he thought. "This roughing it in the boondocks I've been doing in recent weeks must be good for me. I don't think I've felt this good, this fit since . . . oh, hell, since I was in my twenties, anyway."

In the grassy glen beyond the ridge he stopped, dismounted and sprawled on the pebbly bank of the little, fast-flowing rill to drink of its icy water, then gathered a handful of round stones before he arose and uncased the drilling, loading its two smooth-bore barrels with birdshot and its rifled barrel with a hollow-poined .22-caliber magnum. The two shot-loads garnered him as many plump pheasants and a lucky shot from the rifle barrel dropped a peculiar, hornless cervine or antelope—he could not be certain which the creature, little larger than a large hare and equipped with upper cuspids that projected well below the lower jaw, really was, but it was well fleshed and, if Sir Gautier did not immediately claim it, it would make a nice tidbit for Cool Blue.

After very roughly field-dressing his mixed bag, Fitz added them to the load of the motorcycle and headed up the next hill, aware that before he reached the rendezvous at the small, hillside rock-overhang, he would perforce be once again afoot and pushing the conveyance due to the steepness of the rocky ascent.

But when arrive at the rendezvous he finally did, it was to find himself completely alone, neither the 12th-century Norman knight nor the baby-blue lion being anywhere in sight and the ashes in the firepit being dead-cold and dampish. Such supplies and equipment as he had left far back in the shallow cave appeared just as he had placed them prior to his departure, only a canteen being missing.

Shaking his head, Fitz set about doing the necessary—first cleaning out the firepit, gathering squawwood and laying a new fire, then fully dressing the ruminant and the two birds for cooking. He was not in the least worried about Sir Gautier for, if any man could take care of himself in this primitive world, it was certainly that doughty, medieval Anglo-Norman warrior. As for Cool Cat, strands of baby-blue fur showed that the ensorcelled, one-time bopster musician had slept at least once in the rock overhang and most likely was out hunting, his lion-body requiring sizable amounts of high-protein food.

While the wood burned down into cooking-coals, Fitz unloaded the bike and side-car, sorted out the supplies and equipment and stored it in the cave with the shrouded bike at the rear, for his previous sojourn had emphasized the impracticality of trying to use the bike in the broken, rocky, heavily wooded or swampy country that lay beyond to east, west or north. His required journeying must be on shank's mare, perforce.

Taking into account the Norman knight's ingrained senses of honor, duty and loyalty, Fitz doubted that his liegeman had gone far from the rendezvous point and likely would be returning soon, so he would just await that return. Even had he not had a plentitude of supplies, the land abounded with game of all types and descriptions, berries, nuts, wild fruits and other edible wild plants, with springs and brooks and rills almost everywhere. The rocks still were lying nearby with which he could partially barricade the rear area of the overhang at nights so that, with the banked fire and the weapons he always took into his sleeping bag, he felt himself safe from nocturnal predators even without Sir Gautier or the baby-blue lion nearby.

By the time he had done to his satisfaction all that was needful, the first logs were become coals, so Fitz spitted one of the pheasants over the firepit, nestling two canteen cups of water near the edges—one for boullion, one for tea—then sat before the coal-bed watching the bird cook. The other pheasant and the dressed hoofed-beast had been hung high enough to be safe from the predations of anything save insects.

"Odd," he thought, "but after the weeks here, then the last couple of days . . . and the nights—those beautiful, rapturous, very strenuous nights—with Danna; after the stresses and strains of today, even, I'm still not really tired. Used to be, two or three years ago, before all of this started, a normal day of peddling those damned vacuum cleaners would often leave me exhausted. I burned more than one TV dinner through just nodding off in my chair while the blasted thing was cooking."

As he sat, relaxed, watching the spitted fowl brown over the bed of coals, the first tenuous wisps of steam arise from the kidney-shaped steel cups of crystal water, his mind went racing back to the bad old times, when war and mischance had slain his son, made a hopeless alcoholic of his wife, driven his daughter away from their home and then brought her back—drug-addicted, diseased and pregnant. Driving drunk, his wife had had an accident fatal to her and the unborn child. His daughter had been rendered a human vegetable—kept alive only by machines and seeming miles of tubing—and when the greedy physicians and even greedier hospital had made of him a virtual pauper, had taken the worth of the house and everything else he had managed to accumulate throughout a lifetime of work, he had made the opportunity to do that which he had felt he must do: had granted his daughter, the husk that once had contained her, the boon of a dignified death.

They had branded him "murderer," of course, but everyone had seemed to feel sorry for him—a good, decent, hard-working sales executive who had suffered far more than most, for a very long time and completely through no fault of his own—and his very last assets had secured him the services of a competent attorney who had managed to convince the court and jury that so much suffering over so protracted a period had finally brought about a moment of insanity. But the verdict had cost him his job, his position, his career. They had been kind about it: they did not fire Fitz, just retired him, complete with gold watch and pension, for stated "reasons of health." But the sizable loan he had felt constrained to take out with the firm's credit union had had to be repaid, of course, and the monthly installments left damned little pension on which to try to live.

With his record of a felony trial and a finding of not guilty by reason of temporary insanity, he quickly discovered that he might as well forget employment in his previous field and in most others for which he was otherwise eminently qualified. He wound up selling vacuum cleaners on a straight-commission basis out of a rusty clunker of a car, living in a rented, ill-furnished and dilapidated tract-house in a run-down neighborhood, his only companion being Tom, his big grey tomcat, last survivor of his one-time happy family, last reminder of the good times that then seemed gone forever.

Then, to pile Ossa atop Pelion, a sadistic juvenile delinquent armed with at cheap, battered, .22-caliber rifle had senselessly shot Tom. Gutshot and dying in hideous agony, the creature had still managed to make it back to the foot of the crumbling, concrete rear stairs, where Fitz had found his body, the eyes just beginning to assume the glaze of death.

In the back yard of the rented house was a peculiar, oval mound of overgrown earth, said to have existed as long as white men had inhabited the area. Tom had liked in life to snooze atop the mound under a bush, and so, when the grieving Fitz had washed and arranged the stiffening body, had shrouded it in his best, threadbare bath towel, he had sought out a rusty spade and begun to dig a cat-size grave atop the mound, under the bush.

But only a foot or so down into the black loam he had struck stone. Afraid to risk the flaking blade of the venerable spade in any attempt to pry up the obstruction, he had essayed to dig around it, only to discover that it was more than just a stray boulder beneath the soil of that mound. At the end of his labor, he had disclosed a rectangle of worked stones, precisely fitted one to the other by a skilled stonemason. And fitted within that rectangle was a much larger single stone that, he had quickly found, was so balanced as to pivot up and down within its lodgement.

His curiosity piqued, equipped with a flashlight and the old snake-gun from out his tackle box, fortified with a couple of fingers of neat Irish whiskey, he had entered the damp, earthy-smelling stone vault, descended stairs with peculiarly small, shallow treads and arrived at last in a bare, stone-walled chamber well below the surface. Careful search having revealed nothing of any sort in the crypt, his flashlight beginning to dim, Fitz had started back up the slimy stairs, lost footing and balance and felt himself falling backward.

Steeled for the impact of his unprotected head against the hard, cold stone, he had instead landed with a breathless thump on a hard, *but warm*, surface. Even before he opened his eyes he was certain that he was badly injured: lying, despite sensations of warmth and dryness, on that damp, cold floor of the crypt and hallucinating from trauma and pain. Then he became dead certain of the fact.

His vision and other senses indicated that he lay on the sand of a sunlit beach . . . well, at least most of him did. His eyes' testament was that his legs ended abruptly a bit above the knees, beyond the spot whereon his thighs rested athwart a near-buried, weathered and bleached log of driftwood. But he still could move the unseen limbs, could feel with them the cold, slimy stones whereon they rested.

When his mind had ceased to whirl, his incipient hysteria been forced down, Fitz had slid forward far enough to make the discovery that just beyond the log was an invisible portal of some kind—on the one side the cold, stygian stone crypt, on the other the warm, sunny beach—and solid as the stonework appeared to his eyes, he still was able to pass back and forth through it as freely as through empty air.

That discovery made, he decided to just accept the patent impossibility of the situation, to save the reasoning-out of it for another time. After carefully marking the location of the invisible portal on the thick, heavy log, he set out to explore the strange new world.

It had not been until he had left the beach and climbed the high dunes that he found any single trace of mankind. There, partially buried in the sand, he had found a long, wooden ship or rather what was left of one—masts all snapped off, sand completely filling its forecastle and part-decked hull.

However, when he had forced open two doors below the quarterdeck, he had found some artifacts—a big knife and a small, copper cup—in the first. Behind the second door, in the larger of the two cabins, he had found more artifacts . . . and treasure, real treasure, a *cour bouilli* casket almost filled with ancient coins of gold.

"And that," he muttered to himself as he again turned the spitted fowl, "was when all hell really started popping."

Knowing next to nothing about coins, he had taken a double handful of the ones he had found, just what his pockets could easily hold, back to his own world with him, hoping to get only the bullion value of them, perhaps as much as fifteen hundred dollars— enough to pay off the balance of his ailing automotive abortion, get some needed repairs and, possibly, a decent-looking suit from the Goodwill store.

He had driven the miles into the city of his former residence and taken the coins into the shop of a dealer, a retired Army NCO he knew vaguely from the VFW. Then he had come within an ace of actually fainting, right there in the coin shop, upon being given a rough estimate of the true values of the coins—mostly from the Mediterranean littoral, none of them minted less than a full millennium past though some were centuries older than even that, and all in unbelievably good condition for such archaic rareties.

Then it had all just snowballed, happening almost too fast for comprehension. Believing Fitz's spur-of-the-moment fabrication that the coins had been the bequest of some deceased uncle, Gus Tolliver had taken advantage of his guild's far-flung network of contacts to begin to sell and mail-auction the exceedingly rare collector gold pieces all over the world, taking a fee of twenty percent of the profits and giving Fitz the remaining eighty.

The very first thing that Fitz had done with his newcome wealth was to buy the rental house and land outright. Then he had hired a general contractor to convert the decaying edifice into a small luxury home with attached double garage to house the two new vehicles with which he had quickly replaced his clunker.

Next he had paid off the balance of the credit-union loan, which meant that he then began to receive his full retirement pension from his former firm—not that he had any need of so trifling a sum anymore, with money pouring in from sales of the forty pounds or so of golden coins from the casket in the wrecked ship.

In his by then copious spare time, he had spent many full days in what he had come to think of as the sand world, and further exploration of the old ship had disclosed another and much larger cabin behind the two smaller ones, extending completely across the beam of the wrecked vessel. With bits of furniture from the other two cabins and modern items laboriously brought down the narrow, ever-treacherous stone stairs Fitz had fashioned of the sterncabin a moderately comfortable *pied-à-terre* in this world of sea and sand, birds and sea creatures but with no recent trace of man.

The dunes seemed to march on into infinity to the east, the west and the north, as far as he had walked.

It had not been until he had thought to buy and wrestle down the stairs an off-road motorcycle that he had begun to learn more of the sand world, had seen the long, broad Pony Plain north of the dunes and glimpsed the succession of dark-green, forested hills rising on the other side.

He had first brought firearms into the seemingly uninhabited sand world because no matter where he went or travelled within it, he experienced the unpleasant, uncanny feeling that he was being watched, being observed. Even within the locked, barred and shuttered sterncabin he often felt that he was not truly alone, that someone or some *thing* was invisibly with him.

Trouble was brewing in the other, more mundane world, too, coming fast to a roiling boil for him and Gus Tolliver. First came a succession of break-ins at Fitz's house during various of his sojourns in the sand world; although little of any real value was ever taken—save the two artifacts, the knife and the copper cup which had been his first finds aboard the beached ship—he had liked so little the idea of strangers poking about his home that he had taken extreme and very expensive steps to harden up the place and its grounds—steel-sheathed solid doors, special windows and state-of-the-art locks, high cyclone fencing for the perimeter of the entire property topped with barbed wire, floodlights, trip-flares, banshee-loud alarms, the works, the best that money could buy.

Gus Tolliver, too, had had at least one break-in at his shop. Although a good number of silver coins had lain exposed in glass cases and there had been some modern gold coins in the big, old-fashioned, deliberately visible safe that had been skillfully opened, then just as skillfully reclosed, none of this had been so much as touched. Despite intensive, destructive searchings, the location of his hidden safe had never been found. But what had upset the old soldier more than this had been when word had been privately passed to him that certain governmental agencies had been putting pressure on officials of his bank to disclose certain information of a private, financial nature.

That had been when he first had confided in Fitz of his fierce distrust of certain bureaus of the government he had served so long and so faithfully. Furthermore, he had announced his avowed intent of foiling them all.

Fitz had heard his partner out, sympathized aloud, and then simply forgotten the matter, figuring that it had been just one more instance of a disgruntled taxpayer blowing off a little steam. Months later, to his sorrow, he discovered that Tolliver had been serious, dead serious, and that his manner of foiling the Internal Revenue Service had tarred them both with the same brush in the mind of one Agent Henry Fowler Blutegel.

CHAPTER II

Save for a very few modern anachronisms here and there, the room might have been a chamber of a Renaissance Spanish castle: the chamber of a wealthy man, certainly, for everything within it bespoke the lavish sums spent upon its furnishings, decorations and fittings.

Little of the dark-amber wall-to-wall carpet was visible, overlain as it was by a huge, thick, beautiful carpet of Turkish or Persian type. Only an expert could have told that the carpet was a skillful, relatively modern reproduction, for he whose sanctum this chamber was had too much respect for the true antique carpets to subject them to day-to-day foot traffic, the weights of furniture and the hazards of cigar ashes. Those smaller carpets which hung here and there on the dark-panelled walls were, however, authentic antiques and immensely valuable, one and all.

In one corner stood a splendid full suit of fluted, Maximillian-style plate armor, its crossed gauntlets resting atop the pommel of a period bastard-sword. On a stretch of wall not covered by a carpet was hung dog-face bascinet-helm and crossed below it were a medieval battle-sword and a horseman's battle-axe, with a short-hafted, quintrefoil mace hung upright between them. All of these pieces were authentic and of museum quality.

The furnishings looked every bit as old, though outstandingly well kept, as authentic as the weapons, but they were not, none of them; rather, they were painstaking reproductions of tables, chairs and cabinets of the period—all dark woods, leathers, inlays and black wrought-iron or rich bronze. Nonetheless, it was a chamber in which a Renaissance nobleman or lady would have certainly felt comfortable, almost at home.

The desk, chair and console were wrought of the same dark woods with similar decorations, but there the similarities ended. The lamps were electric, with variable intensities of brightness. What might have been two small, carven and inlaid chests on either side of the desk actually housed telephone and an intercommunications device, and another on the console held a tape-recorder and its condensor microphone. A fourth, much flatter chest contained a wide selection of hand-rolled cigars, a box of cigarettes and two lighters.

In the leather swivel-chair behind the desk sat a man who, in period attire, would have matched his archaic surroundings almost perfectly. His hair and moustache were raven's-wing black, his skin-tone saturnine, the backs of his hands and long, tapering fingers black-haired. Only a close approach to the whipcord-slender figure would have revealed that the eyes beneath the dark brows were a piercing blue.

As he often did, Pedro Goldfarb found himself working late at his office, so tied up in a case that he had allowed time, partners and employees to depart the offices unheeded.

Before him, a profusion of thick books lay, some of them open, some of them closed but with scraps of paper marking places in them. One yellow legal-size pad lay aside, filled with his neat, pencilled notes, and a fresh one was already a quarter filled. The stubs of two thin cigars lay among their ashes in a big, bronze tray and a third had smoldered out there. Beside a mug half full of cold, black coffee a crystal goblet of a pale amber liquor sat almost untasted.

The man did not miss even a stroke of his writing when, after a light knock, one of the pair of doors opened and a woman's voice said, "Talk about smoke-filled rooms. Sorry, Pedro, I'd thought somebody'd left the lights on in here. Do you mean to go home at all tonight?"

"Minute, Danna," replied the man. "Important I get this down now, fresh off my brain."

Wordlessly she seated herself in the side-chair nearest his desk and sat, silent and unmoving, until at length he completed his scribblings and laid aside his pencil with a whuff.

"Still on Belcher, Pedro?" she asked. "Or is this that new one, McKiernan?"

He had, as she had been speaking, leaned forward

to bring the mug to his lips, but after only the briefest of tentative sips, he grimaced and declared, "Cold! Hell, I'd rather quaff as much hemlock as cold coffee."

The woman stood and reached for the mug, saying, "Here, Pedro, I can go out and fire up Doris's Silex and . . ."

"No, forget it." He smiled. "Thanks anyway, Danna, really, but if I drink any more caffeine I'll never get to sleep tonight. No, I'll work on this cognac, I think. Would you care to join me?"

Resuming her seat, she replied, with a slight shake of the head, "No, no cognac for me, thank you, but I will have a small glass of your excellent sherry, Pedro."

With a nod, the dark man pushed back his chair, stood and crossed to his commodious liquor cabinet. Then, with a decanter poised over a slender, crystal sherry goblet, he inquired, "Dry or cream, Danna?"

"Not cream, Pedro. Do you still have some of that amontillado?"

When both were again seated, he waved at the clutter atop his desk. "Since you asked: no, not the McKiernans, they're in no real trouble and the agent they're dealing with is a gentleman who goes strictly by the book, young Khoury—reasonable, civil, understanding. No, I turned their case over to Murray.

"But poor Belcher, he's another question entirely. Yes, he's made some mistakes and his halfwitted brother-in-law made some more and far worse ones, and that damned Henry Blutegel rode them so long and so brutally before they came to us that they're both terrified nervous wrecks. But if we can keep them from flipping out and impulsively admitting guilt to things they really didn't do or, at least, intend to do, my researches here tonight just may cost that Czech bastard this case.

"And in regard to Blutegel, Danna: Has your private research project turned up anything interesting on him and his background?"

The auburn-haired woman's lips became a grim line. "Heinrich Blutegel, a Displaced Person from Czechoslovakia, entered the United States in May of 1947 in company with his bride of twelve weeks, an American Red Cross worker née Rachel Feingold. His new wife was a native of Kansas City, a registered nurse by profession and heiress of a modest inheritance. Blutegel was then in his mid-twenties—according to his records which, of course, were backed up solely by his sworn statements, his birthplace and former home village having been completely wiped out and destroyed by the Nazis in the course of the war—so she sent him to college and, by the time he had graduated with a degree in accounting in 1952, he had mastered English, speaking the completely unaccented, colloquial English that he uses today. Quite a feat for the unlettered Czech peasant he was supposed to be, Pedro."

He nodded. "I'll say. He's not married, now; I once heard that he was divorced. Have you been able to contact or talk to his former wife, Danna?"

She shook her head once. "Rachel Blutegel committed suicide in 1958, leaving no note and for no apparent reason. His second wife, a younger cousin of Rachel's whom he first met at the funeral, lost her mind and had to be hospitalized in 1965; when she was declared incurable, hopeless, he divorced her and almost immediately married another nurse, a German immigrant woman thirty years old. She divorced him in 1972, took him for nearly everything he had while he, against advice of counsel, never lifted a finger to contest any of it. She returned to Germany and I'm trying to track her down. At present he lives alone with his bottle in a cheap, furnished apartment; to the best of anyone's knowledge, he owns not one friend and all of his acquaintances are connected with his work."

"Hmm." Pedro gazed long and hard into the glass of pale liquor, then asked her, "It would be very interesting to discover just what the third wife held over his head to keep him from contesting that divorce, that divorce which was so very costly to him, so immensely rewarding to her. Who was his attorney in that action, Danna?"

She sighed. "Bill Smith, Pedro. Another dead end street for me."

"Maybe," mused the dark man. "Then again, maybe not; maybe, rather, a part of a deadly pattern. I knew Bill Smith, Danna, knew him rather well, really. Like all his friends, I could never conceive of him pulling a Dutch, as he was supposed to have done. Dammit, that young fellow had real promise, he was headed places, else old Nussbaum wouldn't have taken him on like he did. The assumption of the authorities was that he was despondent over his personal debts, but it just didn't wash with anyone who knew him at all well. He was on his way up *and he knew it, too,* moreover, he was proud as punch about his little boy, then two months old. Could it be, Danna. . . ? Could it be that our own Agent Henry Blutegel. . . ?"

She blanched. "*Pedro*! My God, Pedro, that's *insane*! Why in the world would even a thing like Blutegel. . . ?" She paused, then nodded slowly, "You think that perhaps . . . that, maybe, Bill might've learned something that could've frightened Blutegel enough to drive him to . . . to. . . ?"

Grimfaced, the dark man nodded. "Could be, Danna, could very well be, all things considered. Tell you something you didn't know, too: Bill Smith wasn't born a Smith. His dad legally changed the family name because he had become so ashamed of bearing his true surname early in World War Two. The name was *Messerschmidt*. Bill didn't tell many people the truth, only his closest friends, that he was originally Wilhelm Messerschmidt, and that he spoke, read and wrote excellent German.

"Now, I've never done any divorce work, myself, but I know the procedure, nonetheless. Who can say that there did not occur some exchanges, possibly very heated exchanges, between the estranged couple? What would be more natural than that, saying things neither of them wished their listeners to understand, they retreated to the supposed safety of a language foreign to said listeners, spoke their thoughts or threats in German? Then, if the dispossessed and not in the least happy Blutegel had in some way learned that his one-time attorney most probably had comprehended all that had been said in his hearing. . . ?

"Danna, this is an order: hand over all your cases to Dundas or Emily or Hammill. Hear? Devote all your working time to this Blutegel thing. Go wherever you need to go, do whatever you need to do: you write the checks, I'll cover them, never fear. It's the very least I can do for the shade of my dead friend, Bill. This slimy Blutegel may or may not be a hide-out Nazi, but right now I can clearly see him as a murderer and I'll be just as happy to see him proven the one as the other.

"But, back to that other, have you heard anything from that man in Austria?"

After a sip of sherry, she replied, "No, not directly, Pedro. I'm just now in contact with a group in New York City that's in some way affiliated with him and his group. I've also been talking on the phone with a young attorney who works for the Justice Department up in D.C., and I've sent both him and the New York people photocopies of my current file on Blutegel, plus the one I sent to Austria and yet another sent to a man who wrote to me from Tel Aviv. Just today, I got two letters—one from Bonn and one from Prague—asking for copies of the file." She grinned maliciously. "Just wait until you see this month's Xerox bill, Pedro, not to even mention the postage meter."

He waved a hand in dismissal. "Forget it, Danna. Like I just said: you write the checks, I'll see to it that they're covered, all of them. Although I warn you, Danna," he grinned, himself, "any written to jewellers, department stores, boutiques or luxury auto dealers are yours, all yours to cover."

Then all at once he sobered and, in dead-serious tones, said, "But, Danna, how ever much it costs in time or effort or money, *get me proof of some kind on that bastard*. It's no longer just his crusade against Fitz and Gus Tolliver now; now the sullied honor of an old friend is in the balance, too. When his death was ruled a suicide, his life insurance holders refused to pay one cent to his widow. I and some others have tried to help her but she's proud, she just won't accept anything that smacks of charity. But as she has no marketable skills, she's growing old long before her time trying to support herself and her kids on the paltry salaries of two menial jobs. She deserves a better life than that, Danna."

Danna Dardrey wrinkled her brows. "She's still a young woman and, as I recall from one brief encounter with her, rather an attractive one. Surely she could find another husband?"

Pedro Goldfarb fielded the question with one of his own. "Is that what you did when your husband died back during World War Two, Danna?"

The auburn hair swirled as she shook her head. "Oh, Pedro, you know better. No, I never remarried, but my own situation was different. I had the home, the security and the moral support of Kevin's parents, who were fairly well off, and I also had Kevin's GI and civilian insurance."

"Nonetheless," he insisted, "don't you think you'd have been better off, more comfortable, more fulfilled in many ways had you found and married some decent, honest, personable man with a good job and income? So why didn't you do just that, Danna? Why didn't you give your sons a new father, at least, a role model to guide their development?"

"Tom Dardrey, Kevin's dad, was all the role model any boy could've asked for, Pedro," she replied. "He exulted in having two new sons to make into the same kind of fine young man he had made of their father. It helped him better to bear up under the loss of Kevin, I think. As to why I never remarried, well, I just didn't want another man, any other man, for many years . . . not until I met . . . until Fitz and I found each other, finally. I was never rich, but I was able to provide all the necessities and even a few small luxuries for me and my sons through my working income and the investment I'd made with Kevin's insurance policies and, later, the modest bequest his father left us. Besides, I just was stubborn enough to need to make it in this world on my own."

The dark man nodded. "Just so. Then can you not believe that perhaps Will's young widow harbors a similar need to, as you just said, make it on her own, unassisted by others, until she comes across her own Fitz, wherever and whenever?"

While she digested the question, he sipped at his cognac, then asked another: "How good is your German, Danna? Can you speak the language at all? Understand it spoken with any degree of accuracy? Read or write it?"

She sighed and shook her head again. "No, Pedro, none at all. Way back when I could've taken German, but instead I took French as my foreign language elective . . . but don't ask me at this late date about that one, either; I can't even recall how to say or to write 'My aunt eats green pencils.' I once read somewhere that one of the hallmarks of the Celtic race is a facility for languages. Well, if so, then I guess I'm something other than Celtic; I even flounder in Latin, and I've been schooled in that since grade school."

Pedro smiled. "There are no pure races of mankind anywhere in this world, Danna. Didn't you know that? All humans are mongrels, a duke's mixture of who knows how many strains and tag-ends of extinct races. The only thing that humanity shares is a generally similar body shape . . . that and an inherently savage, murderous, predatory nature."

"But Pedro," she expostulated, "Mr. Hara says that . . ."

"Ah, yes, the venerable and most eminent Mr. Hara." He nodded. "I had intended to ask how you two were getting along. How is my good old friend Tadahira these days?"

"We had dinner together tonight. He often asks that I pass on to you his regards. He speaks of you quite often, Pedro; he seems of the opinion that, all things considered, you and I are more like each other than we are like anybody else. We've discussed Fitz, too, and Mr. Hara is very anxious to meet and talk with him as well.

"Pedro, how old would you say he is?"

The dark man shrugged. "Probably, exactly as old as he says he is, since I've never known him to lie about anything. But comes to that, Danna, I've never asked his age and I don't think he ever volunteered the information. Why?"

"It's just that he was speaking tonight about having captained a warship during the Russo-Japanese War . . . but, Pedro, as I recall my world history, that was . . . well, at least seventy years ago, and if he'd only been, say, thirty at the time, that still would make him a hundred or more now. Could he be a century old, do you think? He shaves his head completely and apparently has no beard, his eyebrows *are* white, but he certainly doesn't look or move or act like a centenarian."

"Actually," he answered, "Tadahira is probably older than a century, Danna. Ships are not, as a rule, given into the hands of inexperienced officers, so for a thirty-year-old to command a warship would have been most exceptionable in a nation that at that time must have had more than sufficient numbers of veteran maritime officers.

"But how did this subject come up? He never once has spoken of a naval career to me, Danna, and I've known him for quite a few years."

The woman shuddered strongly, rubbed her forearms briskly to lay the gooseflesh that had sprung up upon them, then drained off the remainder of her sherry and said in a low, hushed voice, "It's a long story, Pedro, a . . . a weird story. I . . . *sense* that it is completely true—or that Mr. Hara believes it to be true, anyway."

She did not think it a good idea, then and there, to tell her employer, partner and friend that, using the telepathy that Fitz had so recently shown her how to employ, she had entered just far enough into her ancient friend's mind to ascertain that he was indeed imparting the truth as he knew it in his singular narrative.

Then, of a sudden, she recalled time and place: especially time. "But, Pedro, it's nearly midnight and you've got to get home and get at least some sleep tonight."

Rising, he strode to the liquor cabinet and brought back the two decanters of cognac and sherry, saying, "Whatever Tadahira told you tonight, it shook you, and you don't shake up easily, as I well know. Just recalling it all shook you again, too. So, if you don't tell it to me, here and now, I'd lie awake the rest of this night wondering just what you knew that I don't yet of the gentleman's past. So sip your sherry like a good girl and tell me."

When she had refilled her goblet with the amontillado, she took from her bag a small, fancifully-carved meerschaum pipe, packed it slowly and carefully from an eelskin pouch, then used one of the gold lighters from the cigar-chest on Pedro's desk to puff it into life. Then she began to speak.

"Mr. Hara says that, after the virtual destruction of the Czar's Pacific Ocean Fleet at Port Arthur, the Japanese admiral ordered his fleet to disperse and steam back to Japan. Mr. Hara was commanding a light cruiser—only recently completed and commissioned, new, sleek and modern by the standards of that day—and was very proud of having been chosen to take her out and be her captain during her baptism of fire.

"Steaming homeward through the Yellow Sea, having experienced some minor boiler problems that he feels still were due to the inferior quality of captured Russian coal then stocking his bunkers, his ship had fallen behind the rest of the fleet, even his escorting destroyers. But with those few Russian ships remaining afloat and uncaptured fleeing the area at flank speed, he knew that he and his fine, strong, well-armed and fully-manned warship had nothing to fear, so he proceeded slowly while his crew worked on the boiler repairs and refittings.

"As the sun came up of a morning, with the repairs effected and the coast of Chosen a dim smudge off the port bow on the horizon, he was hastily summoned to the bridge by the watch-officer to view a brace of 'monsters' disporting in the sea some thousand meters off his starboard and almost every officer and man aboard his ship crowding the rails to watch them."

"Does he have any idea what they were?" asked Pedro.

She shrugged. "He says that in his crew there were former fishers and whalers, as well, and that none of them had ever before seen or could put any name other than that of 'sea monster' to the creatures. He says that he viewed them through some kind of range-finding instrument and found them to be both huge and awesome in shape, size and appearance, but exactly what their species was, he cannot say with any degree of certainty to this day, though he got to see most of their bodies as they rolled several times while he watched.

"He says that they were, according to the measuring device scribed onto the lens of his instrument, at least twenty meters long, their thick bodies looking a bit like slightly flattened barrels, smooth skins of a dark-gray color on top and almost white on the undersides."

"How many legs?" asked Pedro.

"No legs at all," she replied, "just wide flippers, four of them. They had necks as thick as tree trunks, he says, and between three and four meters long, with heads a good meter long and wide jaws well supplied with teeth, eyes quite large for their heads and no visible ears. The monsters both seemed completely oblivious of the warship and much involved in what looked much like real play.

"But despite their lack of aggressiveness, Mr. Hara ordered two of his smaller guns manned and loaded to await his order to fire upon the distant, inoffensive creatures. When his intent was made clear to all, one of his crew, an officer who was also a Buddhist monk and, like Mr. Hara himself, scion of an old and noble family, courteously implored his captain not to harm the innocent beasts, warning that if they were harmed by his orders, great calamity was certain to ensue.

"Mr. Hara, with great shame and infinite sadness, told then of how he callously ridiculed the well-meaning holy man, caused all of his other officers there gathered to join in the cruel mockery, then gave the guncrews the order to fire and continue firing so long as the beasts or any portions of them still were visible. Through the range-finding device he watched while his well-trained and experienced gunners blew the frolicking and all-unsuspecting animals into gobbets of bloody flesh and bone. Then, after he had personally congratulated the gunnery officer, he went below to enjoy his first meal of the new, sunny day."

The woman paused for a sip of the sherry, puffed vainly at the now-dead pipe, relit it finally, then went on with her second-hand recountal. Pedro listened in silence, rolling an unlit cigar in his fingers.

"Mr. Hara says that, within turn of the glass, the sun became obscured by masses of dark clouds and the wind metamorphosed suddenly from a gentle zephyr to a half gale, then a full gale, then even worse. The pond-like sea rose up in mast-high mountains of dark water to crash onto and sluice over the ship as if it had been some tiny chip of a fishing boat.

He says that there was simply no riding out the sudden, murderous storm in the proper manner, for no sooner did he see her bow put into the monstrous waves than, by some perversion of the natural order, she would be struck from another quarter by seas no less fierce and deadly.

"The howling winds and crashing seas swept men overboard and did immense damage to the vulnerable parts of the ship, but as he was a master-seaman and had come to know his ship well, he had, despite everything, managed to keep her at least afloat and well-out from the coast of Chosen. But then, all at once, the repaired boiler burst and, denied enough power for any meaningful sort of headway, the battered ship wallowed helplessly until a wall of water higher than any Mr. Hara had ever before seen or even imagined struck the light cruiser on her port side and capsized her. To the best of his knowledge, Mr. Hara was the sole survivor of his ship, though he was to subsequently find that there was one other.

"He has never known just how he survived the diaster, Pedro. He was washed shore on the coast of the Chosen Peninsula, a bit of splintered wreckage having miraculously pierced his uniform coat in such a way as to keep his head and upper body out of the water . . . or, at least, that is what those who questioned those who found him later conjectured.

"But back in Japan, he was given cause to wish that he too had gone down with the ship. His superiors made it abundantly clear to him that, having lost the ship and all her crew, he was in disgrace . . . and that in order that the disgrace be his alone and not that of his family and clan, as well, he must perform the act of *seppuku* in the tradition of his class.

"Obediently, he put his affairs in order and made the necessary arrangements, being offered the use of a cousin's antique swords, his own equally venerable and treasured blades by then resting and rusting beyond recall on the floor of the Yellow Sea. An old friend sadly agreed to serve him as his *kaishaku*, the man who would behead him with the *katana* after he had himself slit his own abdomen with the *wakizashi*.

"What a hideous thing to force someone to do to himself, Pedro. What sort of people would, could, order such an enormity?"

Now it was the dark man who shrugged. "Just your ordinary, run-of-the-mill, savage, bloodthirsty human being, Danna. Mankind was always more vicious than the prey he hunted or even the bestial predators with which he competed. That's why there're so few beasts left in this world that is bursting with humans.

"But, that aside, go on with the tale. It's fascinating. Mr. Hara lost his nerve at the sticking-point, eh? He found he couldn't go through with it, did he?"

Once more the woman rubbed briskly at her forearms, saying, "Oh, no, he did go through with it . . . rather, he did his level best to do so. Pedro, this is where the really weird part starts.

"On the chosen day, at the chosen place, with a dozen witnesses present, Mr. Hara prepared to go about his suicide. But when he put his hand to the cloth-shrouded *wakizashi*, the ancient but tough and razor-sharp blade shattered into countless pieces like length of fragile glass struck with a hammer! After a few minutes of consternation, one of the official witnesses provided his own *wakizashi* to replace the inexplicably broken one, that he still might see the will of the high command properly done in the ritual manner. But no sooner had Mr. Hara touched the point of the blade to his bare belly-skin than that point and a handspan length of the fine steel behind it snapped off cleanly.

Next, his friend, on Mr. Hara's frantic signal, whirled *his* blade up and swung it at the back of Mr. Hara's neck—but that longer blade, the kaishaku, shattered as it was swung through the air, and the poor friend landed flat on his face between his intended victim and the ranks of witnesses.

"At that juncture, another of the official witnesses drew, aimed, cocked and fired a Colt pistol at Mr. Hara. The priming-cap fired, but the charge of gunpowder did not, so the officer cocked and fired again . . . and yet again and again and again until he had tried vainly to shoot five of the six loads in his pistol. With a look of shock on his face, he pointed it at the floor and squeezed the trigger—to see the bullet penetrate the mat and the muzzle-blast set fire to it.

"The frustrated *kaishaku* had, by then, borrowed another *katana*, taken his preassigned post and indicated to Mr. Hara that he once more was ready to accomplish his bloody, painful, but agreed-upon chore. When on this occasion he whirled up the long sword, however, the tang impossibly came free of the hilt and the blade went flying through the air, through a paper wall and was later found sticking in a floor.

"Another try was made with the reprimed and reloaded pistol, an equally futile try. They . . . Can you credit any of this, Pedro? It's unbelievable, completely unbelievable, yet Mr. Hara is completely convinced that it's all true, to the last word."

"There are more things in heaven and earth than are dreamt of in your philosophy," quoted the dark man, nodding and attesting. "If Mr. Hara says it's true, Danna, then I don't doubt that it is, all of it, even the hardest parts to believe. I'll swear by that old man."

After once more getting her pipe going and enjoying one or two puffs, then wetting her lips with a bit of the sherry, the woman recommenced her recountal. "Well, the 'festivities' were put on hold, so to speak, and Mr. Hara, his friend and all of the witnesses trooped off to the senior officers with their weird but fully-witnessed and attested tales. When all had been heard out by three of the superior officers, when the broken weapons and the strangely operating revolver had all been carefully examined, one of these seniors had an orderly fetch back to him a more modern firearm, a captured Russian revolver of larger caliber, fully loaded with metallic cartridges.

"Proferring the big weapon to Mr. Hara, he suggested a self-administered shot to the head, and Mr. Hara endeavored to comply . . . but as before, with the other revolver, all six cartridges failed to fire. A box of fresh cartridges was fetched, the weapon was reloaded, and the senior officer himself fired off two shots that left large, splintery holes in a ceiling-beam, then levelled the still-smoking piece at Mr. Hara and squeezed the trigger only to have the hammer fall on another misfire.

"They ended going through the entire box of cartridges, before they were done; those not aimed at

Mr. Hara fired without exception and with a great deal of noise, smoke and damage to the things the heavy, soft-lead bullets hit, but each and every time that the big pistol was aimed at Mr. Hara, the cartridges did not ignite, for all that the depressions left by the firing-pin were easily evident to the eyes of all the men present.

"Two Imperial Marines were called in, rifle-armed, bayonets fixed. The big, burly men were ordered to impale Mr. Hara on the long blades, only to see the steel inexplicably bend and snap halfway from points to guards when they tried to obey. Other things were essayed—a whole plethora of weapons and means of killing—but with no more success than that first, shattered *wakizashi*, and at that point Mr. Hara was told to return home and wait to hear from his superiors, who would have the unenviable task of retelling the whole, impossible tale to their superiors . . . and trying to convince said superiors that they were neither drunkards, lunatics nor liars in the process."

CHAPTER III

When at last he had snipped the end of his cigar, dipped it in cognac and carefully fired it, Pedro commented, "Now that, Danna, is not a task I would've liked to have to undertake and no exaggeration, either. Were these gold-braid types believed at all?"

She shrugged. "Mr. Hara has never known for sure. He does know that one of his seniors was ordered to suicide and did so according to form. Mr. Hara himself found himself taken by night and in secret aboard a merchant ship; there, he was told never to return to Japan under any circumstances nor to any other part of the Japanese Empire. He was told that he was legally dead of honorable *seppuku* and that his ashes would be put to rest on the very next day, so he was to choose another name by which he would henceforth be known. It was upon that dark night that he became Hara Tadahira. With the morning tide, he set sail upon his lifelong exile from his homeland."

"The poor bastard," said Pedro, feelingly. "But he never told me one word of all of this, Danna, in all the years I've known him. So why did he tell it all to you, an acquaintance of so short a time, I wonder?"

She shrugged again. "I don't really know, Pedro . . . and in a way I wish to hell he hadn't told me any of it."

"Why?" he inquired. "What you've recounted is a most singular tale, admitted, but I can't see any reason that it should've so shaken you up, not the M. Dannon Dardrey I know."

"Oh, but there's more to it, Pedro," she said, softly, adding, "and that's the part that curled my hair and innards."

"Mr. Hara recalls that the captain of that merchant ship was the only man aboard who knew anything at all of his last-minute passenger and seemed a little awed by him; nonetheless, he was eminently practical, too, and immediately he had ascertained that the strange man was a consummate ships' officer and navigator, he was more than willing to allow him to take the bridge on a regular basis, thus making it easier on his own, somewhat shorthanded crew.

"The broadbeamed ship was anything but a speedy sailor, Mr. Hara recalls, and they had been some three weeks at sea on the broad Pacific, far out of sight of any land, when one dark night he was called down from duty-station to supposedly advise on an equipment problem elsewhere on the ship. As he reached the bottom of a ladder, however, at least two pairs of hands lifted him from his feet and hurled him overboard.

"The ship had just then been steaming somewhere, he thinks, near the fiftieth parallel and the water was icy-cold, so he knew that he would not last for long immersed in it, nor did his frantic shouts apparently reach any ears aboard the ship. He could only keep swimming in her direction even as her lights drew farther and farther away to the eastward.

"He says that his body was beginning to stiffen with the deep cold, despite the heat engendered by his exertions, when he suddenly spied a sharp rising and falling. He thought it a mirage until he reached it, felt its solidity and realized that it was truly a half-swamped wooden boat. Once he had hauled himself aboard, he found the twenty-foot boat to be severely battered, oarless and half-full of water, although her hull seemed sound and her seams relatively tight. During his search for oars, he found a scoop and began to energetically bail out the boat. When he had gotten the water level low enough, he decided that this must have been some ship's lifeboat, for a waterproof locker in the bow contained biscuit, water, brandy and some other basic foodstuffs, a German-made flare pistol and a half-dozen flares for it. In a twin compartment at the stern was another supply of fresh water and biscuit, some simple fishing gear, a rubberized raincape and a rainhat.

"But, though provided with water and food, he had no means of propelling the boat and could but go wherever the winds and seas willed. Therefore, after he had partaken sparingly of his provisions, he rolled himself in the slicker—which item, having been cut for a large Caucasian, was more than expansive enough for his shorter, more slender stature—and sank at once into the sleep of exhaustion."

Once yet again, she rubbed at her forearms and said, "Now, Pedro, you can believe this next or not. Mr. Hara believes it and . . . and I do, too . . . I think. But it's screwy and spooky and . . . and . . . Well, anyway, here's what he told me.

"He says that the warm sun on his face wakened him and he sat up to a heart-stopping shock: he was no longer alone in the boat. Not only was he not alone, the man now seated on a thwart was known to him, though he had assumed him dead, drowned with all the rest of the crew of his ill-fated light-cruiser, storm-sunk in the Yellow Sea far to the west. His companion was none other than the Japanese naval officer—the Buddhist monk who had urged him, begged him to forbear from ordering the two great sea-monsters fired upon on the morning before the death of his ship and crew!

"At the first, Mr. Hara believed himself to be dreaming, still asleep or at least half-asleep and dreaming, but then, realizing that he was, indeed, fully awake, he could only sit, stunned, for a moment. Then he politely asked, 'Lieutenant Shimaszu, are you then a *gen,* an apparition come to haunt me?'"

"The man, who was not in naval uniform but rather garbed in the robes of his religious calling, bespoke Mr. Hara in a sad, gentle voice, saying, 'Honorable Captain, I am yet in the body, I too survived the shipwreck; no, I am no ghost, but neither am I truly with you here. You see but a projection of my body, a projection accomplished with the aid of some very learned and holy men. I am come to tell you of yourself, of your future life, that you will give over trying to end it abruptly.

" 'No matter what you may attempt, you see, it will be in vain, for by your deeds you have condemned yourself to life, life that can end only when you have redeemed those cruel deeds by way of actions which are preordained.' "

"Mr. Hara says that he then shook his head and avowed his complete mystification, his utter lack of understanding. He says that the likeness of Lieutenant Shimaszu then told him, 'Honorable Captain, I am forbidden to further enlighten you at this time, for you must gain wisdom that you now lack before you could hope to truly understand. You must seek out and learn wisdom and, in a future time, in a place far and far from here, we two will again meet, meet both in the true flesh. Then you will be told it all and, grown as you then will be in age and in wisdom, you will understand and accept your punishment and your destiny.'

"Mr. Hara says that then, of an eyeblink, the boat again rocked upon the sea, empty save for him. And, Pedro, he firmly believes this all, believes that it really happened, that he truly saw and heard all of it. Can you believe it, any of it?"

His answer was, "Do you, Danna? Do you believe him, his tale?"

She nodded firmly. "Yes, yes, I do. But don't try to probe into exactly why I do, just accept that I have my reasons for believing that old man, unequivocally."

Robert Adams

He shrugged. "Then what can I do save believe him too? For, as I earlier said, I've never known him to lie to me about any single thing. Was that all of it? How the hell did he get out of the middle of the North Pacific Ocean? Did the merchant ship steam back in search of him, then?"

"If it did, it never found him," replied the woman. "No, he continued to drift, helplessly, stretching out his food and fresh water as far as he could. Twice, at the cost of a very thorough drenching, he was able to collect enough rainwater in the rubberized raingear to refill both of his water containers, but he was almost out of food when, of a day, a flying fish—one of a school fleeing predators—plopped into his boat. He said that, although there was not much edible meat on the foot-long creature, he as able to use its guts for bait and thereby catch a sizable tomcod which fed him well for a couple of days, its body-fluids also reducing his need for water from his dwindling supply.

"Mr. Hara says that he can never be certain just how far he drifted in that uncontrollable boat but, as he never saw another ship at any distance, not even a smudge of smoke on the horizon, he knows that he was out of the shipping lanes. Then, of a night, he awakened from fitful sleep to see what looked to be a masthead light bobbing near the limits of his vision, to the southwards.

"Making great efforts to move slowly and carefully, he moved up to the bow-locker, retrieved the flaregun, loaded it and fired a signal high into the starry sky, then another and, finally, a third.

"The crew of the fisher that had found him were a mixture of Polynesians, ethnic Chinese and two third-generation Japanese, all out of Hawaii. They had had the misfortune, in a sudden squall, to lose their half-breed skipper and their rudder. Their mainmast also had been sprung at the same time and they were rather a dispirited lot, more than happy to allow Mr. Hara—who seemed to know what he was about—to take command.

"When he brought the battered vessel back to its home port, the owners decided he was a man worth keeping around, for all that he then spoke not a word of English. And so our Mr. Hara, scion of an ancient and noble Japanese clan, one-time noble officer of the Imperial Japanese Navy and captain of a large warship, became the hired skipper of small fishing boats in a backwater of civilization. He continued this work for more than five years."

Fitz had just finished eating his spit-broiled pheasant and was carefully sipping at his canteen-cup of steaming, fragrant tea when, with the now familiar faint tickling of the mind that bespoke telepathy, a "voice" declared, "I smell fresh meat and like, man, I'm hungry as a lion."

With that, a full-size blue lion strode from among the brush and bushes and rocks of the hillside into the tiny clearing before the rock shelter, facing Fitz across the firepit. His normal, baby-blue hue was closer to a royal blue, which fact told Fitz that he was or had recently been upset about something.

The blue lion flopped down on the rocky ground,

pointedly eying the pint-size antelope hung in the tree. "Hunting like sucked today, man," he declared dolefully, "Old Saint Germain must of like let some of his damn pets loose around these parts, them fuckers like scare all the game away from wherever they're at, you know, they stink as bad as snakes and alligators. I'm like flat bushed and my stomach's growling like I was still a damn old boar-hog, too."

Nestling his steel cup back among the coals, Fitz stood up, paced over to the tree, untied the rope, then took the lowered carcass over to the waiting lion. While the huge beast rent flesh and crunched bones, they continued to silently converse.

"Where's Sir Gautier?" asked Fitz.

"Well, like, man, he nor me expected you back so damn soon, you know. Like, you ain't been gone a whole day, you know. He went off to see could he find the rest his Normans, man. He shouldn't have no trouble there, like, man, he can just follow the stink." The feeding carnivore added, "He should ought to be back in two, three days, like anyway. Hang around, man. You can spend the time like shooting some more of these; they're good eating, see, but the little fuckers are like too fast for me to catch one, usually. I'll be done with this soon, man, hand me down that bird up there, too, huh?"

Fitz shook his head. "That pheasant's my breakfast, Cool Blue. Do you want what's left of the one I just ate?"

"Like is the Pope a Catholic, man?" was the lion's reply, "Like throw them over here; I'm like starving, tramping around these fucking boondocks all day for nothing but a few damn frogs. What'd you like do with the guts and the head and legs and all of this little thing, huh, man? Like they're some of the best parts."

But when Fitz had directed Cool Blue to the spot he had dumped the offal from his kills, little was left aside from bloodstained leaves and stray feathers. The lion's color became almost navy blue and Fitz ended by giving his companion the other pheasant, reflecting to himself that he could breakfast out of the supplies he had brought from the other world, Sir Gautier not being on hand to take a share. Then he banked the fire and zipped himself into his sleeping bag under the overhang, the entrance more or less blocked by rocks, the motorcycle and other gear and the huge, blue lion sleeping just the other side of the firepit.

Hungry as the lion still remained, Fitz doubted that any edible creature would survive long enough to get across the small clearing to the overhang and him, so he went to sleep feeling as secure as if he had been in the soft bed in his other-world bedroom, guarded by multitudinous alarms and a twelve-foot cyclone fence topped with barbed wire.

Nonetheless, he awakened a bit after moonrise to the certain knowledge that he no longer lay alone in the rock recess. Opening his eyes to bare slits, he could see between himself and the lit clearing a shape that was patently feline but clearly not the bulk of the baby-blue lion.

"Tom . . . ?" he projected telepathically, "Puss . . . ? Is that you?"

"Yes, my dear, old friend," came the silent beaming into his mind from the leopard-sized beast, moving close enough to lick at his face with a broad, rough tongue, "I am the creature you once knew as 'Tom.'"

As the hundred-and-a-half pounds of lithe, furry animal lay down beside and snuggled against him, Fitz wondered again—for the umpteenth thousandth time again—if this, any of this, was truly real and, if the events of these last few years had indeed taken place, how it was that they could be real.

And the huge grey cat read his thoughts, half buried though they had been. "Yes, my old friend, my dear friend, it is, has been and is now real. You must accept it, for all that there yet is too much of the mere human left in you to understand it. You must accept it on the faith that you will in time understand it all."

"Mere human, Puss?" he beamed. "If I'm not a human being, then what the hell am I, pray tell? What am I supposed to be becoming? A cat, like you? A lion, like Cool Blue?"

He sensed a gentle humor in the silent reply from the now-recumbent feline form. "When once you have proven yourself of true worth, have met with the Dagda and are come fully into your own once more—you and she who will be yours and the Keepers—then will you know and understand everything."

"What kind of an answer is that, Puss?" he demanded in clear exasperation. "Who or what is this Dagda, anyway? Danna says that in the old Irish folk tales he was supposed to be the king of the fairies. Are you trying to tell me that Danna and I are fairies, too?"

The big grey cat's tail which had been curled and twitching slightly began to swish from side to side with a degree of force, lashing against the sleeping bag and his legs within it. "You are trying my patience, old friend. All right, let me essay to put it in terms that anyone could comprehend:

"A lump of dirty quartz may easily contain as much gold as a shiny coin, but it will not be either beautiful or at all valuable to a human until the raw ore in the quartz has been leached out and refined. Lack of refinement does not lessen the fact that gold is contained in that rock; but only a human with the requisite training or at least experience would know that rock to be different from any other common lump.

"Now, before you first set foot to those stone stairs on the day you went about digging a grave for the husk my spirit had but so lately quitted, before you first entered this land called Tiro-na-N'Og, you were akin to that chunk of dirty rock, seemingly no different from countless other mere humans. But now, after having been within this blessed land for even as cumulatively short a time as you have, you are beginning to become refined metal; you are acquiring powers—re-acquiring them, rather—no human of the common breed could acquire such powers no matter how long he or she dwelt herein. And it is as I have told you in times before this: the longer you stay in, live in and on the water and foods of this land, the greater and more diverse will be the powers you reacquire. In the end, when the Dagda has invested you in the fullest as he alone can, you will be as the bit of pure, refined gold. You will be *Sheedey*, like the Dagda."

"*Sheedey?*" thought Fitz, blankly. "Animal, vegetable or mineral, Puss?"

The tail lashed again. "You are human, as the Dagda and the other *Sheedey*, but you are all more than simply human. You *Sheedey* are descended of the happy breeding between a very early stock of true humans with a few of the last living Elder Race, the beings who preceded you."

"Look, Puss, I realize this questioning is angering you, but if I don't ask, how can I be expected to understand any of it?" said Fitz. "Now this Elder Race, they must've been human too, in order to interbreed with humans, right?"

"Yes . . . after a fashion," was the panther's reply. "They owned the ability—which ability is one of the powers owned by the *Sheedey* when in possession of their birthright—to shift their shapes at will, even to utilize natural materials with which to fashion new or different husks to inhabit for however long a time they wished. The Elder Ones who bred with humans had human shapes . . . mostly. But so well made and accurate to the tiniest of detail were the husks they had fashioned for themselves, to hold their spirits, that the issues of these matings were so human-appearing as to defy human scrutiny. Only the spirits and brains differed from those of the true, pure humans. Among humans alone, without one to waken in them their powers, they might all have lived and died as the pure humans they seemed. But for them the Elder Ones were at hand to show and teach, to instill necessary self-discipline, to begin to channel the abilities of their few offspring and their many half-offspring, as well."

"If they could breed among themselves," queried Fitz, "then why breed with human beings at all?"

"The Elder Race," was the reply, "had exceedingly long spans of existence, old friend—thousands upon thousands of Earth-years did they naturally exist from whence they had come—but this place called Earth was not the place of their origin, and certain of its most common constituents were in ways inimical to their health and well-being. These elements not only shortened their lifespans and somewhat curtailed their powers but lowered their fertility drastically. Even so, it was the best place to reside that they had then found in the course of many lifetimes of searching.

"The exceedingly low birthrate was understood early-on in the earthly existence of this so-wise race, but it was nothing about which they then had much cause to worry—not back then, when so very many of them still existed. However, not even the Elder Ones were truly immortal and, as the courses of hundreds of millennia passed by on the Earth, their overall numbers became fewer and still fewer, as aged spirits flickered out faster than they could produce new carriers of the racial flame.

"Then did all of the remaining ones of the Elder Race meld their minds and decide upon a course by which they might, they hoped, prolong the unique and irreplaceable qualities of their race, if not the race itself. Over a vast span of time, they sought out and subjected to multiple testings a whole host of different creatures, beings native to the place you call Earth. At length, they all decided upon a certain kind of terrestrial primate; you know what kind they chose, old friend."

"Cave men?" thought Fitz, wonderingly, "Neanderthals? Cro-Magnons?"

The big cat answered, "No, those of which I speak now were a far less refined raw material than those of whom you are thinking; ten thousand of the then-generations of human life separated them from those chosen by the Elder Race, who then slowly—allowing almost all of the natural courses of events to take place—guided those chosen, obliquely controlled their breeding, the developments of a culture of sorts, provided them now and then with the germs of technology which could improve their chances of survival.

"In its fullness, time passed. Continents and islands and seas rearranged themselves upon the face of the planet, mile-thick ice-sheets expanded and contracted many times, lands rose above the seas, then sank back beneath them, seas themselves emptied out and their beds metamorphosed into bone-dry deserts or towering snow-capped mountains. A huge assortment of animals of all sorts died out in this time, but the Elder Race saw to it that the chosen species was spared despite their many and blatant vulnerabilities.

"At last, at long last, when the few remaining

Elder Ones felt that, were their long-envisioned plans to have hope of eventual success, they must begin, they went among the various groups of their primates and, again testing, chose those that they found to be the best—physically, mentally, emotionally—and, after bearing them to certain predetermined locations, began to assume shapes and breed with them.

"After several generations of hybrids had been guided and taught that which beings of power must know, the Elder Race determined that, although the hybrids and the get of the hybrids matured faster physically than did the pure get of the Elder Race, their powers were slower to develop and that, although significantly longer than pure humans, the life expectancy of the hybrids was even less than the severely-shortened lifespans of the still-extant Elder Ones. In hopes of possibly breeding to counter these distressing tendencies and traits, the Elder Ones visited the areas inhabited by the pure strains of humans on a regular basis, seeking out and bearing away healthy, young specimens of comparatively long-lived stock and with the best minds that pure-strain humans could be expected to have. In the enclaves, these specimens were bred to Elder Ones or hybrids and, very slowly, the strain was slightly improved.

"When enough mature hybrids were available to make it fairly certain that there would be plenty of teachers for the young they would naturally produce, the Elder Ones—having meantime discovered some large islands which contained fewer deposits of the natural elements which had proven so inimical to their kind—departed the enclaves, taking with them a few of the most promising of the newer generations, added a few more promising pure-strain humans that they gathered from here and there, then began all over again in the newfound, more-salubrious lands."

"Is this place, this Tiro-whatchamacallit, one of those islands, Puss?" asked Fitz. "What ocean is it in, anyway?"

"It is . . . and it isn't," replied the feline. "Once, long and long and very long ago, as humans measure time, there existed an island exactly like to this one in the world from which you came, but shortly after most of the great ice-sheets melted away, it ceased to be, as did the entire archipelago save one island. No, *Tiro-na-N'Og*, wherein we now lie, long ago ceased to exist in the world from which you came, old friend. Fish swim over its bones and sea creatures of the great depths crawl upon them, in that world."

"How did the inundations affect the breeding experiments of the ones you call the Elder Race?"

"The subsidences were mostly gradual, so no lives were lost among the hybrids. Some of them and most of the ever-fewer Elder Ones went to the one remaining island, which had been most northerly of the archipelago. Of the others, small groups roamed here and there for a while among the savage, predatory races of pure-strain humans. Here and there, a few settled amongst their near-kin and, with their powers and relatively advanced technological abilities, became leaders of one kind or another to the primitives they and their get came to rule. But each succeeding generation became shorter and shorter lived and possessed less and less of the powers until, in time, their descendants were only rarely different at all from their fellow pure-strain humans, so dilute had their precious heritage become.

"Other small groups, wishing to keep their heritage intact and pure in their children, sought out and settled in out-of-the-way places—mountaintops, oases deep in vast deserts, in the depths of swamps or the frigid wastes of the ice-lands, all of these places made comfortable to them by their great powers and that capable of being wrought by such powers. But these hybrids owned also great compassion for their near-kin, pure-strain humans, and despite the dangers—for more than just once, that great compassion for suffering beasts and humans has been the eventual ruination if not physical death of them and their get—they moved among their powerless kindred to teach them ways to live better-fed, more comfortably, threatened by fewer natural dangers. They did much to better the lot of the pure humans . . . and sooner or later all were repaid, but always in a hard, bitter coin—suffering and even death being the lot of some."

"Are there any of them still around in my . . . in the world I came from, Puss?" asked Fitz. "Any of the Elder Race or these hybrids?"

The response, though silent like all telepathy, bore a tinge of sadness. "Of the Elder Ones, old friend, no, there are none left in that world of humans and other beasts. But, yes, a few of the descendants of those who survived the subsidence of that archipelago still dwell here and there, though wishing to continue to survive, they have all used their powers to conceal their true nature from their still-savage near-kin, the relatively pure humans."

"These Elder Ones all finally died out, then?" asked Fitz.

"Five remain extant, in this world," stated the cat, "though even the youngest of them is old beyond the calculations of any pure-strain human. But not even the Dagda has knowingly seen or enjoyed converse with one in the space of centuries of human-reckoned time . . . or so I have been told."

"Then just how does anyone know that they are still alive in this world, or just how many they are, if they're not seen or talked to for hundreds of years, Puss?" demanded Fitz.

"They have ways of communicating, old friend," was the cat's reply. "Mostly they enter into the sleeping minds of the Dagda and other *Sheedey*, to explain and advise and teach, as they taught the hybrids of old."

"Why only in their sleep?" asked Fitz, puzzledly.

"Because," he was answered, "the Elder Race discovered, scores of millennia ago in the first generation of hybrids, that the minds of the *Sheedey* are most receptive, most porous, most retentive when generally unconscious to outside stimuli or influences. Also," the feline added, dryly, "in such a state, the pupil only hears, sees, smells and sometimes feels and tastes. He totally lacks the ability to ask endless questions, so the time of the teacher is not wasted in framing responses to trivia."

"Oh, really?" beamed Fitz. "Then if the pupil cannot ask any questions, how does the teacher know that the lesson has been properly and understandably conveyed?"

The tail lashed really hard, hard enough to cause a degree of pain in Fitz's legs even through the thickness of the insulated bag. "The Elder Ones *know*, as do all the *Sheedey* who are in full possession of their mature powers . . . as you will know too, if you will but hurry on to find the Dagda and be fully invested by him. He alone, of all the *Sheedey* in this world or the other, can render you fully awakened, can invest you with your full powers and thus see you become that to which you were born. Moreover, he needs you, he needs you soon; there are still many tests you must survive and precious little time remains.

"As soon as it is light, you must set out. Go east, go west or go north, but go."

"Not north, Puss," replied Fitz. "I tried that, only to end up at what looked like a bastard cross between a rain forest and the great-granddaddy of all swamps. The look of the place would've been daunting enough, but after checking with Cool Blue who said he'd been into it once, I decided there was just no way the three of us, a single Norman knight, a baby-blue lion and myself could handle the monsters Cool Blue says live and hunt in that place."

Once more the tail lashed. "There will be dangers, deadly dangers to threaten you in any direction you go. They are mostly tests and unavoidable, and they are assuredly deadly, but if you are to win to the Dagda's side and reclaim your heritage, you must meet and overcome them. Perhaps I erred in selecting the ensorcelled lion as your guide, but it is done now and soon, in any case, if you survive a few more tests, I will be able to place a second guide with you, as well as direct you to a place wherein you will be able to take possession of certain objects which will serve to increase those powers of which you are already aware and alert you to others you do not know you own."

"Fine," said Fitz, "but I can't start out in the morning, not unless Sir Gautier de Montjoie is back by then. He's gone off looking for his retainers. Besides, Cool Blue hasn't had good hunting and I more or less promised him I'd go down into the glen south of here and shoot him an antelope or four, in The morning. Oww! Damn it, Puss, take it easy with that tail of yours, will you? You break one of my leg-bones with it, and I'll be here a hell of a lot longer than just a few days."

"That man-became-lion," beamed the panther-sized feline, "thinks entirely too much about keeping its belly overfilled. He should know, as long as he's lived here in *Tiro-na-N'Og*, that no creature—from the greatest to the least—ever truly hungers for long here. Food abounds and all are provided their needs. Think, have *you* seen any emaciated creatures here?"

"No." Fitz unconsciously and unnecessarily shook his head. "Every beast I've seen or killed or butchered or eaten was sleek and well-fleshed."

"Just so," said the grey cat. "The lion needs only to apply himself to his hunting . . . unless he can delude another into doing his hunting for him, of course."

"All right," agreed Fitz, feeling like a taken mark, "I'll shove off in the morning: east, I guess. I'll send

Cool Blue to track down Sir Gautier and bring him back here, then leave signs they can follow to catch up to me. I'll head along that glen just north of here; as I recall, it runs roughly east-west."

"Be you cautious," admonished the cat, "for many and great dangers lie ahead along your path to the Dagda. I am forbidden to myself accompany you, as I have previously told you, else I would, old friend. It were better that you go not alone, but travel with at least one other; even the blue lion were better than none at all. So hurry slowly, take no unnecessary risks, leave clear and unmistakable signs for those to follow and allow them time to catch up to you. You mean more to this world than you presently could comprehend.

"Now, sleep."

CHAPTER IV

Fitz did sleep. He slept until he suddenly became aware that he was rolling down a grassy slope, vastly enjoying the feel of the coarse blades lashing at the skin of his nude body, just as he loved the feel of the hot sun and the sweet scents of the wildflowers and herbs that grew here and there among the grasses, the occasional puffs of warm, gentle winds.

At the bottom of the slope, he sat up and gazed out across a plain grown with higher, coarser grasses, dense stands of dark-green bushes and some scattered trees. In the dim distance, a small herd of wild cattle grazed and, closer to him, several cervines browsed on the fringes of a thicket of thorny shrubs.

Fitz had assumed that he was alone, but then a silent, mind-to-mind beaming asked, "Are you hungry, Seos?"

"No, I have no hunger for food," Fitz sensed no

return beaming of "his" body. "But if you do, become a deer, there are more than enough shrubs over there to feed another."

"I am rather going to become a cat and eat a deer," "said" the other. "What about you?"

"Sister-mine," beamed Fitz's body, "do as you wish, indulge yourself, for we two must return soon enough from this lovely place. I think I'll become a young bull and trot over to visit with the heifers of yonder herd."

"You would!" came the response. "Just for that, I should become a lioness and make my meal of young bull flesh, this day . . . but I won't. But before you change, watch me make my kill . . . please?"

"Of course I will, sister-mine. Then I will be able to use some of that kill in forming my young bull."

A few rods away, a slender but well-formed body rose up into the air, moved forward at some speed and then sank, as lightly as a falling feather, into the depths of the thicket around which the cervines browsed. To the mind of Fitz, the sun-browned body appeared to be that of a girl in her mid-teens, as totally devoid of clothing as the masculine body he just now inhabited. Like "his" body, the female's was possessed of reddish-blonde hair, almond-shaped blue-green eyes separated by the bridge of a straight, slender nose. Her face of course lacked the curly, fair beard that his bore, but both owned full lips that smiled often to show the white teeth. Fitz guessed her height at between five feet and five feet four, her weight at a hundred pounds, tops. Her nipples were the same red-pink as her lips and the breasts, though smallish, stood up proudly. Though her hands and feet were on the small side, they were proportionate to her body which, at the distance from which "his" body's eyes had viewed it, had seemed almost hairless, apparently hirsute adornments appearing only at armpits and crotch. The fine bones had all looked to be properly sheathed in flat muscles.

While the cervines browsed on, unsuspectingly, the eyes of the body within which Fitz was visiting continued to watch the base of the thicket, knowing what to expect to see.

Then, with the suddenness of a lightning-bolt, a yellow-and-black, hook-clawed streak launched itself from out the dense dimness of the thicket, landing squarely on the back of a plump doe. One taloned paw hooked under the chin of the frantically plunging deer and drew the head up and back so far and at such angle that the spine was compelled to snap . . . as it quickly did. As the dying doe sank beneath her deadly rider, the rest of the deer scattered at flank speed, making no single offer to fight, as was their natural way unless defending fawns or cornered by predators of any kind.

The cat speeded the death of the kicking, twitching cervine by using strong jaws and sharp fangs to tear out the throat, the torrents of deer blood from the veins and arteries drenching her yellow-gold, black-spotted hide, dripping from her stiff whiskers.

To his own big-boned, hundred-sixty-pound body mass, Seos began to gather and add a vast assortment of natural materials—animal (from the new-slain doe), vegetable (from the plants and trees and grasses all about) and mineral (from the rock-studded soil and that soil itself). Adapting, restructuring and shaping the constituents of all these in the manner first taught by the Elder Ones hundreds of generations before to the first hybrids, the blond young man slowly became transformed into a large wild ox—a bovine that later, much later, generations of humans would call aurochs or *bos taurus primigenius*.

The final creation was, to Fitz, impressive in the extreme. In this dream as in previous ones of similar nature, he was not only participant but observer, and so he could view the formed beast as from a close distance even while he realized that he along with his host-body were actually a part of the beast.

Its color was so dark a brown as to look almost black, which caused the two-inch-wide white stripe down the length of its spine to stand out in startling contrast. The long, thick horns were a yellowish-white, save at the sharp-pointed tips where they were shiny black. Under the glossy hide, the creature was a mass of thick bones, steely sinew and rolling muscles, a good six feet in height at the withers, with the big head carried even higher, the cud-chewing mouth and wide nostrils edged with off-white.

Within that huge, weighty, very powerful and vital body, Fitz noted how much concentration was required on the part of his host, Seos, to maintain his creation in its present shape and to prevent his own mind from becoming submerged in the simpler mind of the beast. Fitz, from his vantage point, could understand how such a thing was done but discovered that his own, human mind owned no words or even speakable concepts to explain it.

Then the young aurochs bull set out across the

rolling plain at a slow trot, leaving the "leopard" to her bloody feast just inside the confines of the thicket, admonishing him telepathically, "Have your fun with those heifers and cows, brother-mine, but be careful, too; big as you now are, you're still not as big as some of the king-bulls I've seen here and there. There still are but few enough of us and I fear that our sire would be most wroth were I to arrive back upon our island with only your well-horned body."

In great good spirits, Seos replied, "You be careful too, my sister-mate. That form you now inhabit is such as to set any male leopard to full arousal, and I think our sire might be equally wroth were you to throw before him a litter of furry, fanged and clawed grand-get. Hahahaha."

Despite the flippancies of the exchanges, Fitz knew that there was real and abiding love between the sister and brother, who also were sexual mates, in the ages-old tradition of their hybrid race, and both love and awesome respect for their sire, Keronnos, ruler of their small group of Elder Ones-human hybrids, resident on the rocky but verdant island in the midst of the sea.

The mind of Seos was as an open book to Fitz, and the man-bull was completely oblivious to the presence or delvings of the "visitor" within him. In the memories of Seos, Fitz could see that island—soaring peaks flung high above broad, long plains, little deep-green glens between hills, large and smaller streams of crystal-clear water flowing from the montane springs to cascade down rocks and race down hillsides and flow upon the plains and feed the lakes and ponds before finding ways to the purple sea—was able to know that, before Keronnos and his kin had come upon and settled it, there had never been humans or even primates thereon. Even now, after the passage of hundred of winters, there were few on the large island—though only a bit over twenty miles in average width, the island's length was more than eight times that distance—for, though the hybrids lived very long as compared to pure-strain humans, their birthrates were very low.

In hopes of partially rectifying these problems, Keronnos and all of the others had taken to seeking out among the smaller clans and tribes of humans in the lands and islands scattered around and about the sea, using their inborn mental talents to try to scry out supposedly-pure humans and find those who might own within them enough of hybrid descent and undeveloped but developable talents to make decent breeding-stock. Those chosen had been taken up and borne back to the island, set down upon it and given all that was needful for them to lead happy, healthy and comfortable lives—hunting, fishing, gathering wild plants, breeding kine and sowing crops in the rich, volcanic soil of the island—while the hybrids got children upon them or from them, guided them into breeding among themselves in ways that would concentrate and enhance their own heritage of talents, and undertook the awakenings and training and discipline of the ever-more-talented young.

Even so, people of any strain still numbered few upon the island and the hybrids still flew out over the surrounding lands and islands in search of promising humans for the carefully controlled breedings they had undertaken.

But this day, this trip to this land, Fitz realized, was not such a search-mission; it was rather in the nature of a romp for the sibling mates, Seos and Ehra, a vacation from the tight strictures of their sire and the other teachers of the young. For, although mature enough for most purely human pursuits, even for breeding, as hybrids their mental and emotional maturity lagged so far behind their bodies' that, in effect, they were only over-grown children. Not only did they naturally embody all the faults and failings of human children of similar mental and emotional development, they could add to them superhuman abilities—and, as their sire and other mentors knew only too well, this combination could, without discipline, sometimes produce devastating if not deadly results. Such unsupervised jaunts into distant lands were thus rare and precious to the hybrid young.

Seos made a good, believable bull, for it was far from his first inhabitance of a bovine body. Where not sown with grain and other crops, the plains of the island gave graze to herds of cattle which, although somewhat smaller, less rangy and much less ferocious, were still obviously the near kindred of the huge, fierce wild oxen that still roamed many of the lands surrounding the sea. Therefore Seos had been able to observe, move among and model the cattle almost since his birth.

Fitz could see in the mind and memories of Seos that there were other beasts and birds he enjoyed—sometimes he became a huge eagle or a monstrous, white swan, sometimes a fierce mountain ram, once a wolf, again, a bear or a boar or a desert lion. On occasion, he and one of his brothers had become long, sleek, black-and-white porpoises and swum through the sea off the island, chasing schools of plump fishes into the waiting nets of human fishers from one of the island communities.

But of them all, among all creatures he had been, Seos still most preferred being that which he now was—three quarters of a ton of big bones, muscles, sinews, speed, ferocity and such horn-tipped strength that not even the hungriest lion, the biggest bear would dare to attack him. Indeed, of all the predators in nearby lands, the mature auroch's in his prime and uninjured seldom fell to any save the increasingly rare long-tooth cats, pack-hunters such as wolves or hyenas or humans, or the almost-extinct dragons. But a herd of aurochs could usually stand off and drive away even these.

The big ox that was Seos-Fitz moved slowly, sampling a few mouthfuls of the herbiage along his way, tail swishing and skin twitching against the voracious, blood-hungry flies that swarmed about him. Along with the mind of his unsuspecting host, Fitz too was aware that, for all his impressive looks, the created bull-body was not quite solid, durable, for the parts of the doe not considered easily edible by Ehra in her leopard-body had simply not provided enough building materials of the proper kinds for Seos to use in creating a good, workmanlike construct.

Abruptly, as the bull crested a low-crowned hillock, he could first smell, then see just what he needed. At some time within the last few days, a largish hoofed animal—either a good-sized antelope or a short-necked giraffid, from the appearance of what the killer-predators and scavengers had left of it—had been slain and mostly devoured in the tiny hollow bisecting two of the grassy knolls. Now all of the flesh and organs were gone, as was most of the hide. All that remained, presently being gnawed at and worried by a brace of jackals, were some of the larger bones, three hooves and a pair of long, pointed horns still attached to the remainder of the skull.

A snort and a few steps of a mock-charge, huge head and black-tipped horns lowered in a businesslike manner, were sufficient to send the jackals scurrying up the opposite slope. Fitz wondered to himself what the matted-haired scavengers thought to watch their feast silently and utterly disappear into nothingness.

At length, everything finally absorbed into the created bovine body, the bull that was Seos and Fitz descended the knoll, trotted across the stained, much-disturbed level surface whereon so much feasting had recently taken place, then set his now more solid bones and muscles to breasting the upward way, the two small jackals scuttling before him, ratty tails tucked between thin shanks. Fitz realized that, had Seos intended to spend more than a few hours in the creation, he would have sought around and about, located more carnal refuse and picked over kills, and used them to give full size, weight and solidity to the bull, but this was but a romp, an outing, for he and Ehra must fly back to the island soon enough.

The bull, unlike Seos, did not see colors, only shades of grey, and his vision was clear only within a relatively short distance. But his olfactory sense was exceptionally keen, as too was his hearing; even from this far away his ears could detect the snarls of the Ehra-leopard, but even had the Seos part of the bull-mind not known just what the cat was, the animal-mind could identify the sounds for the warnings of a feeding feline, not the coughs and growls of a hunting-stalking-attacking cat. And no mere leopard would have dared to essay killing a bull aurochs anyway.

No, he need fear precious few creatures in most lands. True, the smell of lion had lain heavy about that kill on the remains of which the pair of jackals had been gnawing, but having fed so recently, it was doubtful if any save a very large pride would be hunting again so soon. Long-tooth cats liked hillier country than this, as too did the most of the land-dragons, while water-dragons never were seen this far from the sea or at least a sizable river, riverine swamp or deep lake. Smaller predators were dangerous to such as Seos now "was" only in numbers and could often be heard or scented from a distance, especially the two-legged packs.

Fitz could see in Seos' memories the two types of "dragons"—the water-dragon was a large crocodile and the land-dragon looked like nothing more than a lizard, but what a lizard it was. Could Seos' memories be believed, the thing must have been as long as the crocodile—between twenty and thirty feet!—and, although not apparently armored, of a lighter and more slender physique and with a long, tapering tail. The thing stood at least four feet at the shoulder, with a toothy, snaky head on three feet of thick, dewlapped neck, and every line of its scaly body spelled speed. Seos also recalled that there had been a related species— though larger—on the island when first the hybrids had settled it, but as the things were an ever-present danger to anything that lived and breathed, they had hunted them down and completely wiped the species out there. Pure-strain humans feared and hated the things too, and banded together to exterminate them whenever or wherever they were found, so the monsters were becoming exceedingly rare, rarer even than the long-tooth cats, in lands inhabited by humans or hybrids. Nor did it help their chances of survival that the larger of the monsters had an inborn proclivity to chase down, kill and eat the smaller whenever they could.

The young bull had been moving into the wind, deliberately, so that he was ever downwind of the herd and could scent it before his own scent was available to them. This was the cautious thing to do, for if the king-bull grazed with or close to the herd on this day, he was certain to take rather ferocious exception to a strange, younger contender for the favors of his cows and heifers. And it developed to be as well that he had so done, for closer in to the herd he smelled, not the scent of a mature king-bull, but the unexpected—the reek of two-legs, men. When he was come close enough to actually see the cattle, it was clear that they were some generations from the pure, wild strain. These had obviously been bred smaller, with shorter legs and horns, though still were they closely enough related to their larger, wild progenitors that their scent was the same.

Here and there about the far-flung periphery of the herd stood stripling boys and a few older men, some of them leaning on the shafts of long, stone-tipped spears, chewing on stems of grass and watching that their charges did not graze too far from the rest of the herd, while keeping a sharp eye out for any possible dangers.

As the Seos-bull came within sight of the herd, so did he himself come within sight of some of the watchers and these, too far away to themselves do anything about him, signalled to those closer with a series of meaningful whistles. To them, the advent of a wild bull was as dangerous and serious a menace as the appearance of a lion or bear or wolf, for the very last thing they wanted was to have the original size, horn spread and savagery bred back into their carefully nurtured strain of cattle.

Running at full tilt around one end of the herd, an older man—likely about forty, thought the hybrid part of the Seos-creature, with grey in his hair and beard, a profusion of puckered, off-color scars on his hairy limbs and torso, missing an eye and most of an ear moving with a slight but very noticeable limp, of late-middle age for a pure-strain human—took command of the striplings nearby. With a few panted words and gestures he rapidly formed them into a semicircle facing uphill and the strange bull, each of them now with a tall shield on his left arm and his spear presented and menacing. Then he set his troops in motion with a harsh, barked word, advancing on the deadly-dangerous interloper, hopeful of running him off without a fight, but certainly prepared to do whatever it took doing to keep him from their herd.

One of the striplings at the tip of the offensive crescent stopped long enough to take a hide sling from round his neck, load it, whirl it and accurately send a round stone against the near side of the head of the Seos-bull with such force as to bring a bellow of pain from the bovine creature. Seos knew that he had but two options, then: fight and kill all or most of the herd-guards—for they stood no chance of killing him since he was not real, fully-formed flesh-and-blood, only a clever semblance of a beast—or beat a hasty retreat. He chose the latter course, turning and cantering off in the direction of a stand of forest from which came the good, cool smell of fresh water.

A few spears were hurled after him, but the flights of the shafts were short, none of them intended to strike the flesh of the Seos-bull. The herd-guards leaped and cavorted in an almost-dance of victory, they shouted and shrieked and screamed in their guttural language, anything to relieve the tension and express their patent relief at being spared a combat which, had it been well and truly joined, would surely have resulted in the messy deaths of more than one boy or man and the crippling or injury of others. Full-grown wild aurochs of either sex never died easily, the butcher's bill for the hunters was always high, and not a one of the herd-guards was so young or inexperienced to not be fully aware of the grim facts.

The girl half-reclined atop a high rock that was the point of a narrow peninsula of bank jutting out into the stream. The gathering of edibles was usually good in the streambed and along its banks up here above the falls, but the crystalline water that flowed over and among the rocks was icy-toothed cold, telling of the high-mountain snows that spawned the stream, despite its meandering journey across the sun-dappled high plains. And so, periodically, she always found it necessary to find a place to sit or lie in the warm sunlight until the feeling was come back into her feet and legs and the skin of them was no longer all ridges and puckers.

She might not have suffered from the cold in the warmer, deeper waters below the falls, but there she would have been in danger from the water-dragons, which toothy, ever-hungry monsters now and again swam up from the sea to sometimes take their bloody toll of bathers—young and old and of both sexes—despite the best efforts of the priest-chief, the regular sacrifices of goats and all the prayers to the gods of their tribe and of this land.

Besides, her revered father often remarked on how much more tender were the greens from upstream, how much tastier were the shelled creatures she expertly plucked from among the rocks, and pleasing her tall, strong, powerful and wise father was of paramount importance to her, for it was through his loins that she and all her siblings were distant descendents of true gods.

The gathering had not been too good, this day—only some dozen of the shelled water-creatures and even them not so large as many a one she had taken hereabouts in times past, though a fair amount of tender sprouts of various greens—but she had lucked onto something that she knew was certain to bring a broad smile to show through her father's thick, sun-yellow beard.

The round, smooth rock was about as large as her two clenched fists together and might have passed for only another, streambed rock, had not a small chip been sometime broken from off one end to show the white stone within—very fine-grained and about the hue of the fat from a mountain sheep. Her father already owned two axes shod with this incredibly hard and long-wearing stone; he treasured them as he treasured little else, and she knew that he was sure to be inordinately pleased to gain the wherewithal to fashion another.

On impulse, she sat up and looked down into the water at the side of her perch, hoping to see yet another of the rare stones, but the rocks seemed all alike and she ended studying her own reflection in the relatively still pool.

Sighing, she shook her head of thick, black hair. She had always wished that she could have looked more like her father, as did some of her sisters and brothers, and less like her mother—who had been taken in war against a clan of nomads who had tried to seize and hold tribal lands, pushing up with their herds from the southwest, years ago.

All the warriors of the scattered settlements had gathered under the priest-chiefs and had met the invaders on the plain nearest the sea. After a day-long battle, most of the male aliens lay speared or axe-hacked and dead on that plain, with dust settling on their wide-staring brown eyes and their black, oiled, curly beards. Then the priest-chiefs and their still hale warriors had descended on the camp of goat-hair tents, pitilessly slain the old, the infirm and the ugly, then taken the remainder for slaves or concubines or, in the case of the prettiest, more biddable young women, wives.

The girl's sire had taken two attractive sisters and, though one had died in childbirth after a few years, he still felt well served, for he had by then had three sons and a daughter out of her, while her sister still remained healthy and fecund, throwing another child every couple of years as a woman of any value should.

She was just upon the point of arising and descending from the rock back into the knee-deep water to work her way back downstream when she noticed movement in the woods that came almost down to the edge of the stream-bank opposite her and she froze, for wild beasts often came to the stream to drink; she had seen the tracks of their hooves and pads imprinted in sand and mud and atop flat rocks, though seldom the beasts themselves, for most of them moved by night. And she had no slightest desire to meet one of them here and now, armed with only a small cutting-stone and a couple of scraping-stones, especially not one that looked so big as what was on the move through the gloomy shadows under those trees.

The Seos-Fitz-bull knew in its hybrid mind that the spearmen would not pursue him, follow after him, for their responsibility was to the herd and it was their assigned duty to stay nearby it, protect it and keep it from straying beyond easy protection. Of course, they would most likely put hunters on his trail, soon or late, for his huge body represented much meat, fat, horn, sinew, hide and other very valuable items, but by the time the hunters got around to undertaking the tracking of this particular bull ox, he would no longer exist in his current form.

Although the periphery of this wood was of the same thorny brush as the copse out on the plain where Ehra-leopard had killed the doe, within it was true temperate forest—mixed with deciduous and evergreen trees such as oak, maple, ash, pine, larch, walnut, elm and chestnut. Once under the shade of the huge-boled old trees, the bull's hooves sank fetlocks-deep into a mold of damp, dead leaves, wherein a host of insects, worms, mice and shrews crawled and scuttled about their daily lives. Squirrels chattered and scolded from the trunks and limbs of the trees, and a vast profusion of multihued birds occupied every level and flew through the air between those levels. Without exception the denizens of the forest ignored the interloping bull, knowing that they had nothing to fear from him so long as they kept from beneath his big hooves.

Unable to take a direct route to the enticing smell of the water because of the erratic placement of the trees, the bull continued to veer in that general direction and, at last, even his nearsighted eyes could detect the sheen of the sun on a stream. Pacing slowly and deliberately out from the shady concealment of the forest, the bull waded out into the stream and dipped his mighty head down to drink of the clear, cold water, ignoring the cloud of insects that came swarming from every direction to buzz and drone about him.

No truly wild beast survived long without being always on the alert for danger in all its forms, but not even this created facsimile of a wild ox was or could properly be an exception to the universal rule; therefore, when the bull, even as he drank up the water, heard the ghost of a sound, sensed a flicker of motion above and to his right-front, he abruptly brought his dripping muzzle up, snorting, one hoof unconsciously pawing at the water-rounded cobbles that covered the streambed.

On the point of bellowing his awful challenge, the Seos-bull caught full sight of the creature above him, atop the rock. Even with the lack of color perception he could identify the young woman as a stunning beauty of a human female. So much, in fact, did the observance of her lissome form attract and arouse the man within the bull that the hybrid mind let slip its control of the creation it inhabited and first small, then larger and ever larger portions of it began to slip away, slough off into the current to be borne away downstream, an unexpected feast for the water creatures, large and small.

As for the girl, crouched upon the rock with her baskets of gatherings, the cold, trembling, whimpering fear of the great, deadly and known-vicious wild ox rapidly became lost in a degree of awe that left her unable to move when she witnessed the quick transformation from beast into a tall, fair young man, resembling in so many ways her god-descended sire. In the inchoate turmoil that her mind was become, she knew that this could be, must be none save one of the true gods.

The last of the short-lived bull-creation dropped off into the stream, Seos waded through the icy water to the side of the rock, lifted himself into the air to its top and stood on the sun-warmed surface, devouring the recumbent girl's toothsome young body with his eyes.

The skin being darker to start, the sun had taken it to some shades deeper brown than his own, and not only was her head of blue-black hair thick, long, full and wavy, she owned more body-hair than Ehra or most of the other island-women, either hybrid or human—arms, thighs and lower legs having visible black hair, in addition to the thick, dark tangles protecting her pubes and armpits.

The eyes on either side of her large, aquiline nose were of a dark brown, with thick, black, arched brows and incredibly long black lashes. Her face was well formed, the dusky skin unblemished and the full lips of a dark-rose color, like the nipples of her proud, upstanding, pear-shaped breasts, these nipples surrounded by perimeters of black hairs. Though larger than those of Ehra, almost as large as his own, in fact, her hands and feet were both well and symmetrically shaped, while her body constituted nothing less than a broad invitation to a man so lusty as Seos.

Nor was it his accustomed way to even attempt resistance to such natural temptations or pleasures; he fell upon the ripe and ready offering nature had placed before him upon this altar of sun-warmed rock and had his way of her, as was his due.

Although he was helpless but to share the pleasure of the body he shared with the hybrid, Seos, Fitz was appalled at the hybrid's lighthearted commission of what was, to Fitz, an act of wanton rape, almost child-molestation. True, the girl had put up little resistance and had not cried out until she had been entered and deflowered, but the visiting consciousness ascribed that to, most likely, fear.

When he had spent and rolled off the now-bleeding little prize, Seos just lay for moments, breathing raggedly and allowing the love-sweat to dry on the surface of his skin, while his whole being enjoyed the warm, soft, delicious afterglow of successful coition.

At length, he rose up on an elbow to look down at the teary brown eyes of the girl beside him and asked, "What is your name? How are you called, little dark one?"

The girl knew that she must respond to the god's question and, her voice burbling on a gulped-back sob, she said, "Oo-roh-bah, o Sacred One. This one is called Oo-roh-bah, Daughter of the Priest-chief, Tur-ghos of the Two Axes. The mighty Tur-ghos, too, is of the Holy Race, Sacred One."

Something leaped within Seos at the girl's last words. "Is it then so?"

"Yes, Sacred One, God of Wild Oxen," she attested, adding a bit sadly, "Tur-ghos even looks like a god, but I, alas, resemble her who bore me by him, a dark woman of the desert, taken by him in war."

"If the resemblence is marked, little dark one," said Seos, "if the mother looked much like her daughter at the same age, then I well can understand why even a god-descended priest-chief would have felt impelled to take so rare and fair a woman to bear his sons and his daughters.

"But, Oorohbah, you do not understand; the marks of god-descent lie not in light hair or dark, fair skin or dusky, height or lack of it; no, the marks of god-descent are not visible to the eye. Let me enter your mind and . . ."

She whimpered, then, but he laid a hand upon one trembling shoulder to say, "No, there will be no pain to you, not this time . . . and as regards the other," he smiled warmly, "the pain will rapidly lessen and soon there will be none, only the natural pleasure of man and woman."

Only the briefest of delving into her mind raised his joy to fever-heights. Arising to his knees, he first took the girl into his arms, bade her clasp his neck tightly and close her eyes, not to open them until he so bade, then ascended high into the air and retraced his way to the copse of the slain deer.

Having finally tired of being a leopard, Ehra too had sent her body floating in the air and, at the edge of a wood, was watching with amusement the play-antics of a litter of striped piglets as they caroused around and over the snoring bulks of several sows, a huge-tushed boar and the rest of the sounder of older swine.

His voice calling her attention roused the entire herd of wild pigs. The piglets' raucous game broke up at a single grunt from the largest of the shaggy sows and, as they scurried to a place of safety behind her, the old boar and a brace of his almost-mature male progeny trotted forward to the point of danger, snorting, grunting, clashing their tushes, their huge heads down and pure murder glittering from their red eyes.

Floating higher, to his level, Ehra bitterly re-proached Seos, saying, "Now just look what you've done, brother-mine! And I was having so much fun watching those little piglets play. What is so impor-tant about a black-haired human female. Her sex-parts are bleeding, you know, you're all running blood from your waist to your toes . . . but if I know you and your infamous proclivities, you probably deserve it. Did you take her in your man-form? Of course you did, if you'd taken her as a bull the size of the one you were when you left here, you'd be carrying a corpse, not a living girl."

Gravely, he said, "I regret that I had to interrupt your diversions, sister-mine, but I think you . . . and our sire . . . will feel it well worth the cost. Enter this child's mind and tell me what you find therein."

After doing as she was bade, Ehra hissed sibilantly between her white, even teeth, then demanded, "How many like this are there, Seos?"

He shrugged. "I don't know . . . not yet. She avows that her still-living sire is god-descended, or hybrid heritage—however debased, in other words— and she has brothers and sisters all by the same sire and so, hopefully, sharing her mental talents. But before I or you scout out their settlement and try to enter more minds, it were wise, I think, that we bear this sample to father."

CHAPTER V

The clatter of the falling motorcycle awakened Fitz. Still half-asleep, he fingered the fast-release of the sleeping bag's zipper and sat up out of it, the cocked and levelled revolver in his hand, both his eyes and its gaping muzzle facing the sound of the noise.

Moving with an alacrity Fitz had seldom before seen him use, the baby-blue lion leaped backward, frantically beaming, "Hey, man! Like man, hold it, it's just me, the cat, don't shoot!"

Carefully, Fitz lowered the cocked hammer, then raised it enough to turn back the cylinder and leave the one empty chamber under the firing-pin. While doing this, he spoke telepathically to the lion, "Damn it, Cool Blue, to use your hipster jargon, that wasn't a very cool thing to do. What the hell did you knock the bike over for, huh? You scared the tar out of me and you're lucky as hell I like to make sure of a target before I shoot, because even big as you are, I don't think one or two of these forty-four magnums would do you a bit of good."

The lion, which had turned almost navy blue in fright, was slowly fading back to royal blue as he beamed aggrievedly, "Well, I like thought you meant to like sleep all day, man. The sun's done been up over a hour, now, and I'm so hungry I could scarf up cold horse-buns. It's time you went down south, there, and shot me . . . uhh, us, some eatments."

"No, it's not," replied Fitz, as he reholstered the revolver, "The grey panther, Puss, was here while you were snoring last night. She says that I *have* to start out today, not tomorrow, so I'll give you that hung pheasant and . . ."

"No, man," put in the lion, "it ain't no pheasant no more. After you like sacked in, I got so hungry I like chewed through the rope and scarfed that bird up, 'cause I like figgered you could shoot some more this morning, after you'd like shot me a whole bunch of them little antelopes, see."

"Thanks a whole lot, Cool Blue," said Fitz disgustedly, "I'd already told you last night that that bird was my breakfast. Some kind of trustworthy buddy you are!"

"Man, be cool," expostulated the lion, defensively, "Man, I was like *starvin'*, you dig? I was like almost as hungry then as I am now."

"Then why didn't you go off and hunt?" demanded Fitz. "That's what hungry lions are supposed to do, isn't it?"

"Now, how was I s'posed to hunt grub and watch over you while you was sleeping at the like same time, man?" the lion answered. "That's like my *job*, man, like taking good care of you . . . or at least, like trying to. if I'd of left here and a real lion or a bear or something had got you, that weird grey cat would of seen to it. I stayed in this lion getup like forever."

"Thank you for your entirely unselfish solicitude for my safety and well-being, Cool Blue," beamed Fitz sarcastically.

The sarcasm was completely missed by the blue lion. "Aw, hell, man, it's no need to like thank me; like I said, it's my job, man. You gonna shoot us some antelopes now? Just three, four'll last me most of the day . . . and maybe that dumb Norman dude in the steel T-shirt'll be back by then."

As he began to dress, Fitz beamed, "No, Cool Blue, I am not. Since you saw fit to purloin my planned breakfast, I'll eat out of my supplies this morning. That done, I am gong to crest this hill, go down into the glen just north of us and start hiking west.

"You, because with your lion nose you can trail by scent, are going to set off after Sir Gautier. Once you find him, you'll bring him back to this cache long enough for him to take this pack that will be waiting here for him, then you and he and any of his men he could locate are going to set off on my trail at top speed. I'll be moving as slowly as I can and blazing trees at intervals along my path. Understand?"

"Man," exclaimed the baby-blue lion, "you've like flipped your everlovin' wig! You know that? You go around like setting trees on fire, you gonna burn down the whole, fucking woods!"

Fitz sighed. Yet another failure to adequately communicate with the hipster-trumpeter become lion. He asked, "Were you ever in the Boy Scouts, back in the world you came here from, Cool Blue?"

"Aw, hell no, man," was the reply. "I'm like a city dude, man. I like concrete under my feet and flush toilets and showers and all and I have since I was like a little kid, too. I lived in a fucking leaky tent in the stinking mud and slush and snow and all and froze my balls like almost off crapping in a hole in the ground 'long-side of the bush-niggers in the Army in Korea 'cause the fucking Government gimme like no damn choice. But even before then, when I was just a little kid, I wouldn't of like lived like that could I of helped it, and that's the kinds of living the fucking Boy Scouts thinks is the best fucking thing since sliced bread! Like, why, man?"

"Because, Cool Blue," Fitz informed him, while rolling his sleeping bag tightly enough to fit it into its case, "if you had been a scout you would have understood what I said about leaving a well-marked trail to guide you and Sir Gautier when you follow me west. Now, watch."

Taking a machete, he left the rock-overhang and paced across the minuscule clearing to the largest of the nearby trees. With a light, glancing swipe of the sharp blade, he took a strip of bark two inches wide and about six long off the trunk at the level of his chest. A few seconds of whittling at one end of the barked area with the point of the blade gave a reasonable representation of an arrow, its sharp tip pointing uphill.

Turning to the lion, he beamed silently, "That is how you blaze a tree, Cool Blue. I'll be doing that along the way west that I take. All you and Sir Gautier have to do is follow the direction pointed out by the blazes. Okay?"

"But, man," pled the lion, piteously, "I'm like starving! I kept by you all night and now I'm so empty I just like got to have some meat before I can go do anything, you know. What you going to eat?"

Fitz shrugged. "A can of beans, I guess, while I hike; I don't want to take the time to start a fire. I slept longer than I meant to. Why, do you want a can, too?"

"Cold canned beans?" queried the lion, "Oh, God, man, like don't even think gaggy things like that! That's as bad to think about as fucking Yew Ess Army fucking C-Rations is. Like if I wasn't so empty, I'd be like puking my guts out, you know that, man? That's as bad as a gook's been scarfing up stinking *kim-chi*."

Fitz grinned. "I rather liked *kim-chi*, myself, Cool Blue—hot peppers, celery-cabbage, white radishes, plenty of garlic, all nicely fermented in a stone crock . . ."

The baby-blue hue had lightened into almost an ice-blue; the lion looked really ill. "Oh, Christ, man, like stop it . . . *please!* All right, I'll go after your pet Norman dumblock for you. We'll look for them chops in the trees, too, you know. Just promise me you won't never again talk about barfy things like that, 'specially not if I got a full stomach. Like I can't *take* it, man. You know?"

Fitz nodded. "Fine, Cool Blue. You get going, then, I'll do all that's needful here, then hit the trail myself. Be certain to bring Sir Gautier back here to pick up this pack, this belt and the things that are fastened to it, okay? They'll be in front of the motorcycle, just behind the brush and rocks I'll use to close the front of the opening. I hope to see you soon. Good hunting."

"Oh, sure; that's like easy for you to say." Grumbling, his belly rumbling, the big, blue beast set off up the rocky trail toward the hillcrest, but slowly, maned head low, tufted tail barely clearing the ground.

"You like better be careful out there alone, man," he beamed back. "Because if it *is* some of ol' Saint Germaine's pets is loose is why the big game is all hiding or bugged out for safer stompin' grounds, the fucking monsters is gonna be hungry as me and you're gonna look like a nice snack to them and I don't think all the bullets in that humongous rod of yours could stop one of the big ones 'til after it was way too late for you, man. Like 'til I get up to you with the Norman, you better like bed down in trees— big trees, too, thirty feet up in them, anyway, so's them buggers can't just like rear up on their hind legs and sink their choppers in you, man—don't none of them like to climb trees, maybe they can't, I figger.

"Ain't you got *nothing* I can eat before I go? No meat at all, man?"

"How about a can of lima beans and ham chunks, Cool Blue?" offered Fitz magnanimously, maliciously adding, "Or real GI spaghetti in meat sauce?"

The color of the still departing lion paled briefly and he made a noise that the man could not identify —it could have been a growl or a groan. Then the beast was out of sight among the brush and tree-boles and rocks.

* * *

As was his gallant way, Pedro Goldfarb walked Danna Dardrey to the place wherein her car was parked in the cavernous, echoing, near-empty parking-garage. Squinting through the ill-lit gloom, he asked, "Where did you stash your Jag, Danna? Are you sure this is the right level? All I can see is a Pontiac wagon with a flat and that Mercedes sedan over there."

"That's the car I'm driving now, Pedro: the Mercedes, Fitz's Mercedes. The Jaguar needs a new alternator, it had to be ordered from England and the service manager—that slimy little creep—at Gouge and Robb wouldn't even agree to place the order unless I left the car there."

"Ridiculous!" snorted Pedro in disgust. "You should change shops."

With a wry smile, she shook her head. "No such luck. Gouge and Robb are the only game in town. Not too many folks around here drive Jags anyway, you know, and that set of chauvinistic, unhung thieves and lechers own the only authorized repair franchise in this part of the state. I had this same problem every other time I've needed work on it; I guess my vaunted, female masochism is the only reason I hang onto the albatross . . . aside of course from the humble fact that, when everything in it is working right, it's the most responsive and dependable car I've ever driven in my life."

The dark-haired man nodded in sympathy. "I understand, it's your money-hole, like that sailboat I had—when she was good, she was very, very good, but when she was not, which it seemed was most of the time, she was more expensive than you could possibly believe. Well, at least you now have two or three replacement vehicles—the Mercedes and . . . what is it out there, a Jeep wagon?"

"At Fitz's?" she answered. "Yes, a Jeep Wagoneer, this sedan and his Mercedes 450, too."

"Nononononononono!" said Pedro, shaking his head while shaking a finger at her. "You must watch what you say, Danna, Blutegel would be overjoyed to try to hang a perjury rap on you . . . me too, for that matter. The house and property out there, and everything on or in them, are *yours*, including all the motor vehicles! Fitz signed them over to you quite properly and, more important, quite legally, in payment for services rendered. Everything is all duly signed, sealed, adequately witnessed and recorded in all the proper places. Remember what we used to say back during World War Two about loose lips."

"But Pedro," she protested, "just you and me, talking alone in an absolutely deserted place like this at whatever godawful hour of the morning this is? Aren't you getting a little bit paranoid on the subject?"

"Not at all, Danna," he assured her in his normal conversational tone. "Have you read a book called *The Privacy Invaders?* No? Then by all means buy a copy and do so. It's frightening the amounts of state-of-the-art equipment various governmental agencies have at their disposal whenever they want it . . . and they don't always have to have a court order to put the stuff into use. They can sometimes just use it for fishing expeditions against law-abiding citizens they for one reason or another want to get."

She sighed. "Pedro . . . ? Look, I know you're

very tired, just now, but . . . but, Pedro, you're beginning to sound too much like Gus Tolliver used to sound in his endless diatribes against the Department of the Treasury. Coming from him, it was, as Hamill says, just one of Tolliver's kinky quirks; but when I hear the same things from you . . . well, it's scary."

"Sorry, Dana, I didn't mean to frighten you, just to alert you that we two are not really on firm footing in all of this Fitz-business, despite appearances to the contrary, and we have to exercise exceeding caution every waking minute. You know, much of all that Tolliver used to bitch about was correct, pure and unadulterated truth; both you and I and any other tax attorney or CPA worth his or her salt knows that the tax laws of the United States of America are in no way or means fair to the vast majority of the taxpayers. But those unfair laws are on the books and only Congress can change them. And with most if not all of the Congress in hock up to their bushy eyebrows to lobbies and vested interest groups who all profit from the existing laws and situations, don't try holding your breath until anyone up in D.C. does the fair, decent, moral thing and changes the status quo.

"Now, get in your car and warm it up. I'll stay here until you pull out."

"Oh, Pedro," she protested, "you're tired, you need to get home too. Inside the car with the doors all locked, I'll be okay the few minutes . . ."

"No, we'll compromise and do it my way, if you please . . . or even if you don't, Mrs. Dardrey," he

105

stated in no-argument tones. "You are of value to my firm and I always take good care of items of value."

Later, on her drive home through the light drizzle and lighter traffic, she again shivered and took alternate hands from the wheel to lay the gooseflesh on her arms. Should she have told the rest of Mr. Hara's weird tale to Pedro? After all, she did not represent the wizened oriental gentleman, so what he had told her was not privileged information; nor had he asked that she not impart his recountal to anyone else. Could what the aged man had said and—her probings of his mind had proven—truly believed, be true? Not too long ago she would have written Mr. Hara off as an elderly, gentle nut, possibly senile, but that was before she had met Fitz and had, herself, experienced so many utterly impossible things, before she had learned how to use her mind to enter the minds of others and determine whether or not they were lying, whether or not *they* believed what they were speaking aloud.

And speaking of weird, impossible, unexplainable things, no one had taught her how to silently probe minds. Yes, Fitz it was who had showed her how to converse silently, telepathically, but she had come up with the idea of probing for truth or, at least, belief, entirely on her own, as she had lain, thinking and reading in the cabin of the wrecked ship they called their "sand yacht" after the sound of the engine of Fitz's motorcycle had faded into the far distance.

Up there in the office tonight (this morning? whatever), she had rationalized it in her conscious mind that her employer, her dear friend, Pedro, was clearly very tired, despite his apparent animation and energy, and so it would be better to cut the recountal short to possibly be completed at another time. That was what she had told herself up there, then, but now, alone, she admitted the truth to herself. Until she had more proof, more substantial evidence that. . . ?

"That what, Danna?" she spoke aloud in the empty sedan. "That an old, Japanese Buddhist monk or friar or whatever they call them believes—really and truly believes—you and Pedro and even Fitz, a man he hasn't even met yet, to be some kind of gods, real *gods*, for God's sake? Try getting solid proof of *that*, Mr. Ripley! I can just see the headlines screaming out now: Danna Dardrey proved god . . . no, I guess that would be goddess, in my case.

"Mr. Hara believes that a whole race of gods used to live on this earth, that some still do and that he has met two of them so far: first, Pedro, now me. But that's not enough. He says and he honestly believes that he has to meet three gods, has to see them awakened to what they really are, that that's his ordained mission in his present incarnation.

"Wacky sounding? You bet your ass it is! But he's a truthful, honest, very intelligent and very wise old man . . . *and he believes every word of it*. So, where do we go from here, Milady-Goddess Danna?"

She had been halted at a red light and, when it changed, she slowly accelerated into the intersection. All of the time she had sat there, not one other vehicle of any description had graced visible portions of any of the streets, yet she had barely started out when, with horn blaring wildly, a large, battered sedan made a wallowing turn out of an alley and roared through the red light, very narrowly missing collision with her. Half a block to her left, the offending car essayed a U-turn, skidded on the wet blacktop and fishtailed up onto the sidewalk, through a chain fence and crashed into the side of a parked delivery-van.

Shaking her head and muttering disgustedly about drunken drivers, she continued on toward her apartment building, still undecided about whether to tell Pedro all of the rest of Mr. Hara's strange story. She needed peace and quiet in which to think the thing through and she thought she knew just the place in which to do it.

After seeing Danna into her automobile, the engine properly warmed up, the vehicle put into gear, backed out, and headed for the ramp down to the ground level and exit gate, Pedro Goldfarb walked briskly back up to the elevator and depressed the "down" button, his own auto being some levels lower. He waited more than the usual amount of time for such a late hour, then depressed the button once more; but there was no noise of mechanical movement from within the shaft and the level-indicator number never changed or even blinked, so with a shrug the dark-haired man walked the few feet to the door opening onto the stairs and lightly and rapidly descended to the proper level, then pushed open the door and went up the ramp toward his parking place.

There were a few more vehicles still parked on this level than had been on the one above, but even so the impression of the place was one of deserted, lonely emptiness. Therefore it as almost shocking when up ahead an ignition ground briefly, then an engine roared into life, taillights glowed as the auto backed out of a slot, halted, then accelerated down-ramp, all four headlights glaring blindingly in the ill-lit gloom.

Disturbed that the driver of the oncoming vehicle seemed not to be in perfect control of the car, as if he was unfamiliar with it or had steering problems or, more likely, was a few sheets to the wind, Pedro eased a little farther over to his left and quickened his pace, wishing that the erratic driver would hurry up getting past him.

But he was still a good thirty feet from his own vehicle when the almost-new Bonneville suddenly swerved frighteningly close to him, came to a rock-ing stop and two men came out of the nearest doors to confront him. Even in the less than adequate lighting, Pedro could see that one of them, the smaller, was holding a large pistol—a Colt Government Model from the look of it.

Smiling in what he hoped was a disarming man-ner, the attorney said, "Gentlemen, I've something like a hundred and fifty dollars on me. It's in the wallet in the left breast pocket of this jacket. I've used the Colt Auto in combat and I'm not about to try to give you a reason to use that one."

The tall, skinny pistolero nodded at his massive companion and the big black man stepped behind Pedro, jammed hands and arms under the attorney's arms and locked ham-sized hands behind his victim's neck in a full-nelson hold. That was when Pedro decided that this was not a common run-of-the-mill mugging and that he just might be in real trouble this time around. All good attorneys left a trail of enemies in their professional wakes and Pedro knew he was no exception, but he also knew that he never before had so much as seen either of these two men, so most likely they were hired help and could he make it worth their while, then perhaps . . . ? It was, he felt, worth at least a try.

Looking up from beneath his brows, which was the only way he could see with his head being forced forward and down by the thews of the big black man, he addressed the man with the pistol.

"Do you know who I am? I'm Pedro Goldfarb, an attorney. I own a law firm in the Mutual Building. I don't know who hired you on to do his dirty work, I don't know whether you're supposed to beat me or kill me, but I'll guarantee you that I can pay you more *not* to do it than whoever is paying you *to* do it."

"I done thought you 'llowed you dint have but a hunnerd an' fifty dollars, Mr. Lawyer-man?" rumbled the man who was holding him.

"That is all I have *on me*," responded Pedro with alacrity, "but as I just said, my offices are next door and there's more money, there—cold, hard cash-type money. How much is whoever hired you paying?"

The gunman had thrust the big pistol under his waistband and now he stepped closer, saying, "Don't you tell the bastid nuthin, hear!" With that, he cocked back an arm and slammed rock-hard knuckles into Pedro's abdomen, first one fist, then the other.

The punches hurt, of course, but they were not crippling; Pedro was in very good shape, far better shape than most fifty-five-year-old professional men, and he had tightened the dense layers of muscle which protected the organs of his flat midsection. But he had also come up with another plan, since he no longer was so urgently threatened by the big, deadly weapon.

A heightened degree of acting skill is a required talent in a top-flight trial lawyer; Pedro Goldfarb possessed such talent and to spare. At the second blow, he gasped in what sounded like an excess of agony, then slumped limply, allowing the big black to support all his weight. Gasping, speaking jerkily, he informed and beseeched, "Heart . . . bad heart . . . please, nitro . . . glycerin . . . bottle, right side pocket . . . ahhhh." Then he made a gargling noise for emphasis and offered a prayer that it would all work on his assailants.

It did. The man holding him demanded, "Well, what you waitin' for, man? Git the damn heart-attack pills outen his pocket and then put one in his mouf, unner his tongue is what you do."

Wrinkling up his brows and shaking his head slowly, the other just stood, saying, "Aww, I dunno. He could be fakin' you know. And . . ."

"And he could be the best thing to dead right now, you dumb, white-trash, honky fool!" rumbled the black man. "And if he comes for to die here, now, with us here doing what we's doing to him, we gone be charged with capital murder, man!"

"Shit!" burst out the other man, "I ain't hit him hard a-tall, hear. A frigging heart attack ain't murder, you crazy swamp-guinea."

"Yeah, well, my one-time brother-in-law, he was

burglaring a place where the old lady lived there had herself a heart attack and he hadn't never touched her or hardly seen her and he's right now doing hard time, twenny-five years to life, cause she come to die while he's in her house that night," declared the massive black, loosening his hold on Pedro's neck and letting his thick arms, alone, support the dead weight of his victim. "You wanna spend the rest of your natcherl life in the penitentiary or wearing a lowng chain and picking up trash off the innerstates, you gone do it all alone. Now am I gone hafta get the man his medicine my own sef, okay?"

From one of the still-open doors of the Pontiac, a raspy voice demanded, "What the diddly-squat's going on? You-awl gonna work the prick ovuh like we's told to or run your mouths and trade fighting-words or what? Thishere wheels is hot, baby, and I ain't gonna be caught driving this heap in the daytime, hear me?"

"The gennaman's done had him a heart attack," stated the big black man. "Mr. White-ass Knowitall here wouldn't get him his medicine out his pocket, and I think he's dead . . . or closes' thing to it."

"*Sheeeit!*" With no other words, the driver put the big sedan in gear and, with a screeching of tortured tires, he headed for the downramp, open doors flapping unheeded. At the ramp, the left side of the car sideswiped one of the concrete pillars and, all the way down the spiral toward ground level, the nerveracking shrieks of metal scraping against the sidewalls of the ramp could be clearly heard.

"Couldn't keep them big liver-lips shut, could you, boy?" snarled the skinny man. "My paw allus did say didn't none you damn niggers have the *GAARRR-GGHH!*"

That was the sound the man made when the toe of Pedro's fine, Italian-made ankle-boot came into such hard contact with his exposed crotch as to almost lift him completely off his feet. At the same time, the "dying man's" elbow accurately found brief lodgement in the big black man's solar plexus. Both movements were executed so swiftly that even as the gagging, retching and thoroughly agonized skinny man's legs began to fold under him, his erstwhile victim was able to step forward and jerk the pistol from under his waistband.

With the skinny man writhing and moaning and gasping on the hard concrete floor, while the huge black man simply stood, eyes bulging from the sockets, hands lapped over his lower ribs, mouth wide open, making earnest, frantic efforts to again start to breathe, Pedro stepped back a few feet and hurriedly checked the weapon he had acquired. He found one round in the chamber and six more in the worn magazine of the battered, rusty piece, so he engaged the safety and took the cracked grips loosely in hand.

"If either of you types try to run or to hide," he informed the men, "I'll shoot you in the back; that's no threat, that's a promise . . . and I always keep my promises, in case you didn't know. When I was in the Marine Corps, I earned an Expert Badge in this and a number of other weapons."

Having spoken, he strolled down to the emergency wall phone and lifted the receiver. When a voice responded, he said, "This is Pedro Goldfarb. I'm on Blue Level, on the exit side, and I'm holding their own pistol on two men who tried to mug me. Call the cops, huh?"

By the time he got back up to the site of the confrontation, the big black man was painfully taking ragged breaths of welcome air, though he still had not moved at all and did not look very well. "I guess I should watch how much force I put into blows," thought Pedro. "But big as he is, strong as I know he is, I was afraid to try to pull that elbow any."

The skinny man had assumed a foetal position on the dirty oil-stained floor, both his bony hands clutching at his crotch, sobbing, the side of his head and face in the middle of a puddle of his vomitus.

"The police are on their way," the attorney said, in an almost-friendly tone.

"Oh, Sweet Lawd Jesus," prayed the biggest man aloud and with intense feeling, "please save this sinner from going back into the slam!"

"Done time before, have you?" asked Pedro, adding, "Well, you and your buddy here are going to do a lot more time for this night's work. I hope you got paid in advance."

"How come you's thinking we won't just mugging you, mister?" asked the big man, diffidently.

"Because neither of you made a move for my wallet, even after you'd been told where it was and how much was in it," Pedro replied. "No, you were hired and set on me to rough me up, hurt me, for somebody—somebody too cowardly to try to do his own dirty work. I am quite anxious to find out just who paid the freight, obviously. You know that I'm an attorney, I told you that already. I just might be able . . . or willing to help you if you tell me the name or names of the scum who hired you."

The black man gulped. "You . . . you'd let me make tracks 'fore the Man gets here, mister?"

Pedro nodded. "If there's still time. Otherwise, I could help you beat the rap . . . if I felt friendly toward you, that is. What's your name?"

The man gulped again. "Welford Roosevelt Harrison, suh. Whatall you want to know, suh?"

"What is the name of the person who hired you, Mr. Harrison?" demanded Pedro. "How much were you all paid and what were you to do to me for your money?"

Harrison waved at the oblivious, still agonized skinny man, saying, "Thet damn white-trash cracker, there, he hired me, after that chickenshit Junior Jackson, who was driving, had got in touch with me for him. Junior and me done time together back when we's both kids and he knowed I's needing money some kinda bad, too. I tole him I tole Junior I won't gone have nuthin' to do with any killin's for no amount of money, but they said you won't to be killed, just busted up bad and scared off. That and the fifty dollars they promised me was the onliest reason I'm here, suh. And that's the God's honest truth! I told Mr. Meems, there, I'd hold you, but I won't gone hit you none unless you hit me and he said that was a'right 'cause he liked to hit and hurt rich swells like you."

"All right, Mr. Harrison, now comes the question that, if answered to my satisfaction, just may keep you on the street: Who hired Mr. Meems, do you know?"

Harrison shook his head and gulped again. "All I knows, suh, is he was rattlin' on about how the money for me and Junior was ever last cent of it comin' out of his pocket, 'cause of some feller with the Guvamint wanted you hurted but won't payin' none of it. Sounded to me like as how he musta had suthin' on Mr. Meems, is what it sounds like to me, suh."

Though a bit stunned by the revelation of government involvement, Pedro did not show it. "Did Mr. Meems mention a name of this man who wanted me beaten and scared off, Mr. Harrison?"

The big man nodded slowly. "Yessuh, yessuh, he did and it was a damn weird, funny, furrin' -soundin' name, too. But he dint say it but one, two times and I don't remember it . . . I don't think. I'm sorry, suh. Lordy, am I sorry. I . . . I guess you won't let me go now . . . or . . . or try to help me none, huh? I'm sorry, suh." Pedro saw something glistening on the man's dark-skinned face—either sweat or tears, maybe both.

"Think *hard*, Mr. Harrison," he ordered in a command tone, "if you don't want to be looking at the world through steel bars for the next few years, dredge up that name for me. *Now!* What letter of the alphabet did it start with or sound like it started with, Mr. Harrison? *Think*, man!"

The big man gulped yet again, then uttered what sounded very much like a sob, nor was there any longer any doubt that the rivulets of wetness on his forehead and cheeks were both sweat and tears. He started to speak several times but closed his mouth each time, he screwed his eyes tight shut and, at length, said, "Uhh . . . a 'B' . . . I thinks it was a 'B', suh, that that name started out with. But . . . but I still can't remember it all, suh."

Off in the distance, in the quiet, dark, drizzly night, the wail of sirens could be heard, approaching.

Now sweating almost as profusely as his sometime-attacker, Pedro thought hard and fast to cull up names of government types he had defeated or put down hard enough to merit this kind of violent retribution, over the years. "All right, Mr. Harrison, I'm going to call off some names. You tell me if any of them are the name used by Mr. Meems . . . or if any of them even *sound* like that name. Okay?"

The black man's head bobbed. "Yessuh."

Still thinking even as he spoke, Pedro said, "Baxter? Terry Baxter? Bendarian? Bryson? Banduccu? Bloom?"

"Suh . . . ?" Harrison stopped him, hesitantly, "That there last name you named off . . . that won't the name Mr. Meems used . . . but it had a sound suthin like the firstest part of it . . . at least I thinks so. . . ?"

The sirens were getting closer and louder, moving far faster through the benighted, near-empty streets than they ever could have moved during any weekday.

Pedro thought even faster. "Bloom? Bloooom? Blum? Blue, maybe? No, Harold Blue was one I defended, and won, too; so he wouldn't be sending thugs after me. Bloom? Bloo—of course! Of course, that cruel, vindictive bastard will be a long time forgetting—and he'll never ever forgive—what I did to him that day out at Fitz's place, and in front of a woman—Danna—and one of his fellow agents, too."

To the sweating, crying, trembling Harrison, he said, "Here's another name for you: Blutegel, Henry Fowler Blutegel."

"*That's it!*" gasped Harrison, "Oh, thank you dear Lord God, that's the name, suh! Blooot-ehgul, that's the funny name of that feller Mr. Meems said a couple times comin' ovuh here in that car Junior'd done found and hot-wired."

When he had used his special key to unlock the door which led from the parking garage to the Mutual Building, Pedro handed the hulking Harrison two twenties and a ten, plus his business card, hurriedly saying, "Okay, Mr. Harrison, I'm fulfilling my part of our bargain. I always keep my promises, remember that. Get in touch with me sometime after this mess has all cooled down. We may be able to do occasional business, you and I; there are times when a big, strong, intimidating man could come in handy for me and my firm. Now, you take the stairs down to the lobby, make sure the watchman doesn't see you, and go out one of the doors on Fifth Street, that's a long block from here. And try to stay out of trouble, eh?"

He shut off Harrison's blubberingly tearful thanks by firmly closing the door and using the key to once more throw the deadbolt and activate the alarm. Then he trotted back up the ramp to where Mr. Meems still lay moaning and clutching himself at the epicenter of his pain. He had but just reached his victim when the first police cruiser sped out of the up-ramp and onto Blue Level.

Clearing the pistol and expertly locking the slide open, he expelled the magazine and handed all three items over to the first officer to get out of the cruiser, saying, "There he is. I doubt he'll be any trouble for awhile, not after being kicked in the balls as hard as I kicked him."

"Where's the other one, mister?" demanded the second officer, "The feller called us said it was two of them."

Pedro shrugged, shook his head and said, ruefully, "He got away, officer, I thought he was down for the count, too . . . but I must not have hit him as hard as I'd thought I did. Anyway, he just jumped up and ran down the exit ramp. I might have shot at him, under other circumstances, but just look at the sad shape that pistol is in. Would you shoot it if you didn't have to, officer?"

"Could we see some identification, please?" the second one asked in a near-polite manner. "I know who the guy on the phone said you were, you understand, but I need to see for myself, too."

With his identity clearly proven, the two men became much more friendly and almost fawningly polite. They took down his description of the other assailant (not that he gave them a completely accurate one) and, upon the arrival of a second car bearing aboard a sergeant, a search of the premises was ordered and commenced. Of course, said second assailant was not found and it could only be assumed that, in order to avoid the exit gate and guards, he had possibly climbed down the outside from the second or third level to a point where he could safely drop to the sidewalk.

"I 'spect that there boy's long-gone by now, Mr. Goldfarb, sir," averred the sergeant, "but his description's out by now and all the rolling patrols'll be on the lookout for him. Can you go back down to the precinct with me and look at some mug-books, tonight, sir?"

Pedro sighed with a genuine weariness. "Sergeant, I can . . . but I'd rather do it some other time. I have to be in court tomorrow and I think I should get at least a few hours of sleep beforehand."

"Cert'nly, sir." The sergeant proferred a card. "Just you call thishere number and ask for . . ." he took back the card briefly and scribbled a name on the back of it, then returned it, "ask for Detective Langford; I'll have been done filled him in on everthing, sir."

and the K-Bar and odds and
and boots and I'm bound t
damned easily over two-
"Yet, here I am, fi
I was never any ki
nut, either. I
in at the e
vacuum
haust
do

For all that he packed a third again the foods and supplies he had at the beginning of his first hike, only a few weeks before, Fitz still experienced only slight strain in lifting the load and shrugging into the straps, nor did it seem at the outset to weigh all that heavily on him, even with the additional items on his belt and the drilling-gun slung on a shoulder, all three barrels loaded.

"Not too bad," he chuckled to himself as he started off up the brushy slope toward the crest. "Hell, not bad at all for a man of my age, come out of an urban culture in the United States of America, circa 1976; despite what my muscles try to tell me, this pack can't weigh in at less than ninety pounds and to that you add a full canteen, cup and cover—another four rounds right there—about three and a half pounds of pistol and eight pounds of drilling, plus the machete

ends, plus my clothes
                be carrying and carrying
                thirds of my total body weight.
                ty-six years old and doing it all.
                nd of lunatic body-builder or health
                recall that, not too long ago, I'd come
                d of a day of lugging around just a lousy
                cleaner and briefcase abso-fucking-lutely ex-
                ed, so tired it was often all I could do to put
            wn some food for Tom, take off my shoes and coat
and tie and pour myself a stiff drink. Back then, I'd
have needed a dolly to move the load I'm now carrying for any distance, or a wheelbarrow, anyway. Hell,
back then I'd have most likely been huffing and
puffing, wheezing like a ruptured bagpipe and seriously wondering if my heart could take it from just
trying to climb a slope like this carrying no load at
all. So how? Why? What made me different, huh?
It's almost as if I'm growing *younger*, for God's sake,
not older! And Pedro Goldfarb, others too, have
remarked that I'm looking not only more tanned,
fitter, but younger, too.

"So, what brought all this about? Answer me that,
Fitz, my lad. Could that be what Tom . . . Puss . . .
the telepathic grey panther I keep dreaming about
(but am I *really* dreaming at those times? It all seems
so real . . . ?), when he . . . she talks . . . beams
thoughts concerning certain powers I'm in the process of gaining or regaining, is it part of those powers, becoming younger and stronger? Maybe, but
somehow I get the impression that that's not really
what Puss is talking . . . thinking (oh, the hell with
it!) *talking* about, so that still leaves me with the
beginning question not yet answered.

"This island or whatever it is (and I'm starting to think it's not in the real world, the world into which I was born, at all, if any sane man or woman could believe it) is truly, unmistakeably a weird place. Just look at the wildlife, for a for instance, as Mom used to put it in her County Wicklow brogue.

"Starting out where I first started out, back to the south, on the beach, that beach and the miles of dunes that back it, just seems to go on forever; I once rode for almost three days east and never found an end or any real change to it, then did the same thing westward for the almost identical result. It's just all the same, everywhere along it I've been, sand and surf and dunes, gulls of five or six kinds, long-legged beach birds, short-legged beach birds, insects, crabs (good eating, too, most of those crabs, especially those with bodies the size of a football), driftwood and more shells than I've ever seen on any beach, anywhere, plus bunches of seaweeds of several kinds, dried sea horses and sand dollars, strands of shark-egg pouches and what have you . . . but all, every bit of it, natural, not one single bottle or beer can, no disposable diapers, no plastics of any kind, no soggy wads of paper and, with the sole exception of that wrecked hulk of a galley (no, that's right, a dromon), no worked wood even.

"Those fish I've seen or caught by surf-fishing don't seem to be unusual, though there were a few I'd never seen before. I'm sure there're more than a few fish I've never seen before back where I came from, too. The seals that occasionally flop up onto the beach look like seals. But that humongus crocodile, the one Puss calls Kassandra: now, she's something else again—at least forty feet long and with jaws ten or twelve feet long.

"She's the only weird animal I've seen on the beach or among the dunes, but the plain beyond those dunes is different. There're enough strange critters there to make up for the beach and more. And up here in the hills . . . whew! There is up here, in these hills, glens, and plateaus the damnedest mixture, the most jumbled conglomeration of animals I've ever before seen or even heard about. There're more kinds of deer and antelopes than I knew existed in any one place, easily a thousand different kinds of birds, squirrels of sizes and colors I can't find any references to in any of my wildlife books, monkeys, flying lizards like those out on the plain but bigger and more colorful. And Cool Blue's memories show lions (real lions, not ensorcelled beatnik musicians, like him), leopards, wild boar, bears, some kinds of shaggy, horned things that could be bison except their horns are too long, two or three kinds of really big—moose-size or bigger—cervines with unbelievable racks of horns, and some other beasties I can't find described anywhere. Then too there's the thing that scared him out of that big swamp up north of here: his mental image looks like nothing so much as either a dinosaur or an honest-to-God, fire-breathing, mythological dragon.

"North of the chateau of the man he calls the Count of Saint Germaine, the one he says ensorcelled him into his current lion-body, he says there are unicorns, though he never saw any of them. He also says that this man or wizard or whatever he is keeps an assortment of monsters for pets, but I've never been able to find a clear, close-up memory of one of them in his mind.

"Sir Gautier, now, says that he and his bunch of misplaced Crusaders wandered for awhile on and around the fringes of a plain whereon were elephants —he didn't know the name of them but his mental images were of small herds of what looked to me like Indian elephants, the ones with small ears, not big ones like the African elephants have—plus some kind of animals with bodies like big deer but with unbranched horns on their heads and a single, forked one on the nose. Then he saw some things he called 'humpless camels,' but the picture his memory brought up looked more to me like a bastard outcome of crossing a giraffe with the biggest llama you could imagine. The other animal that made a real impression on that doughty knight was, if his memory is as accurate as usual, of a breed to make a lasting impression on anybody—the all-time biggest, bulkiest, hornless rhinoceros's body on a set of legs from a vastly oversize African elephant so that its belly is a good twenty feet of the ground. But he said that the pair of the monsters he and his men came across at the edge of the forest was very placid, just ignored them all and kept feeding of the top-shoots of thirty-foot trees.

"Still, at that time, having Cool Blue's swamp-dragon in mind, I at once thought of dinosaurs and questioned Sir Gautier in some detail, but up close they were obviously mammals of some strange breed. Their skins were wrinkled and in folds at places but not scaled, and they did have hair, though not much of it. The real proof, though, was the one he saw closest: she had what could only have been nipples on her abdomen, four of them, each about the size of my head.

"I hope to God that if I run into anything bigger than those two, it's equally mild-mannered. But, thinking of big beasts, here I've been hiking up this glen for nearly three hours now, and the biggest things I've seen have been squirrels and birds. Where the hell is all of the game? I may just end up eating out of cans again tonight, if this keeps up."

Since Fitz had come down the northern slope of the hill and proceeded westward, the glen had opened up, become much wider, with good-sized expanses of grasses and weeds and dark-green herbs now flanking the broader, shallower and less fast and turbulent stream. But he had been hiking farther up on the hillside, at the brushy fringes of the mixed forest that clothed it, so that he would have tree trunks to blaze as mark of his passage for Sir Gautier and Cool Blue.

It had been his experience that these glens commonly teemed with small game and often larger animals as well—rabbits or hares, racoons, a multiplicity of rodents, odd little animals that Sir Gautier called *desmana*, birds ranging in size from sparrows to wild turkeys, occasionally a colony of oversize gopherlike animals that he had tried, at Sir Gautier's urgings, and found delicious. Sometimes there were to be found one or two or more deer of some variety in the glens, as well as opossums, armadillos, wild goats and pairs of spike-horned gazelles about the size of grown collie dogs.

But even though he was moving far enough up the slope not to spook or frighten animals down below, nearer to the central stream, he had seen few birds of an edible size and no furry beasts bigger than a rat, save for the large and smaller arboreal beasts and birds that all seemed to be staying high up in the trees, not foraging the forest floor as was the normal wont of many of them.

"If it's been like this for long," he thought, "it's no wonder poor Cool Blue was so hungry he ate frogs. Even a good, determined hunter would have trouble feeding himself . . . and I somehow feel that Cool Blue is more determined on finding someone else to feed him than he is on feeding himself by his own efforts. Something has clearly scared all of the game into lying up in the safest places they can find, but I don't think that something was me. So what, I wonder?

"Wait a minute. Cool Blue, yesterday, when he first came into camp there by the overhang, was opining that this Saint Germain character had let loose some of his so-called pets to run in the hills and glens and that they'd scared all the game away. Then, too, last night, what was it Puss had to say about me going on west alone? Something about many and great dangers is all I remember clearly now. But Cool Blue said I should sleep in tall trees, I do recall that, and it sounds reasonable. You can't build a cooking fire in a tree, but if I have no fresh meat to cook, what the hell will I need a fire for?"

He walked onward along the verges of the forest of pine, hemlock, maples, beech, basswood and occasional ginkgo, hacking a mark into a trunk every few hundred yards. He noted that, ever so gradually, the grassy lea downslope was narrowing on either side of the stream and that the stream itself was growing narrower, deeper and faster-flowing. In the distance ahead the wall of trees looked to be solid, but as he neared he could discern the reality.

The glen he had been following for most of the day ended in a narrow, water-filled declivity, the swift-flowing stream finally leaping out over a rocky lip to fall fifty feet into a broad pool at the base of a steep, precipitous cliff. The ground below was invisible under a deep carpet of needles from the towering, straight-boled pines, whose upper reaches had aided in giving the appearance from afar of an unbroken wall of trees.

Fitz looked down the almost vertical cliff face and hissed between his teeth. Glances to right and left through the mists of water spray indicated that at no point was the dropoff any lower than it was here. He uncased and tried his binoculars. Yes, a long way off to the south, the cliff-line did seem to converge with a ridge, but it was a really long way south, maybe far enough to put him back in the range of the Teeth-and-Legs, and this time lacking either speedy transport or his big elephant gun. Besides, that far a passage through even moderately heavy forest and its associated brush-thickets could conceivably take days, even as much as a week, for one lone man to hack his way through, and Puss was certain to strongly dislike the delay.

He peered down the cliffside again; it didn't look to afford a descent any whit easier or safer on the second look than it had on the first. Where not covered with soggy-looking mosses and lichens, the rocks all were shiny-wet and crumbly, like sandstone. There were plants—pine seedlings, vines and herbs—but not a one he could see that looked as if it could bear more than its own weight.

With a sigh and a shake of his head, he doffed the pack and unlashed the coil of rope. On the verge of looking for a secure anchor up where he was, he suddenly snapped, aloud, "Damn me for an idiot! It hasn't been even two full days and I clean forgot what Danna showed me how to do. That's the best way I can think of to get down this in one piece. Of course, how Sir Gautier and Cool Blue will get down is another question, but from what I've gotten to know of that little Normal, I guarantee you he'll find a way to do it."

When he had tied the coil of rope back into place on the pack frame, he removed his pistol-belt and secured it too to the pack, then emptied his pockets of every iron or steel item and stuffed them in a side compartment of the pack. All this accomplished, he closed his eyes for a brief moment, concentrating to recall the exact mindset required, remembered it, and smiled to himself.

Setting his mind just so, he willed the pack to rise. It did not; it just sat there and glared at him. He tried once again. The contrary pack still sat in place on the dead leaves and coarse pebbles. Consciously forcing down his emotions, he carefully ran his hands over his body, finding nothing of the iron or steel which he and Danna had found were inimical to the practice of lifting things with their minds . . . nothing, that is, until his hands reached his boot tops. With the brace of boot-knives stowed away in the pack with the other ferrous items, he tried yet again, wondering just what he would or could do if his newfound talent failed to work this time, too.

But this time the laden pack frame rose. He halted its rise at his waist level, then took a strap in hand and towed it, now light as a helium-filled balloon, to the lip of the cliff; there, he gave it a gentle push and mentally triggered a slow descent. Gradually, as he watched, the load sank until it was pressed deeply into the bed of pine-tags.

After he had released control of the pack, Fitz gulped once, resisted an impulse to sign himself, then bade his own body to rise from the ground. When more than a foot-distance of empty air lay between his boot-soles and the pebbly soil, he willed himself forward, toward the edge of the steep, high, treacherous cliff. All too soon he was past the last of that top, was hanging unsupported over terrifyingly empty air, the needle-covered ground and his pack looking horrifyingly far below his all-too-vulnerable flesh and bone.

Ever so carefully, he willed his body to sllooowlly descend. And it did just that, even more slowly than had the pack. Once again standing with his boot-soles pressed upon hard, solid ground, Fitz realized why his jaws had been aching so severely and with effort unclenched his teeth.

"I DID IT!" he shouted joyously, "By damn, I did it! It works! Dammit, I really can fly! How many other men of my age or any other can fly without some kind of mechanical contrivance, huh? But, by God, old Fitz sure as hell can!"

Feeling suddenly very, very tired, he sank down beside his pack, thinking, "Danna can do it too; she could do it before I could and showed me how, for that matter. I wonder if I can pass it on? I'd like to be able to teach Sir Gautier and Cool Blue and Puss how to do it. If they all could do it along with me, we'd sure get to wherever I'm supposed to be going one hell of lot faster and easier, I'd think."

Reaching around the pack, he unhooked his pistol-belt, buckled it back around his waist, then replaced all of the smaller items of iron or steel into pockets and boot tops before pulling out his canteen and filling his mouth with the water. It was become warm as blood in the closed container, despite the cooling evaporation from the thoroughly wetted cover. He spat the mouthful into the pine needles, emptied the steel bottle and levered onto his feet. Kneeling at the side of the broad pool, he reached out as far as he could and submerged the canteen long enough to fill it, took a long, long drink from it, then submerged it again before replacing it in the cover. On the point of arising, he noted the strange tracks imprinted in the sandy soil right at water's edge.

He thought for a brief moment that they were handprints, there being five digits and an impression that could have been a narrow palm, but then he looked closer to see that the digits obviously mounted claws and that the one on each foot that seemed to be at least partially opposed was on the outside, not the inside of the foot. Where had he seen—and fairly recently, at that!—a print similar to these?

He suddenly remembered, and jumped backward from the pool so violently that he ended up sprawled helplessly on his back for a long moment of terror before he regained his balance and his reasoning took over.

Big as those prints were—they each were much

bigger than his hands—they still were nowhere near the size of those of the nesting crocodile back on the beach. Steeling himself to go back and examine the prints once again, he could easily discern other differences than just size. The digits were, proportionately, longer and slenderer, not intended to bear as much weight; and too, there was no trace of webbing-scuff between the digits. The conclusion to which he finally came was a big lizard of some kind.

"Seems to be nowhere in sight now, whatever it is," he tried to reassure himself. Nonetheless, before he reshouldered his pack and started on westward, he drew the shot-loads from the two smoothbore barrels of the drilling, replacing them with solids—twelve-bore rifle slugs. He also filled the empty chamber in the cylinder of his revolver.

The waterfall and its pool-basin fed a stream that flowed roughly westward, and Fitz followed the waterway for more than two miles beneath a canopy of pines, some of them towering over a hundred feet, he estimated. There was little low-growth or brush to impede his progress, for so deep and dense a layer of resinous tags was sufficient to effectively discourage or choke out most other plants, that and the shade cast by the spreading branches high above the ground; even so, he quickly learned the folly of proceeding onward without probing his footing with the butt of his staff, for beneath the endless bed of needles—in some places, as much as two feet deep—lay such obstacles as fallen limbs, loose rocks and, not uncommonly, whole boles of fallen pine trees. However, there was no dearth of tree trunks for him to blaze along the way.

Near the confluence of another, smaller stream flowing down from the north to join that which he had followed all day, a very large—over three feet to tip of tail, he guessed—and oddly colored squirrel scolded loudly at him from high up in a tree that Fitz thought looked very much like a chestnut. And as he tramped on along the banks of the enlarged stream, he saw the pines slowly, grudgingly yield up their hegemony to hickories, yellow poplars, sweetgums, smaller varieties of conifers and a real profusion of oaks, many of the deciduous hardwoods clearly of great age, incredibly thick-boled.

The sun, though still bright, was approaching the western horizon when Fitz came out into a small, relatively open spot where another small stream, threading through a narrow, brushy gorge between the two rocky hills that lay to the north, flowed down to add its waters to the now fair-sized stream. Some yards farther west stood an oak that he knew must be six feet thick in the trunk. There was no single limb or branch less than the height of the dangerous cliff his new talent had allowed him to so easily master, and some of the limbs above were thicker than the boles of some of the surrounding trees. Proper precautions being taken, any one of those limbs should provide him a safer and secure, if a bit hard and unyielding, sleeping perch for the night, he thought.

In the wake of having seen the possibly sinister tracks by the pool earlier in the day, and recalling the warnings of Puss and Cool Blue, he felt distinctly edgy at again stripping himself of all his weapons beneath the shade of the massive oak, and constantly looked about him, his eyes peering deep into thickets of brush, his ears striving to detect any untoward noises, body tensed to spring for drilling or revolver.

This time, he raised both himself and the pack together, though he suspected that if while flying he was compelled to lay hand to one of the firearms he would drop like a stone and the pack with him, no doubt. How could he find or buy weapons that incorporated no iron or steel . . . ?

On a hunch, Fitz left the pack sitting securely on a thick limb while he rose even higher in search of he knew not what. But when he found it, he recognized it for what it was on first sight.

At some time in the dim past, some titanic force had snapped off the one-time crown of this particular oak and limbs had then grown from out the trunk just below the shattered stump. All of these new-growth limbs had, of course, reached up toward the sun, the source of life, and as they had flourished and grown in length and thickness, putting out branches of their own, they had almost hidden the area which once had been the upper reaches of the oak's main trunk.

Presently, in the heart of the profusion of limbs and branches, there existed a declivity of sorts that was actually longer than the thickness of the lower trunk. It was filled to some depth with dead leaves, acorn, chestnut and hickory-nut shells, squirrel droppings and remains, fleas and other insects.

Fitz considered sinking down to the pack and bringing up the blaze-dulled machete to use in cleaning out this arboreal Augean stable, then, grimacing in chagrin, thought better on the idea—touching the machete with its steel tang and blade, he would lack the power to keep himself aloft and, should he by mischance fall from here, he might not have the time to drop the tool and reestablish weightlessness before he made violent contact with the hard ground sixty or eighty feet below.

Hanging in the empty air, Fitz stared at the decaying, flea-hopping mass of animal and vegetable matter, all become or well on the way to becoming humus. This place would no doubt be more than a little uncomfortable for him through the night, but it could easily be made almost foolproof insofar as falling out of it was concerned and, best of all, he doubted that from the ground his presence therein would be even suspected, far less seen. True, a predatory beast might scent him, but it then would have to climb up at least forty feet of thick-barked bole before reaching any limbs and, hopefully, he would hear and be warned by the rasping of claws as the creature climbed.

But if he slept in this uncleaned mess, he would be a virtual flea circus until he could find a place and time safe enough to immerse himself and wash body and hair free of the maddening parasites. However, to simply plunge his arms into it or kick it out would be to end with the same infestation, so how?

From a crevice between two limbs, the chisel-teeth of a long-deceased squirrel winked at him, grinning at his dilemma. Almost without conscious volition, Fitz raised the small skull from its resting place to see it discolored and porous with the effects of tannin and advanced decay, the antennae of what looked to be a large woods-roach wiggling from out an empty eye socket. Hissing with disgust, he floated the thing and its passenger out into empty air and abruptly released his control of it, watched it plunge to the ground and shatter on impact with a knobby root.

"Goddammit, I'm dense as this tree trunk anymore," he exclaimed. A layer at the time, he proceeded to "think" the years' worth of debris and detritus up from the place of its lengthy lodgement, float it out to random spots among the tree boles and release it to shower down to the ground. When he was down to bark and wood, he floated up the pack, fumbled within it for a few moments, then thoroughly dusted the uncovered area with insecticide. Only then did he begin to prepare for his night's stay.

His meal of canned spaghetti and meat and a handful of raisins washed down with water from his canteen was filling if not very satisfying. As long as there was light, he sat in his aerie and sharpened his machete, but as the light began to fail, he spread his poncho over the floor of the declivity, unrolled his sleeping bag and, after anchoring the bag to convenient limbs or branches with lengths of rope, took off his boots, loosened his clothing and zipped himself in with his knives and his pistol, though he felt safer this night than he had on any other, camping out in this place.

However, despite his unwonted safety, his bellyfull of food, and his overall tiredness from the long day's hike, he could not find enough comfort in his commandeered squirrels' nest to sleep. Rearranging the positioning of the sleeping bag did no good, nor did trying to adjust placement of his body in the narrow cavity on and around the bumps and lumps of the uneven surface. He deeply regretted, now, his decision not to include the air mattress in the pack load, this trip. He even thought seriously about flying back to the rock shelter to fetch it.

Then, "I wonder if . . . ?"

After once again sitting up and partially unzipping the bag, he loosened the safety ropes for a few inches all around, lay back down, rezipped the bag and ordered his mind. Slowly, a bit jerkily at first, the bag rose to the limits of the restraints. With his weight it sagged alarmingly in the middle, nor did he know for sure just how much of the undue strain the fabric and stitching would bear without rupturing in one or more spots.

A bit more thought saw Fitz release the mental injunction on the bag, again unzip it, and leave it long enough to use rope and the tough, surplus poncho to fashion a rude hammock, then anchor the bag both to it and the branches. Of course, the poncho sagged too, but he knew damned well that his mere hundred-and-fifty-odd pounds was not going to even approach tearing the rugged, GI canvas.

"So," he mused, as he at last began to relax in comfort and drift off into slumber, "this miraculous new ability I've found I have isn't always the best thing to use in every case. I'll have to remember that." And, almost asleep, he addended, "If I'm going to be putting weight—mine or that of anything else—on objects I cause to rise, they're going to have to be objects already possessing enough strength or rigidity to hold weight without sagging, tearing or cracking. Like other more mundane abilities, I guess, it's a judgment call of just when, where and how to use it, or whether to use it at all."

The mantle of sleep closed over Fitz, enfolded him in a great, warm, comforting blanket of oblivion. Then, suddenly, he was wide awake, completely aware, and *flying*.

For a very brief microsecond of time he panicked, thinking that somehow, in some way, without really knowing it, he must have released the zipper, floated up out of the sleeping bag and was sailing, sleep-flying, through the nighted forest. But then he fought down the blinding panic long enough to realize that wherever he now was it was not night but, rather, broad daylight, and that below him lay the rolling swells of open sea, not forest. With calmness came too the realization that his mind was no longer in his own body but once more a "visitor" in that of the blond-bearded young man, Seos—he who had fashioned for himself and for a brief while inhabited the massive body of a huge, wild bull; he who had turned himself back into a man and, with his man's body and unbridled lusts, had so horrified Fitz's civilized, Catholic morality by callously violating the virginity of a dark-haired young girl atop a rock beside a stream; he who then, immediately after the carnal crime, the mortal sin, had proceeded to kidnap his child-victim with the stated purpose of bearing her off to where he dwelt, surely for no purpose which would stand scrutiny, Fitz had thought.

And, as before, Fitz could hear, see, smell, taste, feel, even share in the memories and ongoing thoughts of the young man, Seos, but only as an observer. He could exercise no control over his host.

Now the violated young dark-haired girl (Oo-roh-bah, Fitz recalled she had named herself, as she had sat disheveled and weeping in a pool of her own blood atop the rock whereon Seos had raped her that day) flew beside Seos, on his left hand, while the young, blonde woman, Ehrah, was on his right. Fitz had been less than certain of the relationship between Seos and Ehrah, for although they addressed each other most often as "brother" and "sister," he had thought to sense in their conduct one toward the other an intimate if not an actually sexual familiarity; a delving into the memories of Seos had deeply shocked him even before the outrage on the rock by the stream. He had discovered that, for all that Seos and Ehrah were full blood-sister and brother, they not only were a sexually mated pair of long standing, but that this fact—to him shameful, sinful, criminal—was known and accepted and openly practiced by others in their society and of their race. All three of the flyers were clad in thick, hooded cloaks of unbleached wool against the chill of the upper airs they traversed in their journey's transit.

The trio of flyers bore on a true and unerring course of east-northeast almost directly into the recently risen sun. There was no land in sight, unless faint smudges on the distant horizons were truly islands rather than simply banks of foggy mists not yet burned away by the birth of the new, sunny day. Far, far beneath them, the purple-blue sea rolled in its endless, ageless motion. Once they flew for some time over a tremendous school of fish, flashing like polished silver in the sun as they leaped from the swells in attempts to escape the predatory sea creatures which swam in pursuit and among them. The only other signs of life to be seen were occasional birds—gulls, terns; far below, larger birds that looked like pelicans.

From Seos's mind, Fitz could understand that several moons' time had passed since he and Ehrah had borne their chance find, the girl Oo-roh-bah, back to their island home and their sire, Keronnos, who ruled over all there, both pure-strain humans and hybrids. Oo-roh-bah had been examined and put to tests of many sorts by Keronnos and others of the oldest, most adept of the hybrids. She had been found to house within her mind so many valuable, if presently latent, talents that Keronnos and his council of hybrids had decided to first awaken certain of those hidden talents, then send her and her kidnappers back to her home to seek out those of her tribe with equal degrees of hybrid traits and make efforts to persuade them all to journey to the island, that their priceless heritage might be bred even more truly over time—rather than be further diluted by breedings with pure-strain humans until those latent talents had been diluted to no talents at all, as had happened far too often in many a land during the long centuries since the submergences of the islands in the larger sea that had been the homelands of the hybrids and their star-spawn mentors, the Elder Ones.

They had left the home-island of the hybrids with the pale light of the false dawn and flown straight toward their goal ever since. They were speeding to join others of the hybrids who had preceded them. For two moons, now, hidden from all sight by certain of their talents or cloaked in the shapes of beasts or trees or rocks, they had been spying upon Oo-roh-bah's people, delving unsuspected into their minds, searching out the one most strongly possessing hybrid traits. Seos and Ehrah must confer with these scouts before physically appearing before the mongrel tribe of Oo-roh-bah's sire; such had been the firm order of Seos's own sire.

"There will be none of your private games," Keronnos had said in tones that brooked no demur or dissent. "No guises of fish or fowl or furry beasts, for this is serious, racial business this time, not a frolic among the primitive humans. Upon arrival on the mainland, you will seek out your brothers Mikos and Gabrios before you do aught else. They, not you, are my chosen viceroys in this operation, so you will consider the orders given by them, mine own. Do you both fully understand me?"

"But, my father," Seos had replied, with both sulkiness and a measure of aggrievedness in his voice and manner, "it's not fair to put Mikos and Gabrios in charge. After all, it was I who found the girl, recognized what she was and brought her back to you here."

"Yes," Ehrah had put in, "it was we who found her; you would never have known of her and her tribe, Father-dear, had we not borne her back here. It was us, not Mikos and Gabrios, *us*, so we should be in charge, not them."

Keronnos's stern visage had not altered, nor his tone. "No, Mikos and Gabrios are to be in command. Both are almost mature, older, wiser, less inclined to wasting time and talents on childish and sometimes— dangerous frivolities.

"You both feel hurt and that your efforts go unrewarded, unappreciated, now, but in another few centuries, when you too are nearing maturity of both mind and body, you will more fully understand and recognize the necessity of my decision in this grave matter.

"Now go, my children. But remember my words and see that you well heed them."

Seos recalled how the muscles had rippled under his sire's fair, sun-freckled skin as he arose from his seat after he had finished speaking, for though his red-blond hair and beard were beginning to streak with grey, his body was every bit as firm and fit as that of any man or hybrid upon the island. Seos did not know his sire's exact age; the subject was considered of no importance and it had never occurred to him to inquire. Hybrids of as pure a lineage as Keronnos often lived for twenty and more centuries, usually little changed in physical appearance until two or three centuries before death.

With such lifespans, they should have long-since bred enough hybrids to at least conquer, if not actually cover all the earth. However, with the blessing of long life came the curse of slow and spotty reproduction among hybrids of pure lineage. In all of his long centuries upon the island, Keronnos had gotten fewer than a score of get upon his sister-wives, while Seos had yet to get even one upon Ehrah, though he and other male hybrids had proven to the devastatingly potent with humans, wherever and whenever and however these conquests had been found and taken. In fact, the girl Oo-roh-bah even now bore within her still-flat little belly Seos's developing seed.

Seos thought on farther and with remembered relish unhidden of how both he and Ehrah, his sister and wife, had in beast-bodies coupled with wild creatures of the fields and forests, as well as with domesticated animals, to produce progeny that were occasionally not entirely bestial. Fitz was appalled. He wondered just how and why he found himself in the clearly depraved mind of this handsome, ruthless, often childish, human-looking monster.

But then, diving more deeply into his host's memories, Fitz realized that Seos and Ehrah were far from the first of their kind to so comport themselves. The practice was indeed common among young hybrids, whose bodies matured far faster than their minds, talents or judgment. Seos's mind told him that it had been so back almost to the dim beginnings of the hybrid race in some land now lost to the memories of any save the few, scattered, surviving Elder Ones, wherever they might dwell. Keronnos, himself, had told often of how he and his siblings had cavorted and had sometimes coupled with sea creatures, spawning on them more than few offspring that were not entirely of the appearance of either parent, though still denizens of the waters.

Fitz then thought back to the story Cool Blue had told him shortly after their first meeting, of how the Count of Saint Germain's mistress, one Sursy, had aroused the now-lion, then-human's lust for her, then had insisted that, in order to slake his passion, he allow her to transform him into a wild boar and in that form swive the sow she became. Could it be that this sorceress, this Sursy—now, according to Cool Blue, a shocking-pink lioness against her will and by the wiles of the cuckolded and angered Count—be one of these hybrids, of the lineage of Seos and his people? How could he or anyone else ever know for sure? If and when he ever found this man of whom Puss kept speaking, this Dagda, perhaps he would know? Well, it would be at least worth the asking.

The three flew on . . . and on, and on. The sun rose almost halfway to its meridian and a faint, hazy smudge appeared on the horizon dead ahead of them. As they drew ever nearer, the haze dissipated and the smudge became dense, solidified into a line of high, rocky cliffs surmounted by expanses of coarse grasses, herbs and bushes and low trees. Beyond these seaside cliffs, the land descended rapidly to a verdant plain on which grew a very abundance of lush plants of every size and description. One large river cut through this plain within easy sight, several streams of larger and smaller sizes fed the river and distant sparkles of sun on water told of more streams beyond. Hordes of birds and beasts roamed this wild eden. Fish leapt in the river and streams and, along the banks here and there, could be seen the long, thick, scale-armored bodies of crocodiles—called water-dragons by Oo-roh-bah and her people and by Seos and his as well, Fitz had earlier discovered. Seeing them in the flesh, Fitz thought that, though none he could see were as large as the one he had been briefly chased by on the beach, not a few of these sinister creatures were quite large enough to be fairly called dragons.

As far as the keen eyes of the young hybrids could see on either side, the plain stretched on, grasslands alternating with patches of woodland, these latter thin and almost parklike out toward the center of the plain, but growing thicker, denser and with taller trees along the courses of some of the streams and farther northeast, closer to the foothills, purple in the distance ahead of them.

Seos followed the course of one of the river's larger tributaries, and had approached closely enough to the foothills to be able to see tendrils of smoke rising up from a spot too dim with distance to yet be clearly discerned, when a telepathic message reached his mind.

"If you get any closer to that steading, Seos, you'll all be seen. Veer off to the southeast and fly lower, just above treetop level. Do it, now, Seos! You, too, Ehrah! This is serious business today, not recreation."

Gritting his teeth in a brief flareup of his anger at being made a subordinate of his elder brothers, Seos beamed back, "It will be done as you desire, brother-mine. Where are we to find you? Even a scent as rank as yours doesn't carry so far or so high, Gabrios."

"Just fly low, parallel to the line of foothills, Seos," came the reply, "Mikos will meet you and guide you here to our camp."

CHAPTER VII

It was very late in the afternoon following the nighttime attack in the parking garage that Pedro Goldfarb arrived back at his offices after a long, hard day in court. The mirror in the elevator he had taken up from street level had told him that he looked almost as dog-tired as he felt. The receptionist had of course gone, along with the rest of the salaried staff, he presumed, but his private secretary had waited for him in her faithful way to seat him at his desk, serve him coffee, apprise him of all that needed telling, and put into his hands the stack of messages and mail of serious enough import to merit his personal perusal.

"Who's here besides us, Myrna?" he asked after his first sip of the scalding coffee.

"Mr. Jones . . ." she began, then frowned, "No,

he was here rather late, but he's gone now. Ms. Dardrey is still here though, I believe."

He started to reach for the intercom, then inquired, "In her office?"

"No," was the answer, "in the library, when I last saw her."

Picking up his coffee again and sitting back in the embrace of his desk chair, he nodded, "Okay, Myrna, your day is done now, your usual superlative job and I once more am in your debt. Go home. And on your way out, ask Ms. Dardrey to please step in here when she has time. Goodnight, Myrna."

As the door closed behind the black-haired, voluptuous-bodied and almost frighteningly efficient woman, Pedro arose and plodded over to open a hidden wardrobe wherein to hang his suit coat, then across to the liquor cabinet where he selected a decanter of cognac, poured a generous measure into a snifter, then went back to his desk. From the box on that desk, he selected a puro and set one end of it to soak in the cognac before swallowing half the somewhat-cooled coffee, extracted a business card from a vest pocket and dialed one of the numbers embossed upon it.

"Pedro Goldfarb," he said after a moment, "to speak to Mr. Paoli, please." After yet another pause, he answered, feeling just a trifle foolish, "Black, green, granola, orange, nickel. All right, what did you find out here, Pete?"

While listening, he nodded several times, wordless, grimaced once and finally showed his teeth in what was clearly no variety of smile, indeed, bore more resemblance to a snarl.

"Okay," he at last said, "you have yourself a contract. How much down?" He winced. "That much? Okay, come by here tomorrow and you'll get my signature and check. How did I know, you ask? Look, Pete, you don't wait for an answer and I won't ask you just how a man with a record like yours managed to come by a simple business license, much less the others you had to get to operate, agreed? All right, see you tomorrow."

He was just hanging up the telephone when a knock sounded on his office door. "Come," he said in a tone that he knew would carry through the polished walnut.

Danna Dardrey opened one of the doors and moved through it. Pedro noted that she, too, looked tired, drawn—not as tired as he looked or felt, but tired, nonetheless.

"I'd tell you to have some sherry, Danna," he commented, "but you look like even a half a glass would put you down for the full count. I told you to go home and sleep this early A.M., not go carousing in every late-hour bar in the city. Pardon me for saying it, my dear, but you look awful."

She made a wry face. "Thanks a whole heap, Pedro. For your information, I did go home and to bed . . . alone and sober. But then I couldn't sleep, so I sat up reading until it was time to eat and shower and come to work. And by the way, Pedro, pardon *me* for saying it, but you don't look so good yourself; you look, to use an expression I often heard during my college days, as if you were dragged through a wringer by your . . . ahh, nose. So where did you go after I drove off? Out boozing and whoring? Or back here to work until court-time, as you've done repeatedly before? You know, Pedro, you're the heart and soul of this association of ours. Where are any of us going to be if you wreck your health or work yourself to death, huh? You're human, too, you know."

His reply was a cryptic half-smile. "Yes, I sometimes have trouble remembering that last, Danna, that's why I'm so glad I have you and Myrna to stand behind me intoning, 'Remember, thou art but a man.'"

"Oh, Pedro," she snorted, "be serious. I was being quite serious.

"And speaking of being serious, did you know that there was a whole crew of men with all kinds of weird-looking devices poking and prying and snooping and measuring things and taking apart telephones and other fixtures and equipment all over these offices all morning, all lunch hour and part of the afternoon, too?"

He answered simply. "Yes, Danna, I know."

"Well, who the hell were they, Pedro? What in God's name were they up to? When they moved their show into *my* office and took to tearing things apart, I went looking for the head cheese and found him, too. Pedro, that man looks like someone that Francis Ford Coppola would cast as a Mafia thug. His lips don't move at all when he talks and those eyes of his are icy—reptilian, almost. All he would tell me was that he was up here on orders. *Whose,* for Christ's sake?"

"Mine," replied Pedro. "Get some coffee, Danna, and sit down. Your rather uneventful pre-dawn morning was more than made up for by my own overly exciting one. I'll tell you about it . . . it and a few other things you should know."

When he had told her all of the events of that morning, she demanded, "Do you really believe what that criminal you just let get away told you, Pedro? You really believe that Agent Blutegel tried to have you set upon and beaten and robbed? Look, I don't like the man either, not in the least, you know that, but . . . but Pedro, this is the United States of America, not Russia, not one of the Iron Curtain countries, not some dictator-run banana republic, and Henry Blutegel, for all else he is or might once have been, *is* a federal employee. Don't you think that that black man simply told you what he sensed you wanted to hear, told you anything to make you let him go?"

The saturnine man shook his head. "No, I don't, Danna. I think that Mr. Welford Roosevelt Harrison told me the full and unadorned truth as he recalled it—nothing more, nothing less than that.

"Fortunately for us all, as well as for the country as a whole, Blutegel is not your average, normal, run-of-the-mill I.R.S. agent. Rather, he is an aging, probably lonely, alcoholic who is quite possibly mentally ill as well, to judge from some of his behavior at times. Just now, moreover, he knows that it was us who, in collusion with Fitz, got him in a good bit of trouble with his service and his supervisors. Then, to pile Ossa upon Pelion in his mind, I proceeded to lure him out to Fitz's place, taunt his addiction shamelessly, outmaneuver him in his schemes and finally allow you to slap him and myself laid painful hands upon him when he tried to retaliate against you. Danna, a man like Blutegel could never ever forgive those who so treated him in front of a younger agent whom he obviously considers a multiple inferior; so taunted, manipulated, embarrassed, belittled, humiliated, his masculine pride absolutely shattered, a Blutegel could never be expected to forget or forgive, either, and in an ongoing rage that he would rationalize as righteous, he would be capable of doing anything within his still-not-inconsiderable power to avenge himself on me, you, and probably poor young Agent Khoury, too, for that matter."

Shivering, she said, hesitantly, "Pedro . . . look, after all you said just now. Anyway, while I was driving home last night . . . this morning, rather, I sat at one of those looonnng lights, the streets just about empty both ways, you know, and still the light stays red, that kind of thing. Anyway, just as the light changed for me and I started out into the intersection, this big old car zips out of an alley off the cross street, comes tearing down, building up speed, runs the light and comes within centimeters of plowing into me, full tilt. I wrote it off as just some drunk then, and maybe I still would, even now, except for one other thing. After he'd missed me and gone speeding through that intersection and halfway up the next block, he tried to make a U-turn without slowing down, skidded and fishtailed up onto the sidewalk, right through a cyclone fence and into a parked delivery van. But . . . but, Pedro, if he hadn't skidded . . . ? Do you think that maybe he *wasn't* drunk? That maybe, if he'd been able to make that turn, he . . . he might've come back after me? Maybe . . . maybe the man you said drove away . . . ? Maybe, do you think . . . ?" She shivered again.

"What kind of car was it, Danna? What make?" asked the man.

She shrugged. "Oh, Pedro, I don't know all that much about the differences between American cars. Oldsmobile, I think, or Pontiac, or maybe Buick. All I know is that it was big, fairly old, not in very good shape, you know what I mean, full of dents and the vinyl all peeling off the top."

He frowned. "Well, the way he hit that column, then scraped metal all the way down that spiral ramp, then smashed through the gate down below, that Pontiac wouldn't have been in very good shape when it got out onto the street, but that was no aged car, hell, it was almost new.

"Where were you when this incident occurred, Danna; can you recall just what intersection it was?"

She nodded. "Yes, I do, because I'd meant to call the police and report it when I got home. Then I started thinking about some other things and forgot to call; some officer of the court I am. I was driving on Paar Boulevard and the light was at the corner of Paar and Hazelhurst Avenue."

Pedro shook his head. "Then there's no way that the guy who split out of here could have gotten up there in time to be in wait in an alley off Hazelhurst for you. In a helicopter he just might have been able to cover the distance in time; in a car, no way. No, these two were entirely separate incidents . . . not that it's not entirely possible that Herr Blutegel couldn't have been behind them both. Remember, he hates you now fully as much as he hates me."

"Just for slapping him once, Pedro?" she remonstrated. "But I . . ."

"No," he replied, "not just for slapping him once, Danna, though you can be certain that that slap weighs in the balance. No, for witnessing the degradation of his blustering machismo, that is his heaviest grievance against you . . . unless . . . Oh, Christ!

"Danna, damn me for the worst kind of a fool, I should have thought of this sooner. If the man we know as Henry Blutegel is really what you think him to be, what you say you have fleetingly envisioned him to be on occasions and if he has become aware that you are inquiring, prying into his past, then we may have more and far more dangerous enemies about.

"Danna, right at the tag-end of World War Two in Europe, an organization surfaced that specialized in helping Nazis and SS men and, sometimes, even their families get out of Europe or assume new, safer identities while still in Germany. In the years since the end of the war, this organization has hidden under a host of different, innocent-sounding names and acronyms, but its primary purpose has always remained the same: to see to the advancement of the goals of German National Socialism, to aid and abet the purposes of governments and individuals friendly to them and the still-living hideout Nazis and—and listen tight, Danna—to do all within their power to protect these hideouts from detection or apprehension. So, if Blutegel really is a phony Czech, a former member of the Nazi Schutzstaffel, then we just may have bitten off a bit more than we'll be able to chew alone. God Almighty damn! Why in hell couldn't I have thought of this ramification before I just merrily saw you off galloping on your white destrier with your lance and crusader's cross?"

Stunned by his revelations, Danna just sat in silence.

He glanced first at his watch, then at the desk clock and shook his head. "It's too late to now, but first thing in the morning, I'm going to start making some calls, pulling in a few markers, in D.C. and elsewhere around the map. Like I just said, this may have already gotten far too big for us to try to handle alone. But there are more people closer to us than your chap in Vienna who also like to get their teeth into hidden war criminals, and I happen to know at least two of them. They know others and the others know many others."

"But Pedro," she said hurriedly, worriedly, "this thing about Blutegel . . . it's only a hunch, a vague suspicion of mine, maybe bred simply out of my dislike for the man. I've dug up not one supporting fact to damn him, not really even the ghost of one, don't you see? And . . ."

"And," he interrupted her, brusquely, "Henry Blutegel has already damned himself in my eyes, at least, by performing or bullying others into performing criminal acts on his behalf. Admittedly, this time he did them for personal rather than political purposes . . . I hope and pray . . . but one cannot but wonder just where and when and how he learned to think along such lines, Danna."

"Pedro," she said softly but with strength, "think,

please, before you call in others and do something rash; you have only the unsupported word of a hired strong-arm man."

"Not quite just that alone, Danna," he assured her. "I didn't get around to telling you quite everything, earlier this evening. During some of the longer recesses, today, I phoned some police-types, as well as some fellow attorneys connected with the city in one way or another.

"When Mr. Meems recovered sufficiently to be again read his rights, told with just what he was to be charged and came to the realization that—win, lose or draw—he was more than likely going to jail, going directly to jail without passing Go or collecting two hundred dollars, he became most voluble, well before he spoke one word about or to an attorney.

"It seems that Mr. Meems is a tax cheat, a self-confessed tax cheat of some years' practice. About five years ago he was all but wiped out, financially speaking, as outcome of a divorce court's decision. In order to keep his business going, his dozen or so employees employed, he began to do highly creative forms of accounting on his tax records, both personal and business. After a few years of seeming success, he was suddenly telephoned at his office one day by . . . guess who, Danna?"

"Blutegel, of course," she said, grimly.

He nodded. "Yes, give that lady the brass . . . flowerpot. None other than our own renovated and veneered Henry F. Blutegel, Boy I.R.S. Agent, U.S. of A. As matters developed, they had nothing on him then, just a few understandable mistakes on some forms, the kind that anyone other than a very astute and very lucky CPA makes on those paper night-mares the Treasury Department calls simple forms.

"But Blutegel can sense fear more keenly than many, likely because he delights in terrorizing people—I've felt for most of the time since first I met him, dealt with him, that he actually experiences a quasi-sexual joy from the act of creating terror in his victims. Though he just went through the standard operating procedure with Meems on that first day, he apparently kept at it, went after him—digging, probing, comparing statements and other records. Finally, fairly recently, he struck pay dirt, got the goods on Meems. You and I both know what he has been putting the poor, crooked bastard through since then. Both you and I have represented enough other poor bastards who've blundered into Blutegel's clutches to know just what stripe of cold, cruel, inhuman torturer he can be. A cat with a crippled bird is the very soul of compassion in comparison to him.

"Then, earlier this week, Meems's statement reads, Blutegel had a meeting with him on a stretch of deserted road out in the county, at night. There, he offered Meems a deal: I was to get beaten to within an inch of my life by the offices of Mr. Meems and any assistants he chose to hire on. In return for this 'favor' Blutegel would not bring Mr. Meems's heinous transgressions to the attention of his superiors, indeed, he just might be able to so alter the records as to completely cover all of Meems's past misdeeds.

"Quite naturally, all things considered, Mr. Meems jumped at the deal, sought out and secured the services of a former black employee and, through him, found and hired on the muscular Mr. Harrison. And you know what happened after that."

"What are the police doing about it, Pedro?" she asked. "Of course you know Blutegel's going to deny every bit of it. Who'll they believe?"

He looked glum. "Most likely Blutegel, I'm afraid, who'll naturally claim that the accusation is just a case of a tax cheat trying to take revenge on the upright, honest, law-abiding, God-fearing, white knight of the I.R.S. who found him out, unmasked his duplicity, tum-tee-tum-tum-tum and so on; you know that old refrain, they all sing it on occasion when their browbeatings of taxpayers become too noticeable and someone with clout looks like coming down on them.

"No, they'll decide our Mr. Meems is lying through his set of crooked teeth, indict him, try him and send him to the slam, the poor, entrapped bastard."

"Pedro," she demanded, "you're not thinking of . . . Pedro, remember, you're not a criminal attorney, not this kind, anyway."

He waved a hand, placatingly. "No, of course I'm not, Danna. Please, credit me with at least a modicum of intelligence, my dear."

"I'm sorry, Pedro," she said, sincerely, adding softly, "It's just that I well know just how big your heart is. Know how much and how deeply you can feel for, sympathize and empathize with abused, suffering people and . . . I'm sorry, Pedro."

He chuckled. "Don't be, I'm far from infallible; I've made my fair share of mistakes of judgment, too.

No, I'm not going to personally defend Mr. Meems. But that's not saying I'm not going to see to it that he has first-class representation, either. Any victim of Blutegel is, if not necessarily a friend of mine, at least someone who in my book deserves to get the fairest shake he can, and I'm just of the opinion that Meems won't get what he needs from any of this city's P.D. types—long haired, dope-smoking, acid-tripping, draft-dodging, left-liberal boneheads who mean so well but usually can't deliver in the crunch, having spent too many of their college years burning draft cards, relating with their fellow dopers and chanting slogans to ever absorb much law."

"Yes," she said, "I've noted those types. How does this area wind up with so many of them, anyway? Most of them aren't natives of this part of the country, much less this state or county."

He made a rude sound. "It's mostly old Von Fridley, Danna; he's attracted to the New Left because he's of the Old Left. He's also part of the old-strain, New Deal, Democratic machine; furthermore, he knows where so many bodies are buried that his sinecure is a lifetime one, no matter what comes to pass and for all that everyone knows he's so far left that in comparison he makes George McGovern look like the late Joseph McCarthy, philosophically speaking."

"If you feel so strongly, Pedro, you should go into politics yourself. Why don't you?" she asked. "You'd be great."

He shook his head. "No, I wouldn't, Danna, and for one very good and sufficient reason: I am not a crook, never have been, never will be. There is right and there is wrong and I would refuse flatly to compromise my principles in order to win an election or help someone else to win one. You were right in what you said a bit earlier: yes, I do have a soft spot, I deeply feel for some few put-upon human beings, here and there, now and then; but also, Danna, I just as deeply despise the larger number of humans: they seldom fail to disgust me, and professional politicians or hacks like Fridley are quite high on that particular list. So, no, I'd not try politics, for if you once lie down with swine, you are a very long time in ridding yourself of the foul stenches of that in which swine wallow."

He took the puro from out its long, alcoholic soak, snipped off the tip, and meticulously lit it before saying more, while Danna, knowing his habits in this regard, kept silence until the ritual was done to his critical satisfaction.

Suddenly, uncontrollably, he yawned, prodigiously and long. "Sorry," he muttered, "it's not the company, believe me."

"Of course it's not, Pedro," said the woman, "You're almost out on your feet. Do you mean to kill yourself with work before Blutegel and his next set of thugs get to you?"

He grinned. "Just look at who's calling the kettle black, Why, if it isn't the lawyer-lady who sat up all night and all day reading. Which case has got you burning so much oil, midnight and otherwise, Danna? Is it one I know anything about? One of my referrals, maybe? I might be of some help, if it is."

She shook her head slowly, tiredly. "Not a case at

all, Pedro, thanks anyway. No, I spent the night reading a couple of books loaned me by Mr. Hara—oriental philosophy, Buddhist, mostly."

His dark head nodded rapidly. "Good, good. The philosophy is the basis of the only real and effective grounding in any of the real martial arts. Those westerners who try to acquire the latter without more than skimming over the former are, at best, cheating themselves, for the mind must be effectively channeled, disciplined, before it can in turn discipline the body that houses it."

She gave him a wan smile. "Now you sound exactly like Mr. Hara."

His answering smile was broader. "I should, considering how long I've studied under his tutelage and mastery. But what were you doing in our library, here, all day?"

"Reading," she replied. "No, not the same two books but, rather, some others he had recommended. I stopped by the main branch of the public library on my way in this morning, you see, and was fortunate enough to find most of the ones on his list."

"Look, Danna," he said earnestly, "all this is not something you can learn, absorb overnight. One hell of a lot of deep thought has to go into the mental mix before it will even start to jell properly. So don't try to cram; give it time, give it lots of time . . . then give it some more."

The woman frowned, looked down into the old dregs on the bottom of her coffee cup and then, still not looking up at him, said, "Pedro, it's . . . I'm not so much trying to immerse myself in the man's . . .

in Mr. Hara's philosophy and the offshoots, the practical outgrowths of that philosophy, as I am endeavoring, striving with all my might to understand the man himself, to come to a final decision of . . . of whether to really believe all that he says, avers, believes himself.

"You see, last night, here in your office, I . . . well, I told you most of what Mr. Hara had told me, but . . . but not all of it."

She lifted her head then, locked his eyes with her level gaze and stated, baldly, "Pedro, Mr. Hara is convinced that you are a real god, has been so convinced for years, apparently. He has recently come to the conclusion that I, too, am a similar god. . . . For goodness' sake, don't laugh, Pedro. There is no trace of subterfuge in that old man, you know that, and I *know* . . ." she paused for the space of a heartbeat and amended, "at least, I am convinced that he really, truly believes what he told me.

"You see, long years after the events that followed the sinking of his warship and his frustrated attempts at *seppuku*, his exile and the attempted drowning and his meeting with the Buddhist priest in that empty lifeboat in the middle of the Pacific Ocean, he met that man once again, in the flesh, the second time somewhere in Tibet, I think, or at least in the Himalayas.

"Mr. Hara was, by then, himself a Buddhist monk or priest or friar or whatever they call them and had seen, lived, experienced nearly two score more years of life in many different parts of the world. On that second meeting, he was told . . . he believes he was

162

told . . . some very singular things about himself and his future.

"In a solemn meeting with his fellow survivor of that tragic shipwreck off the coast of Korea, as well as with two very aged men to whom everyone in that place deferred, Mr. Hara was told, he says, that he had been, was being and would be denied death and subsequent reincarnation for two reasons. One was as punishment for his willful cruelty in murdering two huge but harmless to him sea-beasts—almost the last of their ancient kind—even after being warned by a well-meaning Buddhist priest.

"That part is spooky enough, Pedro, but now comes the real hair-raiser . . . and that's just what it is, too, I go all goose-bumpy every time I even think about it. The second reason, they told him, was because he was fated to awaken three gods unto themselves, three gods who had been innocently living the lives of, living in the bodies of mundane human beings, never guessing their true divinity or even suspecting their superhuman talents, their intended destinies. He was told that it would be long years into what then was still the future before he would be guided to the first of these three gods, then more years before the second, and that not until he had fully awakened the third and last would his soul be free at last to take leave of its corporeal husk and seek its next one."

She shivered strongly, rubbing briskly at her forearms. "Pedro, I've come to both love and respect that old man within a very short amount of time, yet now I am faced with the very difficult choice of

163

deciding . . . of having to decide whether the utter impossibilities that he tells as believed truth are really true or . . . or that he is only a senile old man who somehow and somewhere has slipped into a form of gentle insanity."

"Danna," said the man, in quiet, restrained tones, "surely there must be some sort of established criteria, signs, if you will, for recognizing godliness in a man or a woman—first, of course, accepting the existence of gods and other supernatural beings or phenomena. Did Mr. Hara give any reasons just why he considers me . . . and you gods?"

"He said . . ." she paused, then interjected, "Pedro, I think he's . . . well, he's at least marginally telepathic and he says that it was in your mind, our minds, that he first recognized the signs that identify us as gods, but he did not elaborate on these signs. He did say that true gods were capable, even without the long years of study, meditation and training of the adept, of performing everything of which adepts are capable and more besides.

"He went on to say that he at first doubted his own . . . ahh, interpretations of that which he had, he thought, discerned in our minds, recognizing of course his own eagerness to find the three who would be his salvation. Therefore, with the aid of other adepts summoned here from elsewhere, he put both of us to certain tests, tests unknown to us, naturally. Then, on the basis of our individual performances, he was able to establish in his own mind and in the minds of the other adepts that you, then later I, were indeed that which we had first seemed to him.

Here, again, he did not in any way, shape or form elaborate as to the signs or tests or results of those tests, and when I asked him for specifics, he just smiled that serene, unworldly smile of his and failed to respond. Do you have any idea what he was then talking about, Pedro? God knows, it's all beyond my depth."

Pedro hissed through his teeth. "Danna, this is quite a can of worms you've broached here. Let's get another cup of coffee, and then be prepared to sit for a spell."

With the coffee steaming in the two refilled cups, he began, "Look, I have felt for many, many years that, if true gods—beings in the mold of the Judæo-Christian mold as opposed to the more numerous anthropomorphic ones—existed or now exist, they could not possibly have the slightest interest in the petty lives and affairs of such savage and disgusting creatures as humanity, whether it or they originally created or bred existing humankind or not. I don't often discuss my beliefs; for one thing, they are highly personal, for another—although I don't make it a practice of running from fights—I long ago learned the utter folly of kicking sacred cows and, since I have to live and work in this society, much of which is indirectly controlled by persons and organizations possessing and jealously guarding vested interests of various kinds in maintaining at least the outward appearances of belief in God Almighty, I make a few genuflections to conformity," he waved at the antique Spanish crucifix hung on one wall, "give to the expected charities in the expected amounts for a man of my income attainments, then assiduously avoid discussing in public such incipiently incendiary topics as religion, politics and the morals or lack thereof of other men's wives. In this way, I have managed to be let alone to live my life in prosperity and relative peace. It's a very good course to follow, Danna, and another good course to follow is that of keeping secret from everyone, even spouses and lovers, any unusual, unbelievable talents or abilities in your possession of which you may stumble upon, for it is a human trait to fear anything they do not, cannot understand, because out of their fear comes abhorrence and hatred . . . that's how witchcraft charges, torture, maimings, *autos de fe* and immolations got their start, you know. You must keep your silence, keep all your own, personal secrets entirely secret until . . . if ever . . . you chance to come across, to meet and to recognize one with the same rare talents you yourself possess; but even then you must study them carefully, take long and long to establish that they are emotionally well balanced and completely worthy of your trust, for what you may well be doing is putting into their hands your very life itself. Danna, turn and look over at the liquor cabinet."

Obligingly, she half-turned in her chair to watch, wide-eyed, as the brass key turned in the brass-framed keyhole, and the two doors swung widely open. A brief glance back at the man behind the desk showed both of his hands resting on the desktop in clear view and unmoving. Back at the cabinet, the decanter of amontillado sherry rose smoothly, lightly from its place, moved from out the cabinet and, accompanied by one of the small, trumpet-shaped sherry glasses, glided through the empty air of the distance separating desk and cabinet to come to rest without a sound beside her coffee cup.

Unable to speak, to even move, she watched, open-mouthed in shock, while the level of the wine in the still-unstoppered crystal decanter sank, even as the glass was filled.

Staring wildly at the man seated across the desk from her, she saw him smile and, although his mouth did not otherwise move and he uttered no audible sound, he said, "Now, Danna, can you put the decanter back into its place without arising or physically touching it? I think that you can."

CHAPTER VIII

Tur-ghos of the Two Axes and his warrior-hunters had of course known that his missing daughter, Oo-roh-bah, had intended to go foraging in her favored place, upstream above the falls, not far from the high-lea, where were pastured the kine of the tribe he ruled. That was where they went, but they found not the girl. Her baskets they found—one in the shallows near the bank, one atop a big rock. Also atop the big rock were traces and stains of dried blood, three stone tools, the workmanship of which telling that they were products of the tribal flint-knapper, Gneeos, and a big pebble of the rare, yellow-white stone of which the finest tools and weapons had always been fashioned.

When first he saw the pebble, Chief Tur-ghos knew that it had been found in the streambed some-where by Oo-roh-bah—ever his favorite, most loved and most loving daughter—and that she must have intended it as a gift for him. It was, he had then thought sadly, her very last gift to her sire.

Of her little body, there was not so much as a trace, unless the blood on the rock had been hers. There was flesh and blood aplenty on the streambanks and in its shallows, however, even after a full night of feasting by scavengers and not a few predators, too, to judge by the signs. The bones and hide and flesh and sinew, hooves and horns remaining were those of a wild ox in his prime—most likely the same one that the herders and herd-guards had had to drive from proximity of the herd just the day before.

Without knowing how, precisely, Chief Tur-ghos was convinced that the death of the wild ox bull was somehow connected with the disappearance of the girl, Oo-roh-bah. He and the veteran hunters carefully studied the spoor and droppings scattered about on the banks of the stream, but found no answers there; the very largest animals represented by those could never have slain so huge and fearsome a beast as a wild ox, bull or cow, not at full growth. A young leopard had partaken of the beef, as well as a pair of small lynxes, a number of highland jackals, eagles, kites, ravens and numerous other, smaller birds and beasts. Of all that sizable aggregation, only the leopard might have been dangerous to the girl, but had she been taken by the cat, they would certainly have found tracks or signs in their wide castings about of which direction the leopard had taken in bearing off her body, and they had not.

So back to the question of what could have killed a prime wild ox, dismembered it, devoured part and then departed, leaving the bulk of the kill to the scavengers? Aside from human hunters, a full-grown, uninjured wild ox in the prime of life had precious few predators to worry about. Tur-ghos and all the other men knew this well.

Ticking the beasts off on his scarred, horny fingers as he thought, the chief pondered. There were the long-tooth cats, of course; any beast, from the smallest to the largest, was their prey, any the slow-footed killers could catch. But what man now living had ever so much as seen one? Well, there were the lions. Yes, but though they lived higher up the mountains in some numbers, none were left on the lower plain and seldom had one been seen of recent years here on the higher plain—and then only in long or severe winters, not in weather like this. The same held true for the big, shaggy, mountain bears. In each succeeding year, parties of young hunters from the tribes of the lower plain had to venture farther and farther up into the high country and mountains in order to seek out and slay the ursines for their warm, valuable pelts and for the rich, fatty meat, the teeth and the claws.

Each year they had perforce to go farther and stay away longer, and they brought back fewer pelts, too, than had preceding hunts. Tur-ghos thought that the day fast was approaching when bears and lions both would be as uncommon, as rare in these lands as was Old Longtooth even now. Without big, dangerous beasts to fear and to hunt—thus proving before all one's courage, weapon-skills and manhood, one's right to a place among the warriors, one's right to take a woman and get children upon her, to be respected,

171

honored in life and in memory—life would be far less exciting, courage and even honor would likely become things of the past . . . but, also, he had thought with a stab of grief, no more young girls and boys, no more foraging womenfolk would be lost to the ravening animals.

At length, they all agreed that Oo-roh-bah must have been taken by a land-dragon—of which there still were known to be a few lurking in the foothills, for all that the nightmare monsters were religiously tracked down and slain whenever and wherever they appeared before men—and either completely devoured on the spot or borne away, upstream.

Bearing back with them all usable parts of the bull the killer and scavengers had left them, the party had returned to their place below the falls and made their sad pronouncement of the fate of Chief's-daughter Oo-roh-bah. According to their rituals and tribal customs, they had mourned the dead girl.

The period of mourning completed, the men of the tribe had mounted a dragon hunt up above the falls of the stream. None of the creatures had been found until they had ascended rather high into the foothills and none of those had been of a size to have committed the killing of a big ox, but they had all been slain just the same, along with a spotted, mountain lionness and a goodly bit of other assorted game—leopards, boar, deer, and the like—that the trip not be wasted effort, for survival was hard and always had been so since the calamitous loss of the Good Land, far away to the west.

After return from that great dragon hunt, things had returned to normal routine in the settlement atop the hill beside the falls, that presided over by Chief Tur-ghos of the Two Axes.

Fitz saw the hybrid, Mikos, as simply a slightly older version of Seos—same red-blond hair and beard, same shade of eye color, same fair, freckled, sun-browned skin, same powerful-looking physique. The age-difference was not at all physically apparent, rather was it seen in Mikos's bearing and recognized in his serious, responsible manner.

He had come into sight, hovering in the air close beside a cedar tree, then had led them upslope where a thick copse of high, twisted bushes masked the locations of a tiny spring and a rock shelter, beneath the overhang of which waited a man who might have been the twin of either Seos or Mikos, save that his hair and beard were both a bright, bricky red, and his sparkling eyes of a shade of hazel. Also he was a couple of inches taller and a bit more slender than the two other male hybrids.

When the newcomers had each drunk from the spring, the red-haired Gabrios sank into a squat and all emulated him, then he began to silently speak.

"These men—the folk of the girl's sire, that is— have not been here long, not as we measure time. They arrived perhaps four centuries ago, maybe less. Before that, they dwelt on some island in this sea—a fairly large island, it was, though apparently not so large as is ours and differently shaped—they had dwelt there for a few centuries, too, interbreeding with the humans they had found there."

"From whence did they first arrive upon that is-land," asked Ehrah, "and have you discovered when, elder brother?"

He frowned. "I have no precise answers to either question, sister-mine; the sleeping minds I and Mikos have entered simply lack the training and discipline to properly chronicle racial memory. Only something less than a third of all the folk we have entered and examined have enough hybrid traits to make it worthwhile to examine them further, train their minds and allow them to breed into purer hybrid stock."

"But what, then, of Oo-roh-bah, oh wisest of brothers?" Seos demanded with something less than respect.

The red-haired man took no umbrage, just answering, "Yes, hers is a truly exceptional mind, but only two of all her siblings are so gifted and even her sire, while well worth bringing to our island, is less gifted with hybrid traits than is she. By far the most worthy we have encountered in all that settlement are a young herdsman and a middle-aged flintknapper. It has been from out their slumbrous minds that we have gleaned the most of the history of the hybrid-humans who founded this settlement and the others on this plain."

"O Mighty One," said Oo-roh-bah, with abashed hesitation, "may this insignificant female speak?"

Smiling, Gabrios beamed, "Not aloud, my child; communicate as you have been taught, with your mind as do we."

She did, beaming: "Gneeos Stone-shaper is known in every tribe and settlement. Even those in places beyond, who are not really people, send things of value with which to obtain specimens of his craftsmanship. He has fashioned cunning tools the like of which no one had ever before seen or even imagined, and he wastes so little stone in useless chips that he can make twice again as many useful things from a pebble of good stone as can any other man within memory. But he is a most secretive man, too. He often does his work alone, apart from even his family, hidden away in his work-hut, saying that his secrets are his and his alone. My sire does not like such behavior, but he also appreciates the value of Gneeos Stone-shaper and the things he creates, so says nothing himself and calls down any who do."

Both Gabrios and Mikos chuckled aloud, and Gabrios beamed, "The man is canny. Seos, he has somehow self-taught his mind to shape stone as we do—with waves of varying intensities of mental force which set up vibrations within the target rock itself. Oh, yes, he is also quite adept, quite artistic in producing blades and flakes in the old-fashioned human way of painful, laborious chipping and pressure-flaking and touching up, and he does only this when under observation, that or grinding. But he uses the quicker, simpler, easier skills in private, being more of mind to be respected as an artist-craftsman than feared as a wizard, another sign of his quick hybrid mind.

"We thank you for contributing information, child," Gabrios addressed Oo-roh-bah, with sincerity, "but Mikos and I already know him better than he knows himself. The man possesses talents that he never has even suspected. Like you, yourself, what meets the eye of him does not look very much like one of us, but his mind is almost pure hybrid."

To Seos and Ehrah, Gabrios beamed, "Now, for all it's seeming size, usable land on our island is definitely finite. A sizable population of fast-breeding humans would find it untenable for a comfortable standard of living within very few of their generations. Therefore, our father has ordered that only the very purest available hybrid stock be brought there, and Mikos and I have selected those who will be borne back westward.

"In the interests of saving both time and effort, as well as sparing the emotions of the pitiful, primitive, easily frightened humans, we are not going to make the sort of grand entrance among them of which you two are so fond: no sudden descent from the sky or the like, no riding up the river standing atop the back of water-dragon. No, you three will simply walk into the settlement with us, the girl will be reunited with her sire, and then we all will talk with him, eat, drink, demonstrate to him our common kinship with him, our shared heritage. Understood, Seos, Ehrah? It all will be done calmly, rationally, and will include no theatrics, no spurts of flames from the fingertips, no objects miraculously floating on air, no sudden transformations into bestial or half-bestial shapes, hear me and heed me, younger brother and younger sister. You must grow up, must mature, and better you do such the sooner than the later.

"Knowing humans and their ways, on one day soon after their lost child's return to them, they will have a feast for us and all others in their settlement. In the immediate wake of that feast, when every human is already sated and drowsy, they will fall asleep, all at once. There are enough of us here to do that by mind-power. While they are sleeping, we will float into the settlement enough of the their fishing craft to hold all those we have selected. The craft then will be lifted and guided by us through the skies to the island."

"And what of the others, those who will remain asleep in the settlement?" asked Ehrah. "What will they think and do, elder brother?"

Gabrios shrugged. "Oh, belike they'll think up some sort of supernatural tale to cover the incident, explain it to the coming generations. Gods stole them all away, or evil demons or some of the hairy near-humans who still live in mountains and wastes. Humans may lack our minds, but they do own vivid imaginations, some of them; they'll think up something, never you fear."

Mikos now put in his own beaming, saying, "For that very reason, brothers and sisters, we are going to have to exercise caution, practice wiles, when we explore the other settlements situated upon this plain, for can we find even half as many worthwhile minds in each of them, our sire's dream of joining and rebreeding our blessèd race to true purity may even come to pass while still we five live. And can we do this, perhaps one of the Elder Ones will then come to live among us, as in times of yore they did in the Good Islands from which came our forebears."

Fitz wakened to light, a narrow shaft of bright light from the risen sun somehow filtering through all of the foliage to lance directly between some of the limbs and branches and fully bathe his face. He had but barely unzipped the bag, sat up and stretched once when he thought to hear, somewhere to the north of his aerie, faint sounds reminiscent of several men shouting; he could discern no words, only the shouts.

"Sir Gautier and his long-lost band of retainers?" he thought, then shook his head. "No, wrong direction. When they come . . . if they come . . . it'll be from the southeast, not the north. Hell, it's probably not men at all, some kind of monkey or other beast, most likely."

But as he went about the necessary chores—arranging his clothing, putting on his boots, rolling his bag and poncho, rinsing his mouth with night-cooled water from the canteen, drinking some of it, then rummaging into his pack for a can of something with which to start the day—the human-sounding noises continued, not constant, but growing ever closer each time they did sound again. Certain now that they definitely were the shouts of men rather than utterances of animals and that they seemed to be bearing directly toward the tree he occupied, Fitz made haste to finish his packing, forgoing breakfast. He placed the full pack in a spot he thought would be invisible from below, then took a position that, while giving him a good, little-obstructed view of the stream confluence and the mouth of the defile to the north of that confluence, afforded him the best available cover and concealment where he crouched with the drilling-gun.

He crouched even lower, sheltering all save his eyes and forehead behind the thick wood, when a crashing and crackling of brush issued from some unseen part of the narrow defile which centered the tributary stream. Abruptly, two really big cervines—large as American elk, both of a rufous hue and neither of them antlered—burst out of the brushy defile, followed at very short distance by another.

The third still was running well, but bore a pink froth at mouth and distended nostrils and was clearly panting with effort, pain, or both together, mouth open wide, tongue quite visible.

The two leaders were out of the defile and galloping toward the stream, the injured straggler followed in their hoofprints, when that happened which caused Fitz to start so strongly that he almost dropped the drilling-gun out of pure shock.

From somewhere it had lain or crouched completely unseen in the bushes and shrubs at the mouth of the defile for who could know just how long, a shape from out of nightmare sprang up and, moving with the speed of insanity, clamped down massive jaws crowded with more pointed, two-inch teeth than Fitz thought any one beast should have high on the straining, rear off-leg of the last big deer.

The reddish-coated herbivore shrieked a sound that was half scream, half bleat and strove mightily to pull free from the grip of those fearsome, tooth-studded jaws, but the efforts only brought more injury and certain agony, for Fitz could see that, while pointed, the teeth also were flattened and recurved, the distal areas of them apparently sharp edges, edges designed for the slicing and laceration of flesh.

All its head covered over in fresh, bright blood, the attacker was pulled along by the frantic strength of the doomed deer until all its four- or five-yard length was out of the bushes and on the clearer area where one stream joined the other. There on the stream bank, unequal to more effort—what with the older injury and this newer—the deer, gasping for breath and coughing up great, frothy masses of red bubbles and even some liquid blood, sank to the knees of its forelegs. The monster hung on stubbornly, silently, unremittingly, through the final spasms of the large cervine, for all that Fitz thought that at least one kick had connected somewhere on the scaly body.

At length, the beast roused itself and shook the deer savagely by the tattered and gory leg its jaws still grasped; the end result of the shaking was the separation from that leg of a huge chunk of skin-covered muscle tissue, a chunk so large that Fitz doubted if even a monster of that size could swallow it whole.

He was wrong. The monster's mouth opened to disclose an expanse of dark blue palate and what looked to the man in the tree like a second row of teeth behind the first. Regrasping the chunk of deer meat, the jaws opened farther . . . and farther . . . and still farther, the lower jaw seeming to completely separate from the upper, both upper and lower jaws of the squarish, slightly oversized head widening even more, along horizontal lines as well as vertical ones. In less time than seemed possible, most of the flesh and muscle and skin of the big deer's off-side ham and hip was out of sight down the monster's gullet and it was clamping teeth in the still-quivering carcass, shaking at it to tear off another chunk of hot, bleeding flesh.

Enthralled by the horror to which he had perforce been witness, Fitz had clean forgotten the earlier sounds in the distance. But now those sounds were no longer distant; they were coming near, very near. He was certain, now, that they were not only of human throats, but that they were something more than simply a spate of wordless cries; they were shouts of words . . . and he was dead-sure he had heard the language or one very similar to it before. It was not English, he knew, but he could not just then say what language it was.

If the monster below heard the shouts, it did not seem to fear or even to heed them; it just kept tearing away at the carcass of its kill, forcing down gobbets of bloody meat that looked to be every bit as big as its outstretched head. Watching the predator from high in the tree, Fitz wondered if the whatever-it-was—it looked a little like the things Seos had thought of as land-dragons, save only that it was not so large as those and its head and neck were significantly different—could gobble up the whole deer and reflected to himself that it just might, for its body was a bit larger than that of the deer, though its legs did not seem as long. He breathed a silent prayer of thanks that the thing down there all covered with blood did not look to be of a build for tree-climbing, for he doubted that anything short of the Holland and Holland elephant gun far away in its case in the rock shelter could easily or quickly stop any creature that size . . . and it just might still be hungry after downing the deer, entire. Fleetingly, he entertained the notion of flying back to the rock shelter and fetching the cased weapon and ammunition, then thought better of it; it could be that he was hiking into territory that these things regularly hunted and he had less than twenty rounds for the double-rifle, so he had better just practice extreme caution and wariness from now on, until he found

181

out or learned a better way to fend the things off. Maybe . . . ? Yes, maybe that thing down there was one of the "tests" Puss kept mentioning. Could be.

The creature had devoured about half the soft tissue from off the deer and was crouching on a pair of thick, flexed but long-looking hind legs, while using its more slender and much shorter clawed forelegs to turn the carcass over, when the oncoming shouts began to be accompanied by sounds of brush crashing in the defile.

At this, the beast raised its large, blood-dripping head, ignoring the cloud of flies and other insects that buzzed and hovered about the feast of blood. From out that lipless mouth, a tongue that looked to be a good two feet long flickered again and again, rapidly; like the lining of the mouth, it was of a dark blue color, shading to blue-black at its two tips.

Briefly, it went back to the task of seeking to turn the carcass, but more and now louder sounds from out the twisting course of the defile again brought up its fearsome head and prompted still more tongue-flickerings.

Then, from out the brush, almost in the same spot whence the deer had exited to the doom of one, ran a near-naked man grasping a long, slender-hafted spear or lance. Spotting the now sibilantly hissing monster, the man halted and, leaning his weapon against one sweat-streaked, dusty-dirty, brush-scratched, yellow-brown shoulder, half-turned to shout back several sentences in that familiar but still unremembered language, using both hands for a makeshift megaphone. He was answered by first one, then another voice in the same language, whereupon he shouted a single syllable, then turned to again face the huge predator, his lance presented, level and steady, while he stood, panting and sweating, regaining his breath.

Carefully shielding his binoculars to prevent sunlight from reflecting off the lenses and thus betraying his arboreal position to knowing eyes, Fitz studied the spearman at the mouth of the defile. He was not big, that was certain, perhaps five foot-four or -five, his weight maybe a hundred and thirty. His skin tones and the epicanthic folds of his eyes identified him as an oriental. His bare feet and his hands were proportional to his height as was his head. His visible musculature seemed well developed, and the rapidity with which he regained his breath and began to breathe normally after what had certainly been a long, hard run over rough country and through thick vegetation bespoke excellent physical condition.

The little man's "clothing" consisted of a strip of greyish cloth that circled the slim waist, had been brought between the thighs and then knotted in place; his thick, shoulder-length, black hair was restrained by another, thinner strip of cloth that covered his forehead, was now soaked in sweat and looked to have some kind of stains in the space over his black-pupilled eyes.

His only visible weapon (and not much of one, thought Fitz, with which to face a terror the size and clear strength and savagery of that deer-killer) consisted of a haft of some hardwood, well finished, smooth, evenly polished and dead-straight, a bit over an inch wide and about seven feet long. But where one might have expected, in the hands of so primitive-appearing a man, a spear shod with stone or bone or antler, one would have been as surprised as was Fitz to see the blade *riveted* to the business-end of the haft. It was slender, four to five inches in length, and shone with the silvery sheen of carefully polished steel.

Then there was another man behind the first, come from out the dense, masking brush. This one, though clearly of the same race, clad and armed identically, was a hair taller, a little more slender in build, and sported thin moustaches and a skimpy chin-beard. Gaspingly, his prominent ribcage working like a bellows, he spoke several sentences or phrases to the first, receiving monosyllabic replies, and Fitz thought to see his face begin to darken in anger, but then two more of the short men came up from behind to begin gasping out their own words to the first.

The blood-slimed monster, meanwhile, none of the two-legged interlopers having advanced on it and tempted beyond endurance by such an abundance of fresh-killed meat, had gone back to trying to get the half-consumed carcass flipped over that the feasting might recommence until the pack of two-legs decided whether or not to try to steal away with the kill. It was long accustomed to the necessity of protecting kills, often then overstuffing itself with the flesh of those of the would-be thieves not sagacious or fast enough to escape its swift wrath, strength and insatiable hunger for flesh.

Up at the mouth of the defile, six of the oriental spearmen had debouched and were standing in the curved line, facing the gorging monster with spears levelled, when another man came out from the brush with still another on his heels. The six spearmen, though they all kept their attention on the monster and their spears pointed in its direction, visibly stiffened and fell silent upon the arrival of the two.

"Brass," thought Fitz, watching warily from the tree. "Can't be anything else. One of these two must be their chief; probably the beefy, mean-looking customer."

The smaller newcomer said something in a low tone to the bigger and that man—not all that much taller, perhaps as much as five-foot-eight, but with more massive bone structure, a wider body, thick, very muscular arms and legs, bigger hands and feet, scarred face and body and a bald or shaven head, also scarred—addressed the spearmen in a growling bark. At this, they all stiffened even more than previously and the slender man, the second to arrive, said one or two words, but fell abruptly silent at a few growled syllables from the big man. Then the first man began to speak.

Fitz chuckled silently. "That big bozo reminds me of some DIs I've had the misfortune to know better than I'd have preferred. Whatever he said to the stringbean, there, probably translates into 'When I want some shit out of you, mister, I'll squeeze your head!' He wants his situation report from the first man on the scene, not from any johnny-come-latelies."

While the first-arrived spearman spoke, answering apparent questions put to him by both the big man and the smaller, seven more of the orientals appeared from out the defile, six of them armed with the lances, one carrying what looked like some kind of axe—a broad, metal head on a haft about two feet long. This one handed something long and slender to the smaller man who had come out with the bigger

185

one, but the bushes were so thick in that area that Fitz could not see clearly what it might be.

After a brief conference between the big man and the smaller who had arrived with him, the bigger one began to bark short, terse phrases and the spearmen formed into two ranks, the spears of the rear rank projecting between the men of the first. At a measured, slow pace, the spearmen bore down upon the predatory monster, the twelve spearpoints winking brightly in the sunlight.

Having just gotten the carcass over to where the other side of flesh could be easily torn off, the beast had to turn from it and make to defend it. It first hissed like an old steam locomotive, then followed that with a healthy roar, but the scavengers did not halt or even pause in their advance, drawing closer and still closer to the contested kill and its defending, rightful owner.

The sun had not yet been up long enough to make it truly warm in this shady place at water's edge, but Fitz's binoculars showed him rivulets of sweat on more than one of those dusty, yellow-brown faces. Yet not one of them hesitated or slowed or even looked like halting and turning back from the mighty, awesome beast; regardless of any justifiable fears, regardless of the rough, rock-strewn ground, the two dressed ranks came on, staunch and steady, blank-faced, spears held ready for the thrust.

"Barbarians, hell!" thought Fitz. "For all their primitive appearance and those spears, those bastards can't be anything but trained, drilled, disciplined troops—veterans, from the performance they're giving out there."

At that moment, as the ranks of ill-armed little men bore down to do battle with the huge, scaly, blood-streaked monster, Fitz finally got a clear, unobstructed view of the hands and body of the small man who had been with the big one and who now strode on a pace or so ahead of him, just behind the second rank of the spearmen. That was when all the bits and pieces fell into place in the watcher's mind.

"Of course," he breathed, almost aloud, "that's why the damned language sounded so familiar. It's been a good thirty years, but God knows I used to hear the bastards shouting and screaming and chattering enough, back then, to remember the sounds and rhythms of their speech for a lifetime. Could these be from that time, that war? How should I know? Considering the time that Sir Gautier came from, the era of the man who became Cool Blue, and the date I entered into whatever this place really is, it could easily be . . . as easily as not be. They could be from an earlier time than the era of World War Two; if they are, that might be the explanation of why they don't have firearms, just what look like handmade spears, an axe and a set of Japanese samurai swords.

"Some of the guys actually learned some Japanese. If only I had, too, I might be able to under— Hey, wait a fucking minute! I forgot, I'm a telepath now. If I can understand, even converse with a grey panther, a blue lion and a eleventh- or twelfth-century Norman, then why the hell not a Japanese?

"But wait another minute. Sir Gautier and his bunch were anything but friendly when they first came across me. I had to end up killing one of them and all-but kill Sir Gautier himself. I wonder . . . can I just enter the mind of one of those men down there without him knowing? Hell, I wish Puss or Cool Blue or somebody would tell me how this thing works, is really supposed to work, not just force me to blunder through everything the way they have. Dammit all, it's not fair!"

He sighed. "Well, the only way to find out whether or not I can is to try it. At least I'm nowhere near as vulnerable to those Japs down there as I was to Sir Gautier and his guys, back when I first met them. I doubt if even those resourceful little Nips would be able to climb the straight, unbranched trunk of this tree easily or quickly should they even suspect that I'm hidden up here. And even if they did try to climb up, I've got enough pistol ammo in it and on my belt to kill them all with rounds left over long before any one of them got within spear-range.

"So the only question remaining now is which one do I start on? The big, mean-looking one? No, he's probably the sergeant, that's what he acts and sounds like. No, the one with the pair of samurai swords is probably an officer; I'll try to get into his mind first. Here goes."

CHAPTER IX

Lieutenant Kaoru Naka might have taken more pride in his commission at such an exalted degree of rank only two years out of the Imperial Japanese Military Academy had he not been painfully aware that he held such rank only because of the exceedingly high attrition of company- and field-grade officers in the Imperial Japanese 23d Army. Nor were the losses confined only to officers and NCOs. The company which he had taken over upon the demise of his predecessor had been at less than half strength even then, and in the months—he was unsure just how many months, anymore—since they had lost contact with battalion headquarters, he had seen his overall strength fall to three NCOs and twenty-two enlisted men.

Other than that they still were somewhere in Burma (for where else could an understrength company of infantry and one attached light tank have gotten to in the elapsed time before he had decided to stop moving about to no purpose and established a more or less permanent camp?), Kaoru had no slightest trace of an idea where they were. His entire packet of maps was meaningless and the radio never produced anything other than static.

Pressed hard and unremittingly by the mixture of opponents facing them—British, Indian, American and Chinese—battalion command's decision had been to shorten the supply lines by dint of a quick night withdrawal and regrouping at a specified and hopefully more defensible point to the northeast. At the briefing of company commanders, Kaoru had carefully marked out on his map the route he and his company were to take, marking also significant compass coordinates in the margins. He and his newly inherited company also had been "rewarded" with the "honor" of escorting and zealously guarding one of the few remaining and therefore infinitely precious Type Ninety-five light tanks with its cart of diesel fuel, lubricants and ammunition.

The company had departed almost on schedule, leaving their vacated positions manned with a skeleton crew of barely trained, ill-armed Korean conscripts under command of a few Japanese and with orders to fight to the last bullet and bayonet for the glory of the Emperor. *Banzai!*

It had been raining, or course, it seemed that it always rained on night marches; Kaoru assumed that that was just the natural order of things on military campaigns. The march had been slow, exhausting and frustrating in the extreme, most of their troubles relating to the light tank. The outmoded track vehicle had sat out most of the preceding two years in some army salvage compound somewhere until necessity had seen it and its mates brought back into field service, and the long neglect and storage under very adverse conditions became more than apparent on the march. Everything that conceivably could go wrong with the motorized abortion seemed to have chosen that night on that wet, muddy, slippery, miserable route to so do.

The crew of the tank had not proven all that much help with their weapon, all of them having been trained and done their fighting on later models; moreover, they tended to treat infantrymen—even while these were performing back-breaking labor on behalf of them and their cranky machine—with scathing contumely, deferring to Kaoru and his junior officers and NCOs because of the varying degrees of rank they held. Had the senior officers not been so adamant about the value of the tank that he and his company were to accompany and guard from harm, Kaoru would have early on had it stripped, boobytrapped and abandoned along the route, but much later he was to find glad that he had not done so.

Company Sergeant Kiyomoto proved the salvation of the problems with the recalcitrant tank. The big, tough veteran had served, it developed, with a mechanized infantry unit in China seven years before, and though not formally trained in automotive mechanics, he was the son of a blacksmith, understood metals, and owned a quick, intuitive mind as well as prodigious physical strength. If one of the crew members could tell him precisely what was the proper purpose of a non- or ill-functioning part or assembly, it had been found that he could almost always restore it to some near-semblence of that function, though usually by way of highly unorthodox methods.

But because of the repeated delays and enforced halts on the march, the dawn had found them still less than halfway to their rendezvous with the rest of the battalion. After he had carefully chosen an off-trail position that was not only easily defensible from ground attack but would be reasonably simple to conceal from air reconnaissance, Kaoru had had the company radio assembled and its generator attached, and had sent the previously agreed-upon, coded message until battalion had responded. Once he had apprised them of his position, he had gone off the air.

Though it was not at all the season for heavy rains, the rain that had so tormented and hampered them on the night before not only continued during the succeeding day but at times increased in its intensity, with periods of heavy drizzle being followed by long bursts of blinding precipitation throughout the whole of the grey, cold, miserable day. Even worse, by nightfall the small stream that they had had to cross to reach their encampment area was become a raging, roaring, white-crested torrent. Two of his men were swept away and presumably drowned while vainly attempting to get a safety line across it.

The tank commander informed him that his vehicle could not possibly ford to such a depth and that a bridge must therefore be constructed. No, he knew nothing about such matters, that was the function of such low-echelon types as engineers and infantry.

The radio was cranked up and activated and battalion, when at last it responded, heard out the encoded problem, then ordered Kaoru to either remain in place until the torrent's waters ebbed low enough for the tank to cross or, better, march cross-country and parallel to the trail until he came across a way to get back on his assigned route of march, but in any and all cases, to arrive at his destination with the tank.

The tank and its mule cart had been enough retardation to any kind of a steady advance on the now-inaccessible track, but trying to get them cross-country was an all-but-insurmountable problem to Kaoru and his part of an infantry company. No one could move any faster than dog-tired men could hack a way through vegetation, haul away obstructions and fill holes or soft places, all the while sweating, tortured by all manner of noxious insects and leeches, having to be every wary of poisonous snakes, scorpions and huge spiders. Edges of machetes and axes quickly became dulled and so close to useless that it was necessary to keep a section constantly sharpening the tools. Ropes snapped and had to be knotted together to await resplicing at a later time. And all the while that so many were striving for them, the tank officer, his crew and two mule drivers sat by in idleness, making rude comments about infantrymen in general and these in particular, while flatly refusing to aid in their own salvation by joining the work crews. Nor could Kaoru do aught to change the situation, since the ever-sarcastic and arrogant tank officer outranked him by one grade.

By superhuman efforts, the column had, by late

afternoon, advanced all of about three kilometers, Kaoru estimated, and when the lead line of axe- and machete-men broke through into a more or less clear area filled with tumbled and overgrown stone ruins, he called a halt for the day. Enough was enough; he doubted his men could endure much more such labor this wet, waning day.

A squad was sent to scout out the ruins and returned to report no signs of recent human habitation. So they went into another wet camp. After he had reported and given the compass bearings of his position to battalion, Kaoru was briefly castigated for making so little distance from the previous night's position, but then he had expected such.

Soon after dark the sky above cleared, stars and moon shining bright and full over the forested hills. The roar of aeroplanes was heard twice during that night, but the camp had been well laid out and well camouflaged, the efforts of Kaoru's force aided by nature in the form of many large trees with thick, overhanging foliage and by the long-forgotten builders of the stone ruins in provision of so many places wherefrom the glows of smokeless fires could not be seen from above.

But warplanes and hostile men were not the only enemies of these Sons of Nippon in the trackless wilds of Burma, circa 1945. In the wan, grey and misty false dawn, a tiger tried to get at the mules and ended by ferociously mauling the guard, whose bayoneted Arisaka rifle made precious little impression upon the four hundred pounds of cat. However, the screams of the man brought the nearby tank crew to wakefulness, and the effect of over a hundred rounds of 7.7mm ball from the hull machinegun rapidly reduced the predator (and the unfortunate guard, as well) into a virtual blood pudding.

When he had examined the scene and taken the reports, Kaoru disgustedly asked of the tank commander, "Lieutenant, why didn't you use the 37mm as well? Then there'd be less to dispose of."

That worthy, engaged in carefully polishing the long, yellow-white cuspid he had had one of his men pry from out the upper jaws of the much-perforated tiger, replied languidly, in his usual, supercilious way, "Because the tube was not charged, my dear Naka, while the hull gun had an opened breech with a belt in place. Any other questions, Naka?"

Seething with rage, but keeping his color and his outward calm intact, Kaoru had politely thanked the despised tank officer and stalked off, in the light of the new rainless day, to send out a patrol or two to hopefully find a quicker, easier way back to the track than would be a climb up than a descent down the slopes of the heavily forested hill that now separated them from their previous route of march. It was either that or backtrack the previous day's march and go back to where they had been when first they had left the track . . . and he had a notion that battalion would not approve that course at all, for all that it might prove the easiest and fastest in the long run.

But just before the patrols returned, neither of them with at all promising information, Sergeant Kiyomoto had come and reported to him in his proper, by-the-book way. He had informed his superior that there was, behind a screening of vegetation, a high, wide opening at the base of the steep hill to the west, the one that separated them from the track. The roof, walls and pavement of the seeming tunnel was of ancient worked stone, and it seemed to run directly through the hill in a straight line, light being visible at the other end of it.

Kaoru had first felt his heart leap, then he had frowned—that cursed tank and mule cart! —and he had asked, dubiously, "But is it high enough, wide enough, to take the tank, Sergeant?"

The opening, when he paced it off, certainly was more than wide enough for the tank, and easily high enough, Kaoru had then estimated. Then, once the highly discouraging reports of the patrols had been received and disgested, he had had a supply of torches prepared and he, Lieutenant Ozawa and Sergeant Kiyomoto had gone almost the full length of the underhill tunnel, often slipping or sliding on the damp, slimy stonework floor, while half-seen things scurried and scuttled and slithered out of their path and away from the dim and flaring light of the torches. The brush and vines and small trees at the western mouth of the tunnel had been too thick for him to get much of a look at what lay outside it save that there was a gradually descending slope and a stream at the base of the hill, as he had seen on his maps of the area. Although he could see only a rise of sorts lined with trees beyond the stream, he knew that the track must lie just the other side of that tree line.

Immediately upon their return, he had set his company to the sole task of fashioning torches with which to light their way in transit of the long, very dark tunnel to the western side of the steep hill.

Then he had gone to impart of this finding of a quick and easy way back to their assigned route of march to the tank commander. He had thought that his information would please the officer. He was quickly made aware of just how wrong he was.

Not even trying to mask his impatience, the armor officer had heard Kaoru out in foot-tapping silence, then he snapped, "Impossible, Naka, utterly impossible, you must put your uniformed aggregation of cretins to the task of finding another way. My tank is of exceeding value just now, to the Army, to the very Empire. It must be given the care you would give a personal possession of the very Son of Heaven, our Emperor, had such been placed within your keeping.

"Why, what if the machine should break down, develop some type or variety of trouble within that tunnel? Do you think it could be repaired by torchlight, even by your hulking, rural blacksmith of an infantry sergeant? I think not!

"Besides, these ruins all are incredibly ancient, uncared for, given any kind of repair who knows how many centuries ago, and that applies to your precious tunnel, too. Naka, it could well be a real deathtrap, for in case you hadn't noticed the fact, tanks make noise, they make a great deal of noise, enough noise that the vibrations of that noise might very well bring the whole of that damned hill down upon us all.

"I must tell you this, Naka, my estimation of your fitness for command—indeed, of your overall intelligence—has not been at all enhanced by this last few days' blunders and real lack of even the bare rudiments of effective leadership of that idiot rabble you choose to call a company of soldiers of the Imperial Japanese Army. And now this suggestion that I take part in your lunacy? No, Naka," he had shaken his head, "I fear that in all conscience, it must be my duty to inform the battalion commander of just how inept you are and rather strongly suggest your quick replacement."

It had all welled up in Kaoru then, welled up with such force and pressure as to defy restraint. But, as was his way, the final bursting forth had come not in physical violence or in shouts of rage. "What's your *real* problem, Lieutenant," he had inquired gently, solicitously, "are you afraid of the dark? Afraid of going through an old tomb? Afraid of Burmese ghosts, is that it?"

The only thing that had saved Kaoru's life at that moment had been that the tank commander's 8mm Nambu pistol had failed to fire—as was common in that ill-designed model—and before he had been able to clear it, the quick and powerful Sergeant Kiyomoto had twisted it from out his hands.

Disarmed, the tank crew and their officer had been marched through the tunnel under guard of the infantry riflemen they so despised, while Sergeant Kiyomoto had trailed the column in the tank, that its exhaust fumes not choke the men and that, in the event of a breakdown, it not block the tunnel to the column and the mule cart. The unquestionable age of the structure of the tunnel and the announced fears of the tank officer notwithstanding, not one stone fell or so much as shifted during the transit of the tank and the column.

They left the camp in the ruins at about ten o'clock

in the morning, under a cloudy sky that threatened imminent rain, but as the tank exited through the space the men had hurriedly hacked and chopped through the heavy growths at the western mouth of the tunnel, Kaoru suddenly realized that it seemed to be—at least to judge by the position of the sun which burned hot upon them there on the hillside—not much more than two hours before sunset. He was certain that the tunnel's length had been no more than a couple of hundred meters, at the most, so how could this time lapse be?

But no one else had seemed to notice and, with so much else of serious import to occupy his thoughts, he just allowed the enigma to remain that and turned to other matters. First, he sent out a platoon-strength probe under command of one of his remaining junior officers—a one-time classmate—to scout out the track that lay beyond the visible line of trees and be certain that no enemies lay in wait to ambush them.

Disastrously, one of his primary problems of the moment was effectively resolved while still the strong patrol was on its way to the stream and the trees beyond. Upon being refused return of any of his personal weapons by Kaoru the tank officer had gone into a livid, frothing rage, shouting vile utterances at his captor the one moment, the next lying upon the ground, writhing, face twisted in obvious agony, hand clutching clawlike at his chest. Then, suddenly, he had gone first board-stiff, then limp, lifeless, unbreathing.

Kaoru would have liked it better to have put Sergeant Kiyomoto into the vacated command of the tank—he understood the vehicle better than any other infantryman, he had proven that he could drive it and, moreover, the surviving crew members all moved in undisguised fear of him—but he was needed too much in the day-to-day management of the infantry company, so the young commanding officer had put the vehicle under one of his juniors.

He would have liked to order the proper disposition made of the newly dead corpse of the tank officer, but he knew not but that the ascending smoke of a funerary pyre would attact the decidedly unwelcome attentions of the enemy in one form or another, so he had the body stripped of all its equipment and most of its uniform, then buried on the hillside near the mouth of the tunnel, taking a compass bearing of the location and noting it down for the eventual turnover to battalion headquarters. Under the circumstances, he felt that he had done his best by his deceased brother officer.

The patrol was gone far longer than the mission should have required and, although Kaoru had made good use of the time by positioning the men out of sight from the ground or air and positioning the tank just inside the mouth of the tunnel with the cart behind it, the company commander was getting more than a little worried when the watching Sergeant Kiyomoto came to report that the missing patrol had been seen recrossing the stream, apparently bearing with them at least one body, either seriously wounded or dead.

While the soldier who had died of a broken neck when he had fallen from a tall tree after being sent up to try to spot the track was being stripped and buried beside the tank officer, Kaoru had occupied the commander's place while Sergeant Kiyomoto had driven the tank over to seek himself for the mysteriously missing track. They had not found it then or ever since. Nor, since setting off to the west in search of it, had they ever again been able to relocate the tunnel mouth or the two graves, despite the carefully noted compass readings.

When diesel fuel for the tank was almost nonexistent, Kaoru had discussed the matter with his two officers, and the decision had been reached that they should make a permanent camp where they then happened to be. It was a place that seemed to offer many benefits; both large game and smaller seemed abundant in the vicinity along with several types of edible wild plants and both fish and crustaceans in the flanking stream.

And there was abundant proof that some other party once had found this spot favorable. On the hillslope about halfway between base and low crown, there still stood the log walls of a structure about thirteen meters long and four meters wide in outside measurements. Two other, smaller, almost square huts of identical construction stood downslope closer to the stream and, farther down still, lay the tumbled logs of still another that seemed to have been wrecked by some flood which had undermined its footings.

The decision being made, the logs of the larger building had been meticulously examined and, upon being determined basically still sound, Kaoru had ordered the interior dug clear of earth and debris. The excavations had, early on, revealed the way in which the collapsed roof had been constructed— interlaced branches holding a layer of turf and itself supported by interior columns and girders of wood.

Beneath the last layers of earth and rotted wood had been found two circular firepits and, most welcome, a fine selection of cooking pots and pans wrought of verdigrised brass, bronze, and copper and some lumps of useless rust that had once been knives or utensils of some nature.

There had also been moldering bones beneath the last layers. At least six sets of them had been human remains—ranging from one that had been an infant to at least three full-grown adults—and some had the appearance of butchered animals bones or bone tools. One, however, that one found nearest to the entry and between the two firepits, had been that of a gigantic beast. Kaoru had been sent for when first the size of the thing had been realized—at least four full meters from tailtip to snout—and had been on the spot throughout its disinterment.

It had appeared to the senior officer that the beast had in some way blundered hard enough against a treetrunk column to knock it out of place and thus bring down the entire, immensely heavy sod roof on itself and all within. The rotted remains of the thick main beam still lay across the skeleton's crushed spine and ribcage, and the column itself lay upon the skull it had splintered just behind the tooth-studded jaws.

Looking at the overall enormity of the skeleton and the size and quantity of the recurved teeth, Kaoru could not repress a strong shudder. He could not imagine just what sort of a beast the monstrous bones had once supported, though the teeth looked vaguely reptilian, shaped a little like those of a python, he thought. Lizard? Possibly so, but most probably not, for not even the oversized monitor lizards of that island near Sumatra got anywhere near this big. He just hoped that he never would see the like of this in the flesh. It was to be a vain hope.

Within the succeeding months, almost all of his officers and men were killed—and sometimes eaten—by living relatives of that huge skeleton found in the old log house. Rifle fire could not stop or even slow the terrible things, and they could run faster than any man, though only for short stretches. Powerful as they were, their attack almost always resulted in the death of at least one man.

Brutal and deadly experience established that the only sure way to kill them was either a sustained and well-aimed burst of machinegun fire, a lucky hit by 50mm mortar shell, 37mm tank gun or grenade, or determined men pinning the thing down with bayonets long enough for another man to step in and sever the spine with stroke of sword or machete or axe. Since the things scavenged as well as predating, Sergeant Kiyomoto had devised and baited deadfalls of heavy logs; one monster had been killed in this way, but none since that one.

Initially, it had seemed to be the two mules that the monsters came seeking—the invaluable mules, without which the snaking of logs from out the forests would have been made far more difficult and strenuous of accomplishment than it already was. And so, until a safe, strong pen and stable could be constructed to house them, the draft beasts had been brought into one end of the big log house when not in use and guarded.

When, of a night, one of the monsters had tried to

break in through the single, thick-planked and heavily barred door, to be pinned down by bayonets and axed and sworded to death on the very doorstep, Kiyomoto had set the men to felling even more trees, stripping them, digging deep holes and setting them in a row all around the log house and enough land for a few other buildings to be erected later. The palisade logs had not been abutted one to the next, but rather left with enough space between them for a man but not a monster to pass through; in this way, only a single gate just wide enough for a mule was necessary.

Kaoru and all his dwindling company had discovered that the fearsome creatures were definitely reptiles, but such reptiles as no one could recall ever having seen or heard described. They also had made the discovery that the flesh of the huge things was not only edible but also tender and tasty if properly prepared and cooked, so the attacking monsters they had had to kill in defense did not go to waste. So fond did they all become of monster-flesh, in fact, that they not only eagerly anticipated another highly dangerous attack, but often tempted one or even set out to deliberately hunt down the creatures, if they suspected the presence of one in the general vicinity.

Not a few men having been lost in this pursuit, their bayoneted rifles having placed them in a proximity to their quarry that had proved deadly in the end, Sergeant Kiyomoto had come up with and—with, of course, the commander's approval—implemented the making of long spears: shafts of ash or oak, knife-edge points fashioned of mild-steel armor stripped from the fuelless tank and cold-hammered into shape by him, then fastened firmly in place by way of brass rivets fashioned from 37mm shell cases. These proved themselves in use, and quickly. They were long enough to allow a man to maintain a safe distance from one of the creatures while at the same time pinning him securely that the men with swords or axes might do their deadly work on the dangerous beast.

Though unspeakably horrified by this callous desecration of their huge, complex weapon by a mere sergeant of infantry, the three remaining members of the tank crew liked to eat monster-meat too and usually kept their peace.

For all their appalling losses and how seldom they won so much as a nibble of flesh anymore, the big beasts still occasionally tried themselves against the deep-sunk palisades, often, oddly enough, by day. In such cases, when most of the men might be some distance away at some task or another, the guards on duty joined to spear-pin and axe the smaller ones and machinegun the largest. They none of them needed orders to aim for the toothy heads and expend only what was absolutely necessary to the job at hand of the steadily dwindling supply of 7.7mm ammunition.

The men, for some reason, took to calling their edible foes "dragons," though they little resembled any representation of a classic dragon, and Kaoru had himself taken up the practice, at least in his thoughts. Sergeant Kiyomoto, on the other hand, had named the monsters "Burma beef."

Toward the effort of maintaining proper morale, discipline, physical conditioning and *esprit de corps* under conditions that were, at best, often very trying, Kaoru had established and seen kept up a correct, military schedule of training and assigned duties for all members of his much-reduced company, nor did even he stick at joining the ranks in the physical and weapons drills most often overseen and conducted by the more than competent Sergeant Kiyomoto.

That had been why, of a morning—early morning, prior to the first meal of the day—he had been in ranks like any common soldier, spear-armed, unshod and in minimal clothing, responding to the snarled commands of the professionally glowering Sergeant Kiyomoto.

When one of the on-duty perimeter guards had reported having seen the unmistakable tracks of a large dragon on the banks of the stream at the place wherein it entered the winding defile—fresh tracks, laid down since sunset of the preceding evening—Kaoru had detailed one of the spearmen in formation to run back to the log house, fetch his swords and an axe (which was the much preferred weapon of Sergeant Kiyomoto) then follow after the rest of them at his best speed. Then he, the company sergeant and the remainder of the drill formation had set off through the long, narrow, meandering, brush-grown defile, set to beard a big dragon.

By purest coincidence, at a point only some third of the way to where the defile would debouch into the open space wherein their smaller stream joined a large (which larger was, Kaoru was certain in his own mind, some nameless tributary of the Irrawaddy River), the leading runners of the hunt chanced to flush a trio of red deer does. Kaoru managed to spear one of the big cervines in the side, just behind the shoulder, but the unbarbed spearhead pulled out as the wounded and terrified creature surged ahead. So the erstwhile dragon hunt suddenly, unexpectedly, became a deer chase, for—as Sergeant Kiyomoto would have put it in his earthy, rural way—meat was meat.

As was usual in running hunts, Corporal Tanuki took the lead, his short but powerful legs churning so fast as to frequently look like only blurs of motion. Also as usual under like circumstances, he was closely trailed by the other corporal—one of the erstwhile tank crew, Tanuki's patent rival in many ways, who despised mere infantrymen as much as had his late officer, and whose presumptive behavior had often brought down upon him the heavy, horny hands of the grim sergeant of company, Kiyomoto—the tall, slim Numata.

When Corporal Tanuki's shouts were heard by the closely bunched average-speed runners, the officer and sergeant included, that not only was the doe down on the bank of the large stream but that a sizable dragon was feeding on her carcass, all the men grinned, took fresh grips on their spears, gasped as deep breaths as they could and did their best to increase the pace of their tired, trembling legs.

As he ran on, just a bit behind the hulking Sergeant Kiyomoto, Kaoru sincerely hoped that the man got up to them with his swords before one was needed; otherwise, someone would have to try to put a spearpoint into the eye of the pinned but thrashing, powerful and still deadly-dangerous monster . . . and not a few of the now-deceased officers, NCOs and men of his company had died while essaying just so risky a task in a hunting of dragons.

CHAPTER X

While reviewing, studying, and scrutinizing the file folders of assorted reports relating to the case of *County versus Yancey Mathews*, David Klein regretted for the umpteenth time getting even peripherally involved in this mess of rural litigation. Against all his prejudices and proclivities, he was beginning to find himself sympathizing with, empathizing with, even agreeing with that cornball, reactionary sheriff, something that he never in a billion years could have imagined he would or could have ever done as little as six months before. The emotions he had begun to feel simply were not proper for a person like him: a true progressive, a proven and implacable foe of the fascist, racist, sexist, imperialistic, bloodthirsty, baby-burning, money-grubbing, red-baiting establishment.

David had not graduated law school anywhere near to the top percentile of his class; truth to tell, he barely had graduated at all. And not only had his father—his pompous, arrogant, hypocritical and disgustingly well-heeled farther—flatly refused to take his youngest son into the family law firm with his elder brothers, an uncle and cousins, but he had declined even to try to use his many contacts to get David into any other prestigious practice.

In their last meeting, his father—looking, in his meticulously tailored silk-and-wool three-piece suit, his gold Rolex watch, his short-cropped, Grecian-Formulaed hair, his Miami Beach-tanned face and his contact lenses, the very epitome of all that his youngest son most hated about the land of his birth—had said, "David, you know well that you were offered the best education that I could afford, the equal of that offered your older brothers and your sister, Raquelle, no less than what your grandfather offered me and your uncle, way back when. From your freshman year in undergraduate school on, you had the use of a good car, tuition, room and board, charge cards and a checking account. All that you were expected to do was to study, apply your known intellect and develop into a fine, professional man like your brothers have done.

"So, with all these benefits, you did what was expected of you? Oh, no, David, not you, not our little Dave Klein, not him! You could have majored in anything you wished—law, medicine, accounting, dentistry, business administration, engineering, psychology even—but you chose to major in revolution, so that it's cost the family thousands of dollars over the last few years to get you into new schools when the old ones chucked you out, more thousands to keep you out of jail so that your poor mother wouldn't lose her mind.

"So, now you've graduated . . . by the skin of your teeth. And you did finally manage to pass the state bar examination. But now, thanks to your extracurricular insanities of past years, you are strictly on your own. With your record of repeated misdemeanor arrests and convictions, no respectable firm is going to be willing to take you on until and if you can manage to prove yourself as something more than an anarchist bomb-thrower. Why, oh why, David? Why couldn't you have ignored the radicals and stuck to the books? You had such great promise, more promise than did either of your brothers at your age."

Bitterly, David had replied, "You're a windbag, you know that, Daddy? You always bragged about being a lifelong Democrat, a liberal, a humanist, and it was all just pure bullshit! Where were your so-called principles when this rotten sewer of a fascist country was supporting a totalitarian dictator in Saigon and all your fat-cat friends were growing even fatter and richer making napalm to barbeque yellow-skinned, slant-eyed children in Vietnam and Cambodia and Laos? Where was your famous humanism when, if we did study hard and graduated, we knew we'd go directly into the fucking Army or something and end up crippled or killed even? What did *you* ever do to try to stop that unjust war? What, Daddy, what?"

His father had shaken his head, slowly. "David, that war is over, done, finished, but you, God help you, are still fighting it and I fear that, until you at long last grow up, that's just what you'll keep doing

I agree that the time and the place, the people we were supporting and the way in which the war was conducted, all were . . . ahh, ill chosen. But unjust? Not at all, David. That phrase, 'an unjust war,' is an infamous Marxist catch-phrase; to them, an unjust war is any conflict that does not, is not intended to advance the goals of Marxism.

"Drafted? David, you know and knew back then that you never would ever be drafted. You're Four-F, son, just like your cousin, Judah. Look, you keep fighting that war as long as you feel you must, but please let the rest of us alone to get on with our lives and our work in the real world. Okay?

"No, I couldn't look your mother in the face if I didn't try to do something to help you get a job of sorts."

He had taken a three-by-five card from under the tooled-leather edging of his blotter and shoved it across his polished teak desk with one manicured hand. "Get in touch with this man. He's your kind of people, David, he used to be a card-carrying CP member and he's as radical as he ever was, it's said, for all that he's now chin-deep in Democratic politics. He really likes perpetual undergraduates, like you, and as he hires P.D.s for that region, he just might be willing to take you on. I do this not for you or for him, but for your mother, understand that.

"If this man does take you on, you can have the Ford wagon as my parting gift. You won't suffer, no matter how small the remuneration, you know it and I know it, for your mother will keep sending you money whether I like it or not. I can only hope and heartily pray to the God of our People that experiencing real life, in the raw, out in the actual world and divorced from the womb of academe, you'll start to grow up. Goodbye, David."

The longer and the better David got to know his superior, the less he liked or even respected the man. He might have seemed a frothing radical to a man as reactionary as David's father, but in David's eyes he was nothing more than a sad, aging, Great Depression Era party-pink, still searching for an attractive woman who really practiced free love.

There was never any doubt in David's mind that the man owned real power in the incredibly corrupt Democratic political machine at state level; otherwise, Victor Owen Niedermeier Fridley would long since have been out on his ear from the civil service job he performed so poorly, and his stable of youngish misfits along with him.

And misfits they all were; even though it went hard against the grain, David Klein had had to recognize and admit to himself that unpalatable fact early on in his enforced relationship with them. Von Fridley had led him to expect a staff of dedicated social activists, highly skilled and polished legal crusaders in constant defense of the impoverished, disadvantaged victims of a callous, brutal, degrading society, and David was certain that that was just how Fridley viewed them and they viewed themselves and each other. But David was realist enough right from the start to understand just what was the truth of the matter.

As compared to conditions in the densely populated and ethnically diverse urban area from which David had come, there was very little crime of a serious nature in that part of the state that fell under the scope of Fridley and his overstaffed office. The bulk of the clientele of his department's young attorneys consisted of beer-bar fights, chronic speeders, common drunks, joy-riding car thieves, spouse beaters, occasional burglars or house-breakers, accused prostitutes, more rarely a bootlegger or a marijuana dealer or grower, and very rarely a case of manslaughter or murder. Unlike the dockets clogged for years by backed-up cases in and around the city of David's birth, the conduct of legal affairs in the environs of his first job was slow, unhurried, done in traditional fashion and presided over by gentlemen judges of the old school, the stripe of jurist that David had been taught to despise. In this small city, suburban, and rural setting, plea-bargaining was quite uncommon, the expected norm being trial by jury even in matters that would have been considered of so little consequence or importance in David's home city as to be heard, if at all, by a police-court judge or a magistrate.

David felt terribly misplaced and lonely in so provincial a setting, but he was also by then aware that he was very lucky to be holding any sort of job in the legal profession. True, by big-city standards his yearly remuneration was a very sick joke, but he knew it to be a third again higher than that of most public school teachers in the locality and, considering the much lower costs of living in these boonies, it could be tolerated and could even have served to support him after a fashion, but of course he could also count on a couple or three hundred each month from his doting mother up north.

It was because of his maternal parent's largesse that David had been able to secure a furnished apartment rather than move into a rooming house like the rest of Fridley's motley crew. But as he always had been surrounded by friends or reasonably friendly acquaintances, owned inbred social graces and usually made friends quickly and easily, he soon found himself feeling miserably lonely and alone in his new home and workplace.

Although they might and did often compete fiercely in court, David's father, uncle, brothers and cousins and their professional peers were almost all friends in private life: belonged to the same clubs, played the same golf courses and bridge tournaments, lunched regularly in the same places, even kept their boats in the same expensive marinas.

That similar civilized civility was the practiced norm of behavior in this smaller city, too, became obvious to David at just about the same time that he discovered that he and any other attorney employed by Von Fridley was automatically beyond the pale, a pariah, barely acceptable as human and then only in performance of duty. Even merely touching his hand or being seen talking to him outside the environs of the courthouse seemed to be further than any of his fellow professionals was prepared to go.

David could not understand the situation into which he had found himself flung, and neither Fridley nor any of the others of his staff had been able or willing to offer any reasons that made sense to the urbane scion of the House of Klein, for he knew of more than one practicing attorney in the city area who was far more of a real leftist than was Fridley but was still treated with personal and professional respect by those with whom he had cause to move in the course of his practice of the law.

It had not been until he had deliberately poured on his not-inconsiderable charm that he had gotten some hard but eminently believable answers from a middle-aged, plump and dowdy but very garrulous court clerk. Once he had heard of the strange types who had worked for Fridley within the past decade, of their at least singular personalities, quirks and generally unenviable ends, he understood the open suspicion, verging upon hostility, with which he and the other P.D.s were being treated.

Mattie Querry knew all and freely told all, gravely but with easily discernible relish in the recountals. She was nearing her retirement date, she knew where fully as many bodies were buried as did Von Fridley and, therefore, she moved and spoke in no slightest fear of the man, unlike many others on the court-house staff.

"And then there was that young Mr. Gluck," she began before stuffing yet another chocolate from the box David had most recently brought to her in her private office, which room reeked of the odor of camomile tea. "He didn't look too odd, you know, Mr. Klein. Really, a body would never of suspected for one minute about him. Well, he was rooming over to Gladys Parker's house, but he always kept his room locked up tight . . ." Another of the chocolates was popped into her mouth. "Gladys, she didn't mind nor make anything of it at all, long as he left his dirty linens and towel and all out in the hall by his door each Friday and took in the fresh, it was that much less work for her and Jewel, her maid then, to do. Likely, she nor nobody would of known anything hadn't come that—" another chocolate met the fate of its predecessors between her dental plates—"during the very hottest week that whole summer, something blowed out in her central air conditioning and this just terrible, awful odor started coming through the door of his room."

As the woman had told more and more of this tale, David had tried to keep down his own gorge and had wondered just how she could tell it all and still keep stuffing herself with the dark-brown chocolate candies.

"Well now, Mr. Klein, the room that young Mr. Gluck had was one of the two at Gladys's house has a private bath and lavatory, the very same one that Miss Fisch has now, and horrible as that smell was, of course, all poor Gladys could think was the septic tank had done backed up and the toilet had overflowed. It wasn't 'til she tried to unlock the door she found out wasn't the same lock on it; Mr. Gluck had put a new lock her key wouldn't fit on it. She got mad, then, and had one of the air conditioning men come up and force the door open. He was my next-door neighbor's cousin's nephew, so I heard both Gladys's side of it all and his, too."

Having exterminated the top layer of the two-pound box of candies, the woman dumped the paper and cardboard refuse in her trash can and began on the lower layer. "Mr. Klein, all it took was one look inside that room for to tell it wasn't no overflowed toilet that awful odor was coming from. Gladys called the police, she couldn't think of anything else to do, just then, and I've seen some the pictures they took in there, too." Politely, she finished crunching the nutmeats and swallowed before she took up her recountal.

"All over that big, lovely room, Mr. Klein—on the bureau, on the windowsill, on the dresser, even on the bedside table—it was piles and pieces of manure, human waste, all molded like children's modelling clay, and in the bathroom it was a five-gallon plastic mop bucket that had disappeared sometime before from the broom closet about half full of more manure. Could you believe it?" So saying, the woman stuffed another piece of chocolate into her maw.

"Well, when it all came to come out and all, old Carver, the janitor—you've seen him, Mr. Klein, the white-headed, light-skinned nigra-boy. Lands of Goshen, he's been here long's me!—he told ever'body about finding pieces of manure all shaped up like them was found at Gladys's house in the men's washroom here in this very courthouse, too."

The upshot of the matter, she had continued, had been a testy conflict of stubbornness and political clout between Von Fridley and Judge Lisburne, which had ended with that jurist's committal of the young attorney to the state home for the bewildered, still his lodging even as she spoke. Wetting a pudgy fingertip, Mattie had probed around in the bottom of the box for crumbs of dark chocolate, while David sat immobile, watching her and wondering if he could hold down his lunch until he had departed her stuffy office.

Other days and additional boxes of candy had elicited more tales of Von Fridley's imported legal talent. One had physically attacked the aged Judge Ben

Green upon being informed that a suit and tie, not a dashiki, was the proper attire for attorneys in his courtroom. Another had been apprehended while trying to smuggle a pistol to a client in jail. Still another, upon finding himself arrested for having added a quantity of lysergic acid diethylamide to the newly delivered refill bottle of mineral water in the attorneys' lounge, had protested that his had been a well-meant act, that all his peers were "too uptight" and much in need of "unlaxing." And one other had taken up an exhibit—a claw hammer—and with it gone after the prosecutor during a trial.

David's immediate predecessor had suicided in jail, while awaiting trial after being apprehended *in flagrante delicto* in a courthouse conference room with the retarded teenager he was just then representing.

However, Clerk Mattie Querry could not be complimentary enough to David, seeing a starry future for this first of Von Fridley's choices that met her critical approval. "It's just so good, Mr. Klein, to get a young man who knows how to be p'lite to ladies and isn't a lunatic or a pervert, who wears decent clothes like he knows how to and whose shirts is always clean and all. I don't know where Von Fridley found the rest over there, but it's plumb easy to tell you come from a good, decent, law-abidin' God-fearin' fambly is all. And you wash every day, too, a body can tell that, and your hair is long like so many mens seem to wear it nowadays, but it's combed and clean and I just wish some the others over there would try to look more like you, that Mr. Mullins in partic'lar."

Having earlier reflected that it could do him no

possible harm to own and continue to cultivate at least one friend in the mostly hostile courthouse, especially one possessing the power and influence of Mattie, so he made no defense of P.D. Morris Mullins. Another part of it, of course, was that in truth he empathized with her as regarded his erstwhile colleague.

Mullins was an immense man—over six feet tall, big-boned and weighing between three hundred fifty and four hundred pounds. He perspired constantly and profusely, seemed basically averse to using much soap and water on either his body or clothes and, on a warm morning in the confines of Fridley's baili-wick, being in forced proximity to Mullins could serve fair to bring up not only your breakfast but even the squib of toothpaste you swallowed after said meal. Mullins apparently could not produce a beard or moustache worthy of those names, so he went smooth shaven, but his hair was almost waist-length and dirty as the rest of him—dull, matted, looking to never have been combed or brushed. Personal ap-pearances and lack of grooming aside, however, Da-vid had quickly discovered that the huge, smelly, grubby man was easily the most knowledgeable and capable of the lot, so far as performance of his job was concerned.

The two other men were real oddballs, but David did not get to learn just how odd immediately. After Fridley had taken him to the courthouse and intro-duced him around, he had suggested that he learn the ropes through working with Amy Fisch. Had he known then to just what that assignment would soon lead, he would have begged Fridley to assign him to any of the others, even to the hulking, stinking, probably louse-ridden Mullins, rather than the plain, but slender and shapely young woman.

Fitz found, immediately he had entered the mind of the slender Japanese with the pair of swords, that his unsuspected occupation—rather, shared occupation—of that mind was different from his dream-sequence occupations of the mind of the hybrid, Seos. In this present case, awake and not asleep, he was aware not only of his host's body and senses but of his own body and senses, high up in its concealed observation point in the tree.

In the mind of Lieutenant Kaoru Naka, however, he was become aware in bare microseconds of all that had led up to this moment on the rocky stream bank, of all the experiences that had gone to shape and determine the young officer's tactics in facing the fearsome monster with his two ranks of spearmen, something that had at his first sight of it looked to the watching Fitz like a projected exercise in a messy form of mass suicide.

Now, however, armed with the young officer's memories of all the many similar encounters of spears versus dragons—some of those bigger even than this one—he was become aware of the fact that, though ever highly dangerous to all concerned, the feat was one that had been done and could be done and would, on this as most of the other occasions, end in a dead dragon and, were the hunters lucky, perhaps only one or two lightly injured spearmen.

As the twin ranks neared the dragon and its partially eaten kill, the monster rushed forward a few yards on all fours, then abruptly rose onto its larger, longer rear legs, hissing very loudly, its long, black-and-blue tongue flickering constantly in and out as its big, square head swivelled on the dewlapped neck and the living, ever-moving cloud of insects swarmed on and around the gore-slimed jaws.

In the portion of his mind still ensconced in his own body, Fitz thought, "Damn, now I know why I thought that thing's head looked so familiar. It wasn't that dream of Seos's land-dragon at all, it was books I read, pictures I saw on my own world, the one I came here from. Standing up like that, that damned creature looks like nothing so much as a scaled-down version of one of the reconstructions of a meat-eating dinosaur, the one they call a tyrannosaurus rex!"

Within a couple of spearlengths of their quarry, the two ranks of near-naked spearmen began to increase their intervals, first to form but a single rank of twice the frontage, then to form an arc which gradually spread about from its tips to completely encircle the towering, hissing beast of prey. Once formed, the circle began to slowly, carefully contract around the monster, the men moving lightly on the balls of their dirty, bare feet, the spears held before them at waist level, readied for a thrust or a slash with the edges.

The dragon lashed out at a spearman with its tapering tail, to gain nothing other than a bloody gash near the tail tip for its efforts, but as the circle contracted more, it did it again, then again, spraying blood each time, but still trying to strike one of the odd, two-legged creatures with the member.

When it suddenly lowered its toothy head and

rushed at one of the encircling spearmen, the man danced back out of the way of the lunge, while others came in from sides and rear to jam the sharp points of spears into muscles and between ribs, then drew them out to stab again or get out of the way of those gnashing jaws, that whipping if tattered tail and the horny claws on the feet.

"A shrewd stroke, Matsuda," growled Sergeant Kiyomoto, adding, "See how the blood bubbles coming out of that hole your spear made in him? You stabbed a lung that time."

The monster continued to turn round and round, its tongue flickering, both eyes and tongue detecting more of the two-legged things with the long, pointed, hurtful claws in any direction and every direction. It had been hurt but was not yet in any way really injured or crippled, and its lunges still were fast as ever, but the luck of the skilled dragon-hunters continued to hold and those at whom the monster lunged were able to avoid his teeth, claws and tail, while their comrades fleshed their waiting spears again and again, driving the steel points through the scaly hide and deep into muscles and internal organs.

After a few furious minutes of the contest, more than just the dragon's jaws and head were bloody; the marks of stabs and gashes speckled his hide in scores, each of them running blood. Ominously, more than just the one of the thoracic wounds now was sending forth bubbly blood, and the monster had ceased to either hiss or roar, needing all the air it could still get for its efforts in the battle against the horde of elusive would-be kill-thieves.

In the course of yet another furious rush at one of

the two-legged things that, like the others before,
always managed to stay just beyond range of teeth or
claws, the monster's gory flank brushed one of the
spearmen hard enough to send his slight, five-foot
body spinning, letting go his spear and deliberately
taking bruises and abrasion in falling in order to use
both hands to give protection to his precious, steel-
rimmed glasses.

Having missed as was become usual catching the
one it had lunged at, the dragon ignored the things
sticking into its body to turn and go after the creature just arising from the ground and lacking its
claw. That was when brawny Sergeant Kiyomoto
plunged into the fray, moving far faster than it might
have seemed possible for so big and broad and thick-
limbed a man. With a full-strength, two-armed swing
of his broad, cleaver-bladed axe, he inflicted a huge
gash deep into the dragon's meaty thigh, and when
the monster next made to put its weight upon that
ruined leg, it collapsed beneath him, its main tendon
now severed.

Helpless to do otherwise, the creature sank upon
its belly, using its remaining rear leg and the two
shorter front ones to support its weight as it still
tried to get at its tormentors with teeth or tail. But
now the spearmen closed in. Following the established pattern, they each moved to a designated spot
and, from that spot, always maintaining maximum
distance from the snapping jaws of the crippled beast,
thrust their spears into enough places to pin down
legs and tail firmly. Others of them stabbed hard into
places they knew from flaying dead dragons were

openings in the bone of the snout and only covered by skin and soft tissues; once they had pierced these, they drove the spears down and down, inexorably, until the steel points sank through the tongue and into the flesh and gristle beneath it to grate on the bone of the lower jaw itself.

And that was when Sergeant Kiyomoto once more swung up his axe and brought it downward in a blur, to cleanly sever the big dragon's spine with but the single blow. That done, a couple of the spearmen left their places and used their bloody weapons to keep the thrashing tail still enough for long enough for the other axeman to take it off near the body. When the taloned feet had all been axed off, the jerking, quivering dragon was rolled over onto its back and the flaying of the torn and multiply holed hide was commenced by the officer, using his *wakazashi* or shortsword. Then the sergeant took over command of the skinning, cleaning and butchering, sending a party back to the stockaded log house for equipment and supplies.

As Kaoru stood off to one side, observing the laboring men and their sergeant, noting the dexterous way in which the big noncom handled the *wakazashi* of the dead tank officer, he once more felt his old frustration that he could not wean the sergeant away from the axe and persuade him to use one of the three spare *katanas* instead.

The oddly shaped axe blade was not made of steel but of some bronzen alloy. It had been discovered during the final cleaning-out of the log house, part of its rotted, oaken haft still in its socket. It had been

Sergeant Kiyomoto who had found the tool or weapon and also he who had first noted and pointed out to the others how the edge of the verdigrised blade exactly fitted into a deep nick in the thigh bone of one of the dragon skeleton's rear legs, remarking that that wound might well be the reason that the heavy creature had fallen so hard against the wooden column as to bring the world-heavy sod roof and his timbers down to crush or smother to death every living thing inside the house.

In his spare time—though the conscientious man did so many things, supervised so many other activities that Kaoru often wondered when he found the requisite time to sleep or to eat—the sergeant had cleaned the last of the oxidation from off the ancient, thick, heavy blade, honed its long, straight edge to a sharpness the equal of any *katana,* then fitted and tried a number of hafts of differing shapes and lengths until he found one that had suited him—just about a meter long and as straight as a *bo*-stave. After that, the axe was his only weapon in dragon-hunts.

When an improperly pinned dragon had bitten off the foot and part of the lower leg of Kaoru's last junior officer as the young man—a former classmate at the Imperial Military Academy of his company commander—had stepped in with his own issue *katana* to deliver the spine-severing blow, Kaoru, after seeing his friend properly cremated, the ashes gathered and stored, had sent for Kiyomoto.

Despite the burly noncom's blank face, Kaoru had, from dint of his long acquaintance with the man, known that he was less than pleased at being told

226

that he now, as second highest ranking man remaining to the fragment of the infantry company, should consider himself an acting officer and, in significance of his new rank, wear one of the three swords available. Also, he would henceforth be required to act the part of opponent in Kaoru's frequent practice bouts with the pair of *katana*-sized and -shaped staves.

Upon being ordered to choose among the available weapons, the knowledgeable sergeant had obediently done so, selecting the pair of fine antique swords that had been those of the tank officer. But therein the thing had ended. The sergeant had worn the pair only when he felt he must for the sake of his duty to obey and demonstrate his respect for his young officer, but when it came to slaying dragons, he still preferred and invariably used his old bronze axe, whether or not he happened to be wearing one or more of the swords at the moment.

And it was all a terrible waste, Kaoru always thought with sadness, for his bouts of army-style fencing with wooden copies of the bamboo "swords" of traditional *kendo* had shown him just how quick, powerful, accurate and deadly a swordsman the big, tall sergeant could easily and rapidly become . . . did he put his mind to it. After many long months of regular bouts, vain encouragements to Kiyomoto to put aside his axe and take up a sword to replace it, only to see the very next dragon axed down even while the sergeant might be wearing a sash holding both *katanga* and *wazakashi*, the young officer finally had demanded to be told of the real reasons underlying Kiyomoto's fascination for the archaic, bronze tool rather than the fine, almost equally antique heir-loom blades that had clearly been family or clan weapons of the deceased tank officer.

The story he had heard in obedient reply to his demand had been an exceedingly strange one, but as no one ever had known Sergeant Kiyomoto to lie for any reason, Kaoru had had no option but to believe him in this instance.

Standing in his accustomed stiff, straight, very military posture, speaking as he always did to any officer or superior, with humble dignity: "My honorable father is truly a smith, as I have often said, sir, but he is that and far more, which last I have left unsaid in times before. For more than six centuries have our ancestors drawn the raw iron from the stones and dirt to produce the finest steel and from that steel to fashion the best of blades. Indeed, the blades of the *daisho* which I now bear at your insistence were wrought by an ancestor; his mark is upon the tangs. Another ancestor wrought your own blades, sir. But to the present issue, these matters are almost unimportant.

"What is important is the fact that, in addition to being a clan of hereditary smiths, my ancestors also are hereditary priests of Fire and Iron. Long, long before that, they were fashioners and priests of other metals as well: bronze and, even earlier, copper. I, too, am such a priest, sir, this is why all metals speak to me, yield up their secrets to my hands.

"Ours is one of the very oldest of priesthoods, sir, it far antedates Shinto, Buddhism or most others that might be named. It has remained active and viable among the select few, passing from father to sons down the endless generations ever since the distant days when true gods did walk upon the earth and breed with beasts to sire the beings we now call men.

"Although these ancient beings looked like men, they were half-gods and, as such, all able to perform true wonders the like of which we mongrelized descendants can only sometimes dream. They could fly like birds, commune silently over great distances even without the machines which we must use to so do. They could make huge, heavy stones float on the air like feathers on the wind and thus easily move them wherever they might wish. They could also shape these stones as easily as a potter shapes soft clay—give round stones sharp angles and edges, make thick stones flat, make rough stones smooth as glass.

"As world ages rolled past, the true gods who had spawned the very first of these man-gods sent silent messages thousands of leagues into the minds of their descendants and thus taught them first how to extract copper from stones and then, long after, how to use tin and other things to make the copper tougher, harder and more durable for the fashioning of weapons and tools with which to replace those of stone, bone, antler and wood.

"But as true men grew ever more numerous upon the earth, in almost all the lands, the blood-heritage of the god-men began to thin, to be all too often diluted by that of the ungod-descended ones who were come of only beasts. Those few clans and families that stayed almost pure and retained some few of their once-vast powers ruled over true-men for long and long or, using the remnants of their inherent godliness in other ways, they made of themselves craft-priests. His Imperial Majesty, the Son of Heaven, Emperor of Japan, is the scion of one of the former of those two lines of god-descended ones; I am come of the other, sir."

CHAPTER XI

Kaoru recalled that he had just sat there in the log house, stunned speechless at that which his two ears just had heard, wondering deep within his mind if he could be hallucinating, or if he truly had just heard the man who stood at the posture of attention before him, clad as properly as possible in a worn, tattered and incomplete uniform of the Imperial Army Infantry, despite his humility and dignity appearing nothing more than the young officer always had considered him to be—an exceptionally effective noncommissioned officer—tell him that he was not only a priest of an ancient religion of which Kaoru had never heard but a few passing references in all his life, but also a living descendant of the old gods and thus akin to the Emperor himself.

Obviously unaware of the mental turmoil his words had wrought upon his military superior, Sergeant

Kiyomoto had continued, saying, "I am not of anything remotely resembling true purity of god-descent, of course, sir, but neither is the Son of Heaven nor has any other being upon earth been for centuries almost beyond reckoning. But the true gods, from wherever they now dwell, still communicate with those with even bare drops of their heritage, in dreams; those with enough innate abilities or those who, like me, have had the benefit of mental training and discipline from birth can identify these dreams and glean from out the imagery the real meanings of them. This is how I came to first join the Imperial Army, sir."

At last able to articulate, Kaoru demanded, "A *dream*? You're trying to tell me that a mere dream of a night impelled you to become a simple infantryman in the ranks? A swordsmith from a family and clan of swordsmiths? Man, you need never have gone to war at all; you and your craft are far too valuable to the Empire to waste."

"I know, sir," agreed Sergeant Kiyomoto in his calm humility, "but it was the will of a true god that I do so, and such will is not to be disobeyed lightly. This dictum was impressed upon me from my earliest memories upon Earth in this body, and when my honorable father heard from me of the dream, he could say nothing but that I must obey the will of the god."

"Exactly when was this, Sergeant?" asked Kaoru.

"In the Year of the Rat, as the Buddhists reckon, sir," the burly noncom replied. "In the next year, I was sent with my unit to China, but I knew even then that long years must pass before that for which I was compelled to seek out foreign lands would occur."

"Oh, how did you know? Did this god speak to you and tell you in your dream?" queried the officer.

The noncom allowed his face to relax in a brief, gentle smile. "No, sir, gods are not so obvious. Early in the dream, there was a rat and, at its ending, a cock did ruffle its feathers, raise up its head and loudly crow. It was in that way that I knew that the time when I must be of service to the god would be in the Year of the Cock, you see, sir.

"Now the time of my service is very near. The dream so long ago told me that, near to the time I would be needed by a god, three precious things would come into my possession. One, the first, would be a very ancient and holy artifact which I must keep always by me until the appearance of the being for whom it is intended. The second and third things were to be works of art wrought long ago by a priest of my heritage," he raised his left hand from his side just long enough to pat the sharkskin-covered hilt of the *katana*, "and that is just what these fine swords are, sir, as I said earlier; under the hilt, cut deeply into the tang, is the personal mark of a priest-smith of my family, a very distant but direct ancestor."

"And did one of your ancestors make the axe, as well?" asked Kaoru in curiosity, "Or can you tell?"

"Yes, sir," answered the sergeant. "It was first cast, then tempered and decorated by some bronze-smith priest. But how long ago? Time beyond the reckoning, sir. Before men had learnt the arts of iron or steel, most likely. Those worn markings which adorn the flats of the blade are not mere aimless, attractive tracery, either. When I was a boy, my honorable father took me up high on the slopes of certain mountains and there showed me huge stones upon which—dimmed and nearly erased by who knows just how many centuries of rain, snow and wind-blown sand—were almost-identical markings, and he attested that they were the writing-signs of a language of such antiquity that the very name of it has been forgotten by even us of the purer heritage.

"Sir, you think of only the spear and the swords as weapons and despise the axe as a mere, commonplace tool, but sir, you do not realize that the axe was weapon long before it was altered to become tool. Indeed, the sword is only a kind of long-edged, short-hafted axe, sir—actually, an amalgam of knife, axe and spear, that is the *katana* and, especially, the old *no-dachi*, the sword of the olden days, with the longer, thicker, wider, heavier blade.

"This bronze axe and the one I fashioned of steel from off the tank for Private Ota are in no way mere woodchoppers' tools, for all that they can be used in butchering carcasses of dragons and other large game; they are weapons. In addition, however, I am certain that the older one, the bronzen one, is also a godrelic, a talisman, wrought in incredibly ancient times in some distant land by a god-man for himself or for another of his sacred ilk. Where it has travelled since that day in the dim past, how it has travelled to at last come to rest for just how long beneath the bones of that dragon, these are questions that only a true god could answer.

"But soon after it had been found and I had cleaned it, restored its edge and properly hafted it, I had another god-sent message in a dream."

"And where did this dream order you to go, pray

tell?" asked Kaoru. "Did it by chance tell you just how to get through these damned, unmapped Burmese hills and valleys back to where we can find our battalion before we're all listed as missing in action or even as deserters in the face of the enemy? Sergeant, I'm still a young man; I could enjoy life far more I think than I'd enjoy *seppuku*."

"I am to go nowhere else, sir," said the sergeant, gravely. "A god is on his way here, toward this place. The axe is intended for him, for his holy use, as was long ago foreordained."

"On his way here, is he?" commented Kaoru, "And just what does he look like—Japanese, Chinese, Burmese or what? How are you supposed to know him when you see him? Will he have *G*O*D* in fine calligraphy upon him somewhere, Sergeant?"

Kiyomoto shook his head slowly. "The how of recognizing this god was unclear, as dream-messages often are, sir, but I trust the true god who sent the message. I know that it will all be made clear to me in the true god's own time; I will be shown, will know, this god who is to receive the bronze axe.

"But, sir," he dropped the level of his voice, for all that they two were just then the only men in the log house, "although I have said nothing, even intimated nothing of it to the men, I am certain that we are no longer anywhere in Burma . . . or even in any part of that world in which lies the countries known as Burma, Japan and China."

"*Whaatt?*" the officer burst out, clean forgetting his rank and its dignity, "Sergeant, are you ill? Did you sample some strange new plant, perhaps? You're not going mad, I hope, for the company needs you.

You should make the time to get more sleep, you know, you do and try to do too much, and extended loss of sleep can cloud the mind and the judgment, that was taught to us in the Imperial Military Academy; at a battle called Five Days in the American Civil War, a rebellious general called Jackson Thomas Stonewall did not sleep and so misjudged the . . ."

"Sir, no, please do not worry yourself on my account," the noncom interrupted, hesitantly. "I have good, sound reasons for believing as I do about this matter. Does the honorable lieutenant choose to hear me?"

At Kaoru's nod, he said, "First, there was the matter of the maps, sir. Back in the place of the ruins, we still were in our own world, for marks on the maps matched marks on the face of the land. But when we came out from that tunnel, nothing upon the land has ever since even faintly resembled the markings on the maps and, in this place, none of the compasses will behave as they should, a thing that I never saw good, Imperial Japanese Army compasses to do in all my nine years of service to the Son of Heaven.

"Then there is the matter of the animals. Sir, there are no animals like these dragons in any place that I have ever been and in no place that I ever have heard anyone describe. Also, we have in our journey about these hills and valleys seen and often killed and eaten animals that never roamed the land of Burma or even China, India or Tibet. Who ever saw or heard of a tailless rat weighing at least thirty kilos in Burma, sir? Yet we have killed and eaten and tanned the pelts of no less than three of them, over the years . . ."

"Oh, Sergeant," said Kaoru, "enough is enough. Besides, we've not been here much more than one year. That's my estimate. We're none of us any older than we were when first we came out this end of that tunnel through that hill."

"Sir," asked Kiyomoto, "what of the mules? Why does the most honorable lieutenant think they died?"

Kaoru shrugged. "I cannot really say. I know very little of anything pertaining to animal husbandry. Perhaps a lack of the proper foods? Maybe the hard work to which we had to put them?"

"No, sir," Kiyomoto demurred. "None of those things. Those two mules, when they and the cart and tank joined our column, I examined closely. They both then were young, strong, healthy animals, in good flesh and as well cared for as can be any draft animal under combat conditions. Their army ration was hay and millet and what they were fed here was, if anything, a better, more varied and nutritious diet. If the honorable lieutenant will care to recall, after we set up camp here, we did have cause to use the mules for snaking out logs and many other draft purposes, but after that, once the palisades were up, it was seldom that we needed or used the mules.

"You are correct, sir, you are no older than when we all came here, none of us is. Indeed, I feel now much younger than a man of nearly forty years has any right to feel. Apparently, men do die here, but they do not age. Not so mules and other beasts, however. The mules, when they died despite all that I or their driver could do for them, were the very same pair of mules with which our column set out on the night march, the very same pair of young, strong mules. But when we cut up the carcasses of those two dead mules to use for dragon-bait, sir, it was apparent to both the driver and me that they were very elderly mules. How old were they? I would say, at least thirty years, maybe more."

"Impossible!" snorted Kaoru. "Had any such amount of time passed for us, we'd know it . . . I'd know it, realize it. Yes, we have been here for some time, but I last estimated that time at no more than fifteen to eighteen months, Sergeant. And what kind of a country would this, could this be to hold such properties, anyway? Tell me that!"

Kiyomoto sighed. "Of my own knowledge, I cannot, sir. However . . . there are old tales, legends of long ago, coming from many, many lands and races and realms, that tell of the cruel fates of men who found such lands and returned from them to tell the tales and, invariably, suffer most cruelly.

"It is said that, just before the most honorable Hideyoshi invaded Korea, long ago, a man named Shengin was sailing with his followers to join the army of his *daimyo* when a strange and sudden tempest blew the ship far, far out to sea. The ship was so badly damaged by lashing winds and crashing seas that it almost sank, but it did not and, with the abatement of the tempest and the calming of the waters, Shengin and his surviving followers set to effecting repairs and bailing out water. But they still had little control over their small ship when they saw that the sea was bearing it and them fast upon what clearly was a line of fearsome, rocky reefs, a beach lying beyond them and tall trees beyond the beach.

"When certain death of both Shengin and his followers seemed imminent, a fortuitous swell rose up under the ship, lifted it over the reef and deposited it safely within the quiet waters just beyond, and a gentle current bore it toward the sparkling beach until its keel grated on sand. All of them exhausted and some of them injured from their long, harrowing ordeal, Shengin and his followers dropped overside of their beached ship and waded through the warm, shallow water to the waiting shore.

"After they had rested long enough in the shade of the trees to somewhat restore them, Shengin ordered two of his *samurai* and their servants to take containers from the ship and proceed inland in search of fresh water and fruit, or whatever else they could find that men might eat, most of their own stores having been either lost or damaged in the tempest.

"The two *samurai*, each with his servant, went off in different directions and the youngest presently returned with a cask filled with fresh, cool water and another cask full of strange-looking but tasty and wholesome fruits. It then was long before the return of the elder *samurai* and his servant, and they did not come back alone or empty-handed.

"The folk who dwelt in that land called it *Hai-bara-zir*. They were not a people who in any way resembled Japanese, Koreans, Chinese or any other people Shengin had seen or heard described by others. Tall were they, taller than any of Shengin's men, and well-formed of body; though tanned by the sun, their skins were white and their hair and beards were none of them darker than a soft brown or dark red, their eyes either blue or grey or hazel or green.

"Many of these folk bore weapons—strangely formed

swords, spears, axes, dirks and odd bows—but they were more than merely friendly to the shipwrecked men. They all spoke a Japanese as good as Shengin's—his own, regional dialect, in fact—and they conducted Shengin and all his followers to their city, where much was made of these strangers. They all—from Shengin even to his lowliest *go-kenin*—were housed in luxury, feasted endlessly on myriads of strange but always delicious viands. Though mostly larger of body than Japanese women, with much larger breasts, the females of that city were nothing less than willing bed-partners to the party of Shengin, more than merely complaisant and fantastically stimulating in their actions. Available for but the asking, too, were both beverages and foods that could soothe body and mind to gentle languor, others that could quickly give energy and renewed strength and vigor to even the most exhausted.

"Not ever a willingly idle man, Shengin and his *samurai* did ask for service as warriors, only to be told that warfare did not exist, only hunting, fishing, farming and the gathering of wild-growing foodstuffs. He was told that there were but few folk in all the vast lands—seven cities, the inhabitants of all of them related and always friendly one toward the other. Few strangers ever came to *Hai-bara-zir*, they averred, and those that did were always treated well and allowed to stay or go, as they wished.

"Shengin was also told that the folk had once lived in another land, far, far away, but when threatened by a huge and most savage horde of barbarians, all had left their homeland, flown to *Hai-bara-zir*, settled, built their cities and since lived in peace and harmony. He was advised to forget all his arts and skills of war, as had they, and learn to enjoy life for the sake of living.

"But poor, loyal, dutiful Shengin could not so do. Nothing that he did, nothing that he ate or drank, no delicate pleasure that his body enjoyed could take from his mind the fact of his oaths given to his *daimyo*, his duty to honor them."

Kaoru waved a hand preremptorily. "Yes, yes, Sergeant, I recall that hoary old children's tale now; 'The Far Traveller' is what I remember it called. I heard it as a child in a slightly differing version and I'd forgotten it as I've forgotten so many of the fantastic fictions we then were told.

"When this character finally arrives back in Japan and goes to his home, his grandson rules there and the only one of his generation still alive to recognize him—although feeble with age and almost blind—is she who had been his youngest wife. After suffering many slights and injustices, he finally goes mad and, after somehow—I forget just how, now—acquiring a small boat, he sets sail eastward and is never again seen.

"But what does this errant nonsense have to do with anything, Sergeant? Or is your mind slipped and just rambling?"

"I must beg the pardon of the honorable lieutenant," said Kiyomoto, respectfully, "but the tale called 'The Affair of the Far Traveller' is no mere legend, though many today think it such. It is at least part truth. A man who called himself Abe Shengin, the same man of that clan who was thought to have been lost at sea during the time of Toyotomi Hideyoshi, did arrive in Japan in the third year of the Shogun Tokugawa Ietsuna; this is fact. Although appearing to be of no more than perhaps thirty years, he claimed to in fact be the grandfather of the then-family head and he bore the swords of that very man, assumed by all to be more than sixty years dead, he and all his war band.

"No one believed him, of course, and he suffered many, many indignities and vicissitudes first at the hands of the man he claimed to be his grandson and that man's housemen and servants, then at the hands of the head of the Abe clan. And he might well have finally been killed had not his informants in the land gotten word to the Shogun at Edo of these strange happenings, and ever a curious and enquiring man, the Shogun ordered that the man who called himself Abe Shengin be brought to tell his tale to him.

"When Tokugawa Ietsuna had heard the man out and had also questioned him at length and in great depth, he had the lands searched thoroughly for any still alive who might have known Abe Shengin prior to his supposed death. Two such were at last found, sir. One was an aged, almost sightless woman who had been the youngest wife of Abe Shengin for two years before he went away bound for the marshalling of the armies for the Korean Invasion; the other was an even more venerable priest-smith who had forged swords for Abe Shengin. This man was at the time of his being summoned to Edo by the Shogun Ietsuna more than ninety-three years of age; he also was one of my ancestors.

"Upon arrival at his court, both of these aged people were received and treated most graciously.

They were asked to dictate questions that only the real Abe Shengin could have been expected to be able to answer accurately, and this they did. Yet, when the Shogun, himself, put these questions to the far traveller, almost all of his responses matched the list of proper responses dictated by the most venerable man and woman. Then the two were brought before the mighty Ietsuna and asked to pass among those men there assembled, all garbed and accoutered and armed in the fashions of six decades past, and choose he who was most like the Abe Shengin they recalled. They hobbled about for some time, then sadly told the Shogun that the man, Abe Shengin, was not anywhere in the room. All thought that Tokugawa Ietsuna would be angry or, at the least, show some disappointment at these words, but he did not, seeming neither angry or sad. He ordered that certain members of the court not in antique garb be told that they might return to his presence.

"When these men entered, the mighty Ietsuna waved casually at them, all clothed and equipped in the height of the court fashion of that day, and suggested that perhaps the man, Abe Shengin, might be found in their ranks. Again the two elderly people went from man to man, staring long at faces, studying gestures, but again they had to sadly report that none of the courtiers could be the Abe Shengin they remembered. At this, the assembled all thought to see one of his properly feared rages coming upon the Shogun, but when he finally spoke, he sounded only a little sad and he ordered that the servants waiting with the gifts of appreciation for the old smith and the widow of Abe Shengin be summoned.

"When the majordomo came leading the servants and they came to stand before the two aged ones, the smith cried out, while the old woman screamed and would have fallen, save for the quick action of a courtier. When the Shogun demanded to know why their sudden cries, they both told him that one of the humble, plainly garbed servants was none other than Abe Shengin . . . but Abe Shengin almost exactly as he would have looked sixty years agone, having aged hardly at all in all those years.

"At this, the mighty Ietsuna showed much pleasure, as too did the whole of his court and household. He proclaimed that the Shogun was completely satisfied that, fantastical as it might seem, the far traveller was in truth none other than the original Abe Shengin, in the flesh and almost unaged in over six decades of elapsed time.

"My ancestor was thanked, most generously rewarded for his service, and carried home by servants and *samurai* of the mighty Ietsuna. At her request and that of Shengin, the old woman was allowed to stay at court with her long-lost husband until her death, at which time the Shogun had produced a rich and elaborate funeral for her and personally provided a very valuable, antique urn for her ashes.

"Shengin remained a favored and always honored guest of the Shogun for eleven years, travelling whenever the court travelled and otherwise making his home in Edo. Then, shortly after his aged wife at last had died and upon receipt of word of the death of his grandson by a fever, he asked of the Shogun permission to return to his family home, that he might present to his great-grandson the *daichi* that he had himself born for so many years.

"Tokugawa Ietsuna, regretting for all to hear that the press of official affairs would not allow him to himself accompany his long-time guest, friend and confidant on so old-fashionedly honorable and dutiful a journey, sent Abe Shengin off with his best wishes, in a style which would have befitted a powerful *daimyo* of an earlier time. On the very eve of the cavalcade's departure, Ietsuna summoned Shengin to wait upon him and at that time presented to him a *daichi* to replace that which he meant to pass on to his great-grandson. That *daichi*, sir, is one of the finest and most richly ornamented produced by my ancestors in that period; it still exists as an Imperial Treasure, at the Imperial Palace complex in Tokyo.

"But once the deed of honor was done, Abe Shengin did not go back to Edo. He sent the most of the cavalcade back, bearing a letter of explanation to the Shogun. Retaining only some horses, a handful of servants and two *samurai*, he travelled on about the countryside, visiting lands and places he had known so very long before, grieving within his own heart about the ugly changes that had come to pass, seeking out the very eldest of folk of every rank and class that they might talk to him of things that once mattered in life and did no longer in a world become crass and unknowing of honor and the proper obligations of duty, or oaths sworn, of the now-unheeded responsibilities of the holders of rank and power and wealth in the land.

"After a year of this, he sent back the servants, most of the horses and one of the two *samurai*, this one bearing not only another, final, letter for his sometime-patron and friend, the Shogun Tokugawa

Ietsuna, but word that the beautiful, precious *daichi* would be left for the Shogun in the trust of the family which had forged the blades. Then he and the last of his *samurai* travelled directly to the home of my ancestors, anxious to begin the final leg of his long, long journey.

"The eldest priest of my family at that period, sir, was one Kawabe. He of course welcomed his esteemed visitor, whose clan had, from the very earliest days, always been appreciative of the skill of mine, treating us both fairly and generously—not always the case with which the powerful deal with humble craftsmen.

"Obedient to his guest's request, Kawabe accepted the gift-*daichi* to be held in trust for the Shogun Tokugawa Ietsuna; then showed him available wares, and Shengin purchased of him a fine but less splendid *daichi*, that he might not go upon his planned journey unarmed. Then he asked that Kawabe find him a boat with a sail, but small enough for two men to easily handle, for the last of the Shogun's *samurai* insisted that the constraints of his honor and his oath-sworn duty compelled him to accompany Shengin on his full journey, wherever it might lead, however long it might take. Touched by the modern warrior's antique sense of honor and duty, Shengin had sadly accepted him into his service.

"However, when Kawabe had seen the boat secured and prepared and provisioned, Abe Shengin had had little gold left with which to repay him and so, after giving him all that he did have, he brought out and presented to my ancestor a singular stone. Black is that glass-smooth stone, looking like jet in strong light, but as the light grows dimmer about it, it lightens in hue and thin bands of many different colors can be seen dimly, moving about just under its surface; then, in full darkness, it becomes of a milky translucency, all the colored bands stronger, brighter, moving more swiftly, while the stone itself exudes a soft light, a radiance. I have seen and even handled this stone, sir; it is a treasured possession of our priesthood now, and although our agents have searched for hundreds of years in every nook and out-of-the-way corner of all the world, anything like it never has been found. We have long believed it to be not of the world of men, but of the world of gods. And Abe Shengin told my ancestor, Kawabe, that the peaceful folk of that land whereto the tempest winds and seas had borne his ship used larger examples of such stones, which there were most common, to light their homes of nights. I believe, sir, that this land here is that land or one much like it, a land of the gods."

"Is that why you are always selecting pebbles from out the stream beds and polishing them, Sergeant?" demanded Kaoru. "You imagine you'll find a stone such as that you describe in some Burmese watercourse? Perhaps, if you are very, very lucky, you might find a garnet or even a ruby—such things have occurred at rare intervals in Burma, they say—but not anything remotely resembling the wonder that you say came down from your distant ancestor."

At that juncture, Kaoru recalled something had come up in the camp-area that had required the presence of Company Sergeant Kiyomoto, and the two had never gotten around to resuming the discussion.

Fitz shuddered uncontrollably when he delved into these memories in the Japanese officer's mind, for he had seen a stone very much alike to the one the sergeant had told about. It had been while he and Cool Blue and Sir Gautier were hiking back south from the fringes of the dangerous, wide-spreading swamp which had blocked their northern progress and impelled them to retrace their steps to change direction.

As the fire had died to embers on the moonless and cloudy night, a dim radiance had been seen coming from a mound of boulders and earth. Curiously, Fitz had cleared away enough of the soil and pebbles to reveal a rock giving forth a misty light, with threads of a dozen or more colors looking to move about within it and just below the surface of it.

When he had called their attention to the phenomenon, Gautier had muttered of demons and devils, signed himself and begun to mutter prayers in Latin. But Cool Blue had just yawned widely and remarked, "Man, like he's sure superstitious, ain't he? Them rocks that lights up in the dark, like I seen them before, lotsa times, you know. Ain't too many around here, mostly, but like it's places they's all over the fucking place, man. Believe me, man, 'cause like since I been in the lion getup, thanks to old Saint Germain, the gut-butcher, I'm like hep to wizards and witches and all and ain't no magic in none them rocks, see, man, they all like natcherul, you know."

Fitz would have like to have taken the "natcherul" lamp along with him, but when uncovered in the morning, the glossy, black boulder that Cool Blue confidently assured him was what the light-producing stones looked like in sunlight was almost as big as his pack and far too heavy for either he or Sir Gautier to have packed any distance.

Was this a land of gods, he wondered? If it truly was and if he hung around long enough, despite the grey panther's endless insistencies that he hurry to pass his tests and meet the Dagda, would he get to see this·god who was supposedly coming to take possession of the bronzen axe? If he did see him, perhaps he would also be able to speak to him and, conceivably, get some straight answers out of him, not just go on forever tramping through these end-less woods and hills and valleys to no apparent purpose.

"But I'll be damned if I'm going to spend all that time up in this tree," he muttered to himself. "I wish to hell Cool Blue and Gautier, with or without his stinking pack of Norman cutthroats, would show up, so I could camp on the ground like normal people."

Kaoru, part of Fitz's mind still without his knowl-edge exploring his own, wandered idly west along the bank of the larger stream while Kiyomoto and the men butchered the dragon and what it had left of the red deer. Neither the host-mind nor the guest-mind even suspected that deadly peril waited hidden in the brush around the very next bend in that stream.

CHAPTER XII

Although he felt compelled to indicate foot-dragging reluctance to go, David Klein had truly felt overjoyed to get away from the city and the increasingly kinky and aggressive Ms. Amy Fisch.

When first he had "gotten to know her, really" (as she had later put it) on the day that he had watched her lose a client's case by turning an objective judge into a hostile judge by way of a screaming tirade after she had been referred to by a witness as "the lady-lawyer," he had not suspected just how odd she actually was.

They had arrived back at Von Fridley's establishment to find it mostly darkened and filled with the resounding snores of their colleague Morris Mullins. The immensely fat man sat at one of the sheet-metal desks, his long, lank, dirty locks and his cheek pillowed on the open pages of a reference book, his arms resting on his more than just meaty thighs. The rest of the desk was littered with carry-out containers from the nearest Chinese restaurant and the combined smells of soybean oil, soy sauce and spring onions almost—but not quite—masked the unwashed reek of Morris Mullins.

Nothing, no light in Fridley's office, David said, "Look, why don't we just unload here, then drive down to Scales's place for a drink?" At what he took for a look of uncertainty on her face, he added, "Let's dump the stuff and get out of here quick, before Mullins wakes up and invites himself along, huh?"

But in his Ford wagon, as he had sat warming the engine, she had said, "Klein, after that mess in court this afternoon, with that fat, fascist farmer-judge and that chauvinistic pig-turd witness—I knew there was a good reason why I always hated goddamn bankers! —I'd just as soon not have to go into Scales's and have to even sit in the same room with that *herrenvolk* bunch of neo-nazis from the courthouse. Have to sit and pretend I can't hear them all snickering at me and saying that it's my fault that that black-robed motherfucker found that poor, disadvantaged young black man guilty . . . and it would hurt because they're right about that, but that's not going to be the end of it, you know, Klein. I think, with someone else handling it, an appeals court just might consider today to be grounds for declaring a mistrial." She giggled and added, "I'll have to remember to blow my cool more often in these jerkwater courts, Klein."

"Then you want me to drive you home?" he asked.

She had nodded. "Yeah, you do that . . . wait a minute, you have your own apartment, don't you, one somewhere in the new Darby section, isn't it? Okay, I'll tell you what to do. Drop me off at my place, then drive on down and turn right onto Vine Street. Go to the pizza place and get us a pizza with everything and double cheese. Then while you're waiting for that, go across the street, there, to that Little Giant Market and pick up a half a gallon of Gallo Pink Chablis and some Oreo cookies.

"I'll change clothes and pick up a few things, then we'll go to your place and fuck, okay? That way, Klein, you'll get your rocks off in me for a lot less bread than a restaurant dinner and enough booze to get me sloshed. You got any grass or pills or acid?"

He hedged. "Uhh, I haven't been in town enough to make a connection . . . but I do have a few grams of pot."

The sentences handed down in the courts of this semi-rural backwater for simple possession of something so innocuous as plain marijuana had early shocked David out of the easygoing complacency of school, grad school and the more liberal state from which he had come down to work in this archaic, near-medieval place. Therefore, he felt that he could not confess to actually holding much of anything until he had gotten to know this strange woman better, in more depth.

And more than six months after that evening, sitting in a vacant office in a rural, mostly farming community, studying the various file folders connected with the case of one Yancey Mathews, his client, he wished to hell and gone that he never,

ever had gotten to know anything more than had been absolutely necessary for his working relationship with her of the kinky, clearly demented, hung-up and quite possibly really dangerous Amy Fisch.

Glancing at yet another of the terse, concise reports of yet another arrest of Yancey Mathews by deputies of Sheriff Vaughan's department, David reflected that his feelings for and about the big, scarred, no-nonsense lawman had moved almost a hundred and eighty degrees in the three weeks he had been up here. Despite his patently adversarial position in the case of *County versus Yancey Mathews*, the sheriff had bent over backward to make many aspects of David's life and work in the area easier, had sent out deputies to ride with him and direct him to places whereat he could find those men and women to whom he wished to talk and try to learn more than mere dry records could provide about his client in order to build some sort of a defense.

When David had indicated that he would prefer living in the area rather than commuting as needed from the distant city—he had told Von Fridley, by phone, and both Mike Mills and the sheriff in person, that he felt he needed to try to absorb the "feel" of the surroundings and inhabitants and their culture, and since he asked no more than the pitiful (by modern standards) per diem proffered by Fridley, there had been no objection from anyone and not a little praise for such dedication from Fridley; of course, the real reason he chose to exile himself was neither dedication nor Yancey Mathews, it was Amy Fisch— Sheriff Vaughan had seen a vacant office in the new courthouse turned over to him, equipped it with basic items of furniture and a telephone, stuck a tag on the bumper of his wagon that would allow it to legally occupy county parking slots, then warned him which bars and restaurants in the general vicinity were best avoided did a man wish to avoid stomach and bowel distress. The lawman also had pointedly added a new china mug to the row ranged above his office Silex.

David could not prove it, of course, but he was sure that it had been a word from Vaughan that had caused the owner/manager of the Honeysuckle Motel to suddenly find it necessary to shift his guest to the bridal suite—two-bay bedroom with a king-sized bed, a larger-screen television set, better and newer furniture, deeper carpet and a bath with dressing table, massage-head shower and a separate, pink marble tub equipped with Jacuzzi jets—at the same price he had been paying for a commercial single.

His first night in the new and sumptuous quarters had also been the night he had told Amy by phone that no, she definitely could not take a bus up to spend the weekend with him. He got shakes as bad as those of his client with a hangover just thinking about trying to explain to the live-in owner of the motel about the nocturnal noises that sex with Amy always produced.

A bit later, as he relaxed in the imitation-marble tub filled with blood-temperature water and let the pressure jets soothe his muscles while the contents of the plastic tumbler of scotch-rocks soothed his innards, he thought back to that first night with his colleague Amy Fisch, hang-up girl of the century, so far out in left field that she had started him wonder-

ing just what he was doing anywhere near her, wondering, if he stayed around her too long, her condition
would infect him, too.

When she had come down the steps of her rooming house to get into the wagon with him, the hot
pizza, the jug of wine and the package of cookies, she
had exchanged her severe courthouse attire for the
uniform of her generation—faded, ragged jeans, worn,
none-too-clean sweatshirt, thong sandals and an army-
surplus backpack which sported the faded outline of
a hand-drawn peace symbol.

She said little in the car on the drive to his apartment building, one of a block of several identical
buildings in a newly developed suburb of the city.
Shrugging into the pack straps, she carried the pizza
box, following him up the stairs and entering behind
him after he had unlocked the door.

While he was locating relatively clean glasses and
pouring them full of the pale red wine in the eat-in
kitchen, she had begun to unload the rucksask onto
the scarred cocktail table, and by the time he came
back in with glasses brimful of wine, a couple of
hastily rinsed and dried forks, paper plates and nap-
kins for the pizza, the table top held an assortment of
items. There was a medium-sized brass hookah or
waterpipe, a handful of small vials that David recognized—"poppers" of amyl nitrate—a big glass jar
about half full of several kinds of pills—uppers, down-
ers and unknowns—a much smaller glass jar containing some white powder that David was certain was
not the powdered sugar it most closely resembled, a
dark green dropper bottle, a cheese knife, a box of
Swedish matches, a tube of stick incense and a brass

holder for them, and, peeking shyly out from its aluminum-foil wrapping, a dark brown chunk of enough hashish to keep a herd of elephants stoned for a week. There were other items, too, but David had no eyes for them at that moment . . . though he was to keenly recall them later during that weekend.

Taking a deep, deep breath and carefully setting down the wine and other items wherever there was space on the now-crowded table, he asked, in the calmest voice he could, "You mean you actually keep all this stuff in your room, in a place you can't lock in a damned rooming house, for the love of God?"

Amy Fisch had just shrugged and nodded, "Sure, why not? Oh, I'm not dumb about it, most of the stuff is always locked up in my footlocker and nobody's tried to rip me off yet. Besides, whenever I fire up the hookah, I always burn lots of incense before, during and after, and I leave the window open, too."

"Holy shit, woman!" David managed not to exactly shout, "Don't you read the local papers or follow other peoples' cases? The Stinker just last month had a twenty-two-year-old client sent to the state prison for forty years for getting caught holding a couple of lousy dime bags of low-grade pot. Think about it, huh? You're an officer of the court, they'd nail your ass to the wall, crucify you . . . and the way they all seem to feel about Von and the rest of us, simply love doing it, every minute of it!

"Oh, sure, I keep a little stuff around, pot, but it's not anywhere it could be unqestionably pinned to me, either, there are forty other tenants in this complex, you know. I don't want to even think of getting caught holding or using in this state. But the way you're taking chances, it looks like you *do* want to get busted." He stopped when he ran out of breath, then demanded, "What the hell you think you're doing, woman?"

"What's it look like, Klein?" she answered calmly, the cheese knife in her hand continuing its steady, even strokes as she shaved hashish off the chunk. "Why don't you turn on that air conditioner, get the air circulating in here, and you can light a couple of those patchouli sticks, too, the purple ones. Then you can get out of that damned suit and all, I wanta see what size basket you've got inside those pants. I just hope you can get yours harder and keep it up longer in action than that damned over-the-hill Von Fridley can."

When he did not move at once, she paused in her task and looked up at him, a faint smile on her thin face and malicious mockery in her voice. "Well, Klein, what're you waiting for? Are you just shy or did ums mommy tell ums not to let anybody see his weewee? Hmm?"

"The . . . uhh, the pizza," he heard himself stuttering, "it'll get cold and . . ."

She dropped the knife and slapped the palm of her hand down hard on the stained and battered table, snarling, "Screw the goddamn pizza, Klein, I wanta see your cock! I wanta see it, feel it, smoke some hash and then eat it, okay? Or . . . ?" she choked, then demanded, "Or are you another fag like Czernako? Please, tell me you're not gay, too . . . or better, show me you're not."

"God, what an idiot, what an utter dunce I was

that night," thought David, sipping another sip of the strong scotch as he lay there in the pink marble tub. "That was a perfect out, right there and then, and if I'd only known then what I know now, I'd have told her I was queer as a three-dollar bill. And she'd be stalking some other poor bastard by now, but better him, better any-fucking-body than me!"

He sighed and took another small sip of the smoky nectar. "She gives good head, though, the best I've ever had. That first time, now, there in my living room, on the floor, *God*! What an experience. With the hash and the amyl and her tricks, I thought I'd just keep coming until . . . until my toenails came out or my heart stopped or my fucking brain exploded or all three at once. If only she wasn't so damned weird, otherwise . . . I wonder if she really did make it with her own father, a rabbi, or if it's just some kind of damn Electra thing whirling around in her definitely fucked-up brain?

"Of course, if everything she's told me at various times is all true, if she's done as many drugs as she says she has for as many years as she says she has, her brain couldn't be anything but a bowl of oatmeal. I wonder how anybody that all-time screwy managed to get through pre-law, even, much less law school. I damn near didn't, and I wasn't into a tenth of the stuff she's been—seventy or eighty acid trips? Holy shit!—she must of been in the pants of every dean and prof on her campus is all I can figure. I wonder how the dyke she said she roomed with liked them apples? Or maybe she was a bi acid-head and fast-track doper, too.

"But the big question is how can Mrs. Klein's little

boy, Dave, get out of this unholy godawful mess he's screwed his way into before he winds up in serious deep shit or in a coffin at Weinstein's Chapel, where all his father's high-powered buddies can take a last look and murmur lies about how tragic it was and how a promising career was cut short. And I can't stay up here, can't drag this case out forever.

"No, once Mathews finally goes before a judge . . . and, God and the state bar forgive me for even thinking it, but from all I've learned about the bastard so far, I think the sheriff is right, I think a prison farm or a chain gang is the best place for him . . . and it's all decided one way or another, then I'll have no choice if I want to keep my job, such as it is, than to go back to the city. And then my ass will be grass and Amy Fisch will be the fucking lawnmower."

The salvation of David Klein, Public Defender, was yet to come, but he did not yet know of it, of course.

Half-zonked with hashish, a couple of lines of coke, wine and then more hashish, David had not demurred when the woman had asked—no, demanded—that her wrists be tied for sex, and due to the fact that the wooden bedstead included a row of three-inch spools along most of the middle of the peeling headboard, there was no trouble finding a place to which to secure the length of rope—it being furnished by Amy from out her rucksack. At her direction, he left enough slack so that she could get one hand—the one clutching the popper of amyl—to her nose.

It had been all that he could do to drag his weary, burnt-out carcass back up the stairs on the Sunday night of that ill-recalled weekend of sex, hash, sex, wine, sex, coke, sex, bennies, sex, cookies and cold pizza, sex, reds, sex, whiskey and then sex. He had not been worth a damn on the following Monday, and Amy had not come into the office at all.

When she had come in on the Tuesday morning, she had nodded to him as she stalked back to Fridley's private office and slammed the door behind her. Whence loud, angry voices presently could be heard to emanate, their decibel rates steadily climbing, though still lacking in clarity due to the sound conditioning of the smaller office and the noises of the thirty-six-inch floor fans in the larger room.

"Oh, shit!" Morris Mullins had muttered, heaving his bulk up from out his desk chair and beginning to frantically stuff his peeling briefcase. "Whenever that shit starts up, anybody with any sense says bye-bye until it's over and done with. Those two'll drag anybody that's around into it, and you don't want any part of that, Klein, believe you me, buddy. It's a 'heads you lose, tails you lose' proposition."

A few minutes later, ensconced in a booth at an eatery favored by the city police and so avoided by Fridley, who called it "The Pig Pen," David sprung for coffee and doughnuts and was related some facts by another of his fellow employees, Gregor Czernako, Mullins having lumbered out and away ahead of them.

"We should be safe in here from that dust-up back there, David . . . may I call you David? Good. I'm Greg," said the slender man with his singular, ash-blond Afro, a full beard but no trace of a moustache. "You spent the weekend with our Amy? Of course you did. Welcome to the club, David." He smiled. "This sort of thing happens every time Amy sets out after a piece of fresh meat."

Czernako took a swallow of the coffee, licked the doughnut glaze from his fingers, then continued, "Amy and Morris have been here longer than any of those still around and they've outlasted not a few who came after them, you know. Morris is good at what he does, you've seen that, he knows his law, and what he doesn't know, he's not long in researching and absorbing. Our Amy, on the other hand, is real bad news for any poor fucker so unlucky as to draw her to represent them, but she also has obviously got poor Von by the balls in some way and so she not only stays here engaging in what amounts to continual misrepresentation of her luckless clients but she gets away with bloody murder in other ways, too."

"I got the impression, from her," said David, *sotto voce*, "that she and Von had been an item for a while, some time back."

"Ahh, poor, poor Von," sighed Czernako, sadly, "for two thirds of his life, he tried to find a good-looking, progressively minded young woman who practiced free love and, when he finally found her, she was too much for him. I had a very dear friend once, a Jesuit, who used to say that when God really has it in for you, He gives you exactly what you think you want. That's been the case with our feckless leader, I fear; unquestionably powerful a man as he is, in a political and bureaucratic sense, Amy is his superior in all else. The sad old man still thinks her his mistress, for all that she's openly, flagrantly put horns on him with nearly every man he ever brought into the office, at least half the local cops, and God alone knows who and how many others. She even tried it with me once, but I'm not her type, thank God." He smiled again. "I'll turn on with her anytime, naturally; I'll never turn down good hash or grass or coke."

Even more softly than before, for all that the few other diners this early in the morning were clustered at the counter some feet away, David asked, "That's another very troubling thing, Greg. In a place as uptight as this is, how in the hell has she stayed out on the street with all the stuff she holds and does, not even making much of a secret of it? And how in hell can she afford to buy shit like that on the pitiful salary we're paid? Do you know?"

"Like I said, David," replied the blond man, "she's got some kind of a lock on Von and Von has great power in certain quarters; also, as I said earlier, she's got a whole string of conquests on the cops, hereabouts, all ranks and divisions. As for where she gets the money for the shit, maybe from Von or some others I don't know about. I wouldn't put a wee tad of blackmail past a woman like our Amy. Hell, David, she could even be turning tricks on the side, for all any of us could know. Morris says that if that woman had as few as half as many sticking out of her as she's had sticking in her just since she'd been here, she'd look like a prickupine." This time, he grinned widely enough to show every crooked, yellow tooth as he added, "Of course, he could truthfully say the same thing about me, God be praised, and that's what *I* like about the South, David."

263

* * *

Mike Mills, who had had David sent out to the county to give representation to Yancey Mathews, was of about Von Fridley's age and had been in state politics for about as long, but there the similarities between the two bureaucrats ceased. Mills was tall, robust and bronzed, looking nearer to forty than his actual age of sixty. He was a hunter, fisherman, horseman, skeet shooter, and one-time army officer, and his office furnishings and decorations reflected all these interests and pursuits.

Despite his affable, somewhat folksy manner, David accurately sensed a keen intelligence as well as an unidentifiable something that made him feel strongly that he would not at all like to have to face an angry Mike Mills, most particularly were he at all the cause of that anger.

Having been asked to please step over to his office, David had found himself greeted warmly, offered whiskey and had settled for coffee. Leaving his cluttered desk, Mills had waved David to one of a pair of worn, leather wing chairs, then seated himself in the other, the dark mahogany coffee table between them holding a humidor of the tobacco he favored, big ashtray, pipe rack and their cups.

"David," he said without preamble, "are you ready to take this Mathews case into court? Is there anything else you want to do, any more tests you want run on him, any more folks you want to talk to? I don't mean to rush you, son, but it's been more'n three weeks you've been up here, now . . . ?"

David sighed; the jig was up. "No, sir. I guess I'm

as ready as I'll ever be on it. I'll be facing you, then?"

Waiting until his ancient, blackened and knobby briar was well lit, Mills shook out the wooden match and shook his head of dense, brown hair. "No, no, son, not me. At my age, I can afford to give small stuff like this to young fellows to do. No, Harry Robins—I introduced you two, you recall?—will be representing the county opposite you. It's his baby, I'm not and won't be at all involved, win, lose or draw, that's my way.

"I serve you fair warning, though, son: young Harry's good, he's out of U. Va. and I trained him here. If you can outmaneuver him, you'll be able to figure you earned your salt that day. But win, place or show, son, there's more than just the Mathews case I want to talk to you about today. More coffee?

"David, in the time you've been out here with us, you've made a real impression on some of us, a good impression, a real good impression. But I'll get back to that in a minute.

"When I went off to war, back in '42, David, the county seat, here, was called a town on the maps, and that was about all. Besides the old courthouse, there were a Baptist church, a Methodist church, a gas station, a general store, my uncle's feed store, a tourist court and restaurant where the Honeysuckle Motel is today, and no more than a handful of houses; just outside what was then the town limits there were three big estates—one raising beef cattle, one raising thoroughbreds, and the third one, where some reclusive English gentleman lived, that didn't raise any cash crops that any one ever knew of. The whole rest of the county was wall-to-wall farms and woods and more farms, small farms, mostly. The big road, the interstate, hadn't even been thought about then and the city was half a day and more away, if you had a car, an overnight trip by wagon, or you could get over to the crossroads before dawn and wait on the Greyhound bus.

"By the time I came back, though, in '47, two of the estates had been sold and the land developed and the town limits had been expanded to take in the plant that had been built during the war and the rough housing that had been put in to give the workers a place to live. All kinds of small businesses either had started or were getting ready to start, and plans were all drawn up for the beginning of what ended up as this complex based on the courthouse.

"But we still might've just stayed a small town, wasn't for the interstate, David, that and the way the city keeps growing. Son, within another ten or fifteen years, we here are going to be to all intents and purposes a suburb of the city; smart money from there is already feeling out things along either side of the interstate between here and there. I've even joined in buying the options of a few select parcels here and there myself, come to that.

"What I'm getting at, my boy, is this: We're not exactly the countrified backwater that we seem to be, out here. One whole hell of a lot of big-money business is going to be conducted in this county over the next few years and that could mean a good living for a good, young, sharp, friendly lawyer who could see whatall is coming and got himself set of it."

"Mr. Mills . . ." asked David in consternation, "do

I understand you? You want *me*, on only three weeks' acquaintance, to enter into private law practice in your county? You don't really know anything about me . . . do you?"

Mills shrugged. "I judge a man by what I see in him, mostly, David, and I like what I've seen in you. But I did do a little wee tad of investigation, too; after all, you do work for, were bought into the state by, Von the Red. But I liked what I found out, mostly. You're third generation of a whole family of attorneys, and you went to good schools. You appear to have gone a bit overboard in extracurricular activities to the detriment of your grades, but that is most likely an indication of your energy—how I wish I were your age again with the boundless energy of youth." Mills sighed, commenced to probe into the depths of his pipe bowl with the butt of a kitchen match, but spoke on while so engaged.

"As regards private practice, that's all up to you, son; you certainly can if you want to, but it wasn't exactly what I had in mind. No, I thought you could work with me, here, for a while. Judge Hanratty, he means to leave the bench within the year—but you keep that under your hat, David, it's not common knowledge yet—and he's going to set up offices here in town, and when he does, you'd go over and work with him, you see. Then, when I retire, end of the current year, we'd become Hanratty and Mills, while young Harry Robins takes over my county job. You work with us for one or two years and then, if you like what you're doing and we three seem to get along okay, we'll start calling ourselves Hanratty, Mills and Klein. How does that sound to you, son?"

David felt just then as if he'd been clubbed, felt as fuzzy-headed, as utterly divorced from reality, from the world and all in it as he had back in '70, during the Days of Rage, when that District of Columbia pig had downed him with a swipe of his baton. He couldn't speak, he just sat there, his eyes a little glazed over.

"David? David, boy?" Mills leaned forward, concerned patent in his voice and manner. "Are you okay, son? Let me get you a drink, a little bourbon never hurt anybody."

But as Mills started to rise, David at last found his voice. "No, no thank you, Mr. Mills, I . . . I'm all right, it's just . . . well, all . . . everything that's gone down in here this morning. Look, you're not putting me on, man, are you? No, forget I said that, of course you're not, you're not that kind, none of you people down here are. I'm honored, of course . . . more than that, really. But look, Mr. Mills, you . . . you don't know all you think you do about me. I don't know as much law as I should, you know, I damned near didn't even graduate, that's why my father and uncle wouldn't take me into the family firm . . . that and some of the things I did while I was in school, my politics and . . ."

"Hold it, David," said Mills. "Just hold on, boy. There is an arrogance in your generation, you know. You all think you're the very first nonconformists, the very first crop of wild-eyed radicals this country ever produced. Oh, how very wrong you all are. Why, David, when I was a freshman in college, I came within a hair of leaving school, going to Spain and enlisting in the Loyalist army to fight the

Falangists, and I was far from alone, too. All intelligent, sensitive, caring folks are, in their undergraduate years at any decent university, inclined to being ranting, left-liberal egalitarians, crusaders all searching desperately for a crusade to join in, and I would imagine that that's how it always has been and always will be, too, David; it's just the nature of young folks, it seems.

"What your politics are is your business. National politics only concern this state every four years, mostly. Rest of the time, it's state politics and, though the state is mostly ostensibly Democrat, like all the other southern states are, it's a whole heap of difference between our interpretation of that party label and the brand of such states as Massachusetts, Michigan, Minnesota and a lot of other northern and western states.

"So what do you have to say, David? Think you'd like to live and practice out here in the sticks? You probably need time to think on it, but . . ."

"Yes, I do need some time to think, Mr. Mills," agreed David. "Besides that, I'd like to talk to my father about it, get his opinion, you know."

" 'Course you would, David." Mills nodded, smiling. "Shows you've got brains, it does. The offer's been made and it'll stay open, too. So you just take your time; last thing I want you doing is jumping into anything you might have cause to regret later, son. You want to, you can go back after the judgment's in on the Mathews case and talk to Von Fridley 'bout it . . . but just don't bring up anything about Judge Hanratty, hear, that's got to be just 'tween you and me and the gatepost for a while yet."

Mention of Fridley's name and the phrase concerning jumping into things and later regretting the plunge triggered the thought of Amy Fisch and having to go back into that sinister circus of hers in the city. David asked, "Mr. Mills . . . if . . . in the event I did decide to go to work for you . . . when could . . . would I be starting? I mean, when would you want me to move down here? I'd have to give Von notice, I guess, and find a place to live and . . ."

"Now don't you worry your head one bit about Von, David," said Mills in reply, "you won't be the first youngster's been stolen away from him by a county or another department of the state government; I'll take care of all that. Oh, he'll yell and scream and bitch like you wouldn't believe, but as much power as he's got in some quarters, he still knows who his masters are.

"So far as a place to live goes, don't you worry 'bout that either. You can just stay at Honeysuckle until we find a place you like. That tract the Mathewses live in, out on the east end of the old Dabney estate property, some of them are kind of ratty and run-down, true, but it's a lot that aren't and I own some of those, the bank owns some others and the sheriff owns some, too. Between us, it's for damn sure we can fix you up proper.

"How much have you got to move down here? You think a truck made to haul six horses would be big enough to hold it all?"

David smiled. "Sir, I own no furniture or major appliances; back in the city I live in a furnished apartment. My effects consist of clothes, mostly, some books, tapes and a player, a few kitchen items I've had to buy and some sheets and towels, nothing that I can't get into my station wagon with room to spare."

"Well, then," Mills grinned, nodding, "you just think on it, son, and talk it over with your dad, up north, and if you decide you want to be one of us country-boys, you give me a call, day or night, and let me know, and if you can't get a hold of me, call the sheriff and give him the message, then you pack up and drive on down here and you'll go on the payroll the next day, hear. And son, you haven't asked, but you should know that the county pays a tad more than Von Fridley gives his wage slaves, and it's cheaper to live out here, too . . . unless," he grinned again and more widely, "your tastes run to French cognacs and champagnes, escargot, Beluga caviar and Kobe beef, as mine do, unfortunately. But more fortunately, I've never had to try to live on my county income, either.

"You're not married, never have been, I hear, but you once were affianced. Are you still? Or planning to be?"

At David's headshake, he said, "Well, then, if you do decide to move down here, we'll have to get you initiated into the hunt club, our homey version of a country club. It's out in what used to be the Dabney mansion, though it's been gussied up some over the years since that old man went away. That done, it won't be long until you'll be fighting the girls out there off with a club, good-looking young fellow like you."

"Uhh, Mr. Mills . . ." David began, hesitantly, "I'm Jewish, you know . . . ?"

Mills just stared blankly at him for a long moment,

then said, "And I'm Methodist, son. But out here, it's like I said earlier about your personal brand of politics: your religion is your own business and nobody else's. Oh, wait a minute, I get you now. I'll just bet that all your life you've been pumped chock full of all kinds of scurrilous propoganda about how terrible things are in the South. Right? Of course you have, else you wouldn't have said what you just did and when.

"Well, you just sit tight and listen to me, Mr. David Klein, I am not an unworldly man. Yes, I was born and a good deal of my rearing was in this county, but I've lived in, travelled in some other parts of this country and the world, for that matter. And I'll tell you this much: you'll find more real racial, ethnic and religious prejudice up north than you will down here. Oh, yes, there are enclaves of white trash scattered here and there, brainless wonders who march with the Klan and raise a hooraw every so often, but you've got their like up north, too; their kind occur world-wide.

"We southerners are largely caste-conscious as old hell, comes to birth and breeding and how long your folks have been in America, but David, you find that kind of thing in the north, too: Boston is infamous for it. 'The Lodges speak to the Cabots and the Cabots speak only to God.' Ever heard that quote, son?

"But since World War Two, as the South has begun to become less rural and agrarian and more urban or suburban, more industrial or business oriented, the old order has been changing and, in more recent years, those changes have been accelerating. For all that some folks in some places try desperately to keep up the old forms, the old ways, they're as deluded as old King Canute was in ordering the tide not to flow in; the Old South is as dead as a mink stole. It may be mourned by some, but no one can ever bring it back any more than a man can unscramble an egg.

"What I'm telling you, son, is this: in this county and the most of this state, for that matter, you'll be judged based on what sort of *man* you are, not on the religion you practice, the political views you espouse, the color of your skin or how you part your hair. For far too many years, right many of the best and brightest of our young folks have left the state, gone north to make their mark in life, so what you now are in is sort of like the frontier used to be and, like the builders and the planners back then, we'll do our level best to attract young folks from elsewhere who look like they'd made us good citizens, who'd work hard with us toward the tremendous things that are coming to this area sure as horses drop road-apples. You're prime, David, whether you know it now or not, and I want to get you before some other county does. Have I made myself clear this time, son?"

David placed the call to his father immediately he got back to his borrowed office and, after a delay, the elder Klein came onto the line. He heard his son out in silence save for a few, probing questions, then asked, "David, just why did you telephone me?"

Taken aback, his offspring stuttered, "Why . . . to . . . I thought I needed advice . . . your advice and . . ."

"Advice, you want? *My* advice, David?" was the response. "Well, maybe, just maybe, your uncle and

273

brothers are wrong and you're going to grow up, after all. All right, you want advice from me, you get advice from me.

"David, you thank that man, Mills, on your knees, you thank him after you've thanked God. Then you accept his offer and you work, you *work* for him harder than you've ever thought of working before. I don't know the man, but I do know about Hanratty. Hanratty was one of my Uncle Saul's students, years back, and he so impressed Uncle Saul and your grandfather, too, that they tried everything short of kidnapping to get him to stay up here and join the firm, but he went back down south, instead.

"David, please hear me and believe me. If you accept this opportunity and foul it up as badly as you've seemed prone to do in recent years, then do not ever, ever phone or write or wire me or the firm again for any reason. Goodbye, David."

CHAPTER XIII

Once she had gotten over the shock, Danna Dardrey had found that the knowledge of psionic powers she shared with Pedro Goldfarb had definite advantages. Having consciously realized that he owned the abilities, and having used and experimented with them for years, he had been able to show her a much wider range of uses for her own powers than she otherwise might have suspected. On the other hand, it had been her joy to show Pedro how to lift himself, something he said he never before had thought of or considered, for some reason.

In answer to his questions, she had told him which abilities Fitz owned and had warned him of the strange fact that items made of ferrous metals in even the slightest contact with the skin had the quality of completely damping everything except telepathy.

Pedro had nodded. "Yes, I learned that a long while back; that's why all of the metal items I customarily carried around are of gold, silver, copper, bronze or brass. I even managed to find an all-bronze pocket knife, made in Thailand, and it takes and holds quite a nice edge, too. It's also one of the reasons why I don't go around with a hideaway revolver or pistol, as an increasing number of our professional colleagues seem to be doing these days. You do, don't you?"

She nodded. "Yes, but in my purse, in a special holster I had sewn into it—a Browning twenty-five caliber." Upon seeing his frown and grimace, she hurried to add, "Yes, I know, it's not much of a self-defense weapon; both Fitz and my shooting instructor told me that early on, but that three-fifty-seven weighs a metric ton in comparison and I just couldn't see lugging it around all day when I'm out of the office. I don't own any other handguns."

"Oh, yes, you do," said Pedro. "You forget fast and easily, lady. Out at your country house there are enough handguns, rifles, shotguns and ammo to start a banana-republic revolution, at the least. I looked them over, once or twice, and I'm sure I recall seeing at least one Walther PPK or PP. Compared to the three-fifty-seven, of course, or even the thirty-eight special, the three-eighty the PPK fires is a weak, ineffectual cartridge, true, but compared to the twenty-five . . ." He raised his eyebrows and shrugged, then added, "And the PPK is not all that big or bulky and not too heavy either, Danna.

"But whether you have the Browning, the PPK or the revolver, always remember this, my dear: Never

ever draw the weapon out of your purse until you are absolutely convinced that there is no other choice, that you'll certainly be killed or hurt if you don't shoot your attacker. And when you draw it, Danna, *use it immediately*. I know of far too many sad cases wherein well-armed people tried to use their weapons as a threat or a bluff long enough to have those weapons taken away and used on them. A handgun, any handgun, large or small, is made for one purpose and one purpose only: that of expelling hunks of lead alloy with considerable force along a relatively straight course. If you're not prepared to utilize it for the purpose for which it was designed and manufactured, then don't buy it at all, or keep it unloaded in a locked display case, not in your purse or on your person."

Then he chuckled. "Sorry, I do get preachy sometimes, don't I?"

She smiled. "No more than Fitz or my shooting instructor, Pedro, and I appreciate it, I really do; feminism is all well and good, but a woman who really likes men also usually likes being looked after, it's just the nature of the beast, I guess.

"I'll tell you, I'll drive out to the house this weekend—I'd thought about doing that anyway—and I'll look around for that pistol and the ammunition for it. Can you show me at least a picture of one so I'll know what I'm looking for, Pedro?"

He nodded. "Can do, lady. I've got some gun books at home; I'll bring one in tomorrow. One of the best things about the PPK is that you can safely carry a round chambered in it, release the safety and fire off the first load double-action, no need to have to use your other hand to pull back the slide, as with your little Browning.

"Oh, and Danna, you'd better get in touch with Fitz, too, this week sometime, if you can. I just may need to talk with him soon."

Danna grimaced. "Blutegel?"

"No." The man shook his head. "The I.R.S. thing is still hovering over Fitz, of course, but we've done about all that we can for the nonce. I still wouldn't advise him to make a big public thing of coming back to this country if he does come back, but Blutegel's superiors now know that certain monies are in an escrow account, so they're not as likely to get a federal warrant for Fitz as once they were.

"No, this is a new can of worms that's unexpectedly popped open, Danna, or rather an old can that's showing new life after a lengthy hiatus . . . and I just may have been part of the reason it's now reraised its ugly head."

"What in the world are you talking about, Pedro?" she asked. "How could you have gotten Fitz into more trouble?"

"Simple," he replied. "Completely unintentional, of course; I like everyone else thought that the U.S. Customs-Interpol aspect was over and done, long ago. But it now appears that the powers that be in those two groups have never been completely sold on the Irish provenance of the gold coins and those artifacts, and my recent release of that batch of coins Fitz had had hidden in his freezer in that bucket of stewed squid has set them off again.

"The first I knew of it was when a Customs agent, one Evan Stilton, rang me up earlier today, asking

278

Fitz's whereabouts. I told him the usual, that Fitz was on safari, whereupon he demanded to know exactly where he was hunting, saying that an Interpol type could question him wherever he was. They want, it develops, to search the house and grounds—the grounds in particular, or so it sounds—but they want to do it with Fitz's permission, sans a warrant."

"Looking for what?" she queried, blank-faced. "As Fitz tells it, the first bunch of them broke into that house on at least two occasions and searched it rather thoroughly on both visits. And why the grounds? The only thing that can't be seen clearly from almost any point outside the back fence is the interior of Fitz's fallout shelter, that and the crawlspace under the house itself."

"Beats me," he shrugged. "But my experience with these kinds of bureaucrat is to try to at least give the appearance of bowing to their requests before they reach the stage of demands, no matter how petty, silly, meaningless or quasi-illegal those requests might seem to be. I told him that, although I was not at all certain just which country Fitz currently was in, I could arrange for him a meeting with the owner-in-fact of the property. He has an appointment with me, here, for tomorrow at two. He mentioned that he would be bringing along a couple of his professional colleagues. We'll get them in here, hear them out, then take us a little stroll through their minds and find out just what they're really up to—what they know, what they think they know, what they suspect, what they hope to find out by searching that place out there in the county.

"And, recalling the last bunch of these types, should

we find that they're up to something other than official business . . . ? Ah, then you and I just might play us a little psionic game or three with them, Danna."

Even as the dragon rushed from its place of concealment, hissing, tooth-studded jaws agape, Kaoru's *katana* left its case and the tip of its blade took the reptile—which had chosen to attack on all four feet, in this instance—directly across the hinges of both sides of the jaws, severing the powerful tendons there as well as deeply gashing the ultra-sensitive tongue, but even as the beast screamed and swerved its hard-lashing tail took the man's bare legs from under him and he fell, his head coming into contact with a rounded boulder half buried in the soil, whereupon his mind became a momentary blur of bright red, then a blank nothingness.

In his aerie up in the towering oak tree, Fitz willed himself to fly to the assistance of the now-unconscious Japanese officer, for he knew that the lizard or dragon or whatever was not anything approaching dead and, although only about ten or twelve feet long, could doubtless still do fatal damage to the senseless and near-naked body of the little man. He willed, but nothing happened, nothing at all.

"Damn me for a fool!" he thought, furiously, then began to strip himself of the iron and steel items. His next mental willing worked and, pausing only long enough to lift the drilling in one hand by its leather-and-brass sling, he sped through the air in the direction of the imperilled officer.

Among all the laboring, blood-smeared Japanese

infantrymen, only Company Sergeant Kiyomoto saw the flying man . . . and his heart seemed to stop. Then, dropping the *wakizashi* and grasping the haft of the ancient bronze axe, he shouted exultantly, "He has come! The god has come! We must go and greet him!" Then he set off along the stream bank at a dead run.

The men just looked at one another, then dropped their work and their implements, retrieved their spears and followed in the noncom's wake. None of them could imagine what his strange shouts had been all about, but he was the sergeant and if he said to follow him, then that was clearly their duty.

Cool Blue had not had to go far. In the next vale over from that Fitz was even then following westward, he had encountered Sir Gautier and had very nearly been speared by one of the Norman's retainers into the bargain. The knight had found six of these—every one of them scruffier and smellier than the one before, the blue lion had thought, disgustedly.

Giving Sir Gautier Fitz's instructions, the lion had seen the Normans well on their way toward the rock shelter, then had set himself to hunting for flesh to fill his gaping void of a belly. This day he had been successful, and more quickly than he had even hoped. Then, with his belly full of hot meat and blood, he had valiantly resisted the almost overpowering impulse to lie up somewhere and take a lengthy snooze; instead, he had set off after the Norman knight and his stinky retainers as fast as an overstuffed, basically lazy, baby-blue lion could travel, consoling himself with the thought that the Normans would doubtless camp at the cache overnight and he could sleep there.

He was wrong. The knight and his men, with so much daylight yet remaining and who knew just how far to go to catch up with Fitz, had divided the load and set out following the blazed trees. Indeed, Cool Blue never even got back to the rock shelter, for as he had come down into the vale up which Fitz had travelled, he had smelled, then heard the Normans headed west along the vale and set out after them.

Night had come on them still in the vale and they had camped there, dining well on fish from the burn, a plentitude of snails and an abundance of plant foods. At dawn, they had set out once more, guided by the white slash-marks on the tree trunks, and at the moment that the man they sought was flying to the defense of a man he had never really met, the seven Normans and the big blue cat had arrived atop the waterfall-cliff.

Kneeling, Sir Gautier used the butt of a spear to test the weight-bearing capacities of several of the spray-slickened boulders that projected from the vine-covered face of the cliff, but two out of five, when subjected to any meaningful amounts of pressure, pulled from out their seats to fall in a shower of damp earth and bounce down into the deep bed of pine tags below.

"We could always try joining our sword-girdles, I suppose," the knight mused dubiously, "but I doubt me that a mere seven girdles would own the span to lower a man far enough that he not still suffer sorely upon dropping the remaining distance. What think you, Master Lion?"

Gazing down the face of the cliff, Cool Blue beamed, "Like I could prob'ly jump down okay; it down look like no more than 'bout forty feet, you dig? But any you cats try that way, you gon' be like crawling the resta the way. Must be a way 'round it, but how far is all, you know."

Just then, a short, squat, but muscular towhead tugged at his forelock and addressed the knight, saying, "My lord, know you not this place? Down in that pine grove is where we first found us when we were chasing the camel up that stone-dry wadi . . . and it please my lord."

The knight suddenly struck his fist into his thigh so hard that Cool Blue winced. "Of course! I must be losing my memory. Well done, Rollo, well done! And if it be so, then . . ."

With Sir Gautier leading the way, the Normans and the lion retraced their way far enough upstream to be able to wade across the rushing, icy burn, then proceeded back down the opposite bank to the north side of the falls. Here the cliff-top was rocky and uneven, and it grew higher the farther north they went.

"Man," protested the blue lion, "like not even me in this like lion getup could jump down that far. You guys wanta try it, like go right ahead, but them iron tee-shirts and steel pots ain't gonna help you like one damn bit, you know. But if you like do it, at least I won't have to do no huntin' for a while, is all, you dig?"

"No need to remind me that you do not stick at eating the flesh of good Christian men, you heathen beast," said Sir Gautier. "Were we not both sworn retainers of our puissant Lord Fitz, I'd certainly set upon you with spear, axe and my good sword."

"Any time, buddyroll," replied the lion, "any-fuckin'-time, 'cause like you know, you and them stinkpots of yours ain't my idea of good cats to do no gig with, neither. But forgetting that, you got any real idea how the fuck we gonna get down this mutha, man?"

The knight nodded. "If in truth this is the place wherein we—me and mine—did arrive in these climes, and not merely some place than beareth a resemblence to it, then there is a way. I need but seek out and rediscover it, then we . . . Aha!"

When at last the seven men had carefully and very laboriously descended the height by way of a copse of pines that grew hard against the cliff-face, they were running sweat and Cool Blue—he having made his way back across the burn and jumped down from the spot where the cliff was much lower—was waiting for them.

As the men dropped their loads and their weapons, first to drink deeply and long from the pool at the bottom of the waterfall, then to sprawl out on the soft bed of pine tags, the lion lied to Sir Gautier.

"Look, man, like we should oughta be catching up to Fitz soon, and like he told me was you to find any your boys and bring them along, you know, it was plenty of soap and shampoo and all in that pack and he wanted them and you to be clean, like you know. And like this here's as good a place as any with that there pool and all, you know. Humans smells bad enough when they're like clean. You dig? You and your bunch, man, I've smelled dead skunks had been rotting out in the sun and was full of worms and maggots smelled better'n you do, now."

"I knew there was soap, Master Lion," replied the knight, a bit stiffly, "I smelled its exotic fragrance when first I did gape the pack and right gladly will I relish that cool water upon my body. The men now . . . ? Well, they all are good retainers, obedient and loyal; they will do my will, obey my dictates, even if not at all happily, to begin."

Because the other two-legged, warmblooded prey-beast seemed to have fled, the huge, scaley predator forgot about it, for there was meat to fill its belly in the one that his lashing tail had felled. Approaching its stunned and immobile prey, the lizard sent out its long, forked blue-black tongue to explore the full length of the meal-to-be. When still it made no move to either fight or flee, the predator moved in closer still, close enough for teeth to close in the warm, soft, unscaled flesh of the helpless creature . . . but they would not. Try as the nightmare monster might, strain as it might to bite down, all that the beast accomplished was to cause itself increasing degrees of pain and accelerated blood-loss in the jaw-tendons and muscles almost severed by the shrewd, circular slash of the long, sharp *katana*.

The reptile backed off, hissing its rage and frustration at being unable to even begin to consume so much fresh, hot meat. Lacking the reasoning-abilities of even the most primitive mammalian brain, the monster could not understand why it could no longer snap its toothy jaws shut, so once again it sent the long tongue out to examine its "kill," relishing the feel-taste of the hot, red blood flowing from the scalp which had impacted with the stump of tree-bole.

Then, suddenly, its senses told it that another of the prey-creatures had appeared nearby; hissing, it spun about to face the menace to its ownership of the meat.

Fitz held the weapon suspended by the leather sling and made sure that both his feet were planted firmly on the ground before his skin came into contact with any steel portion of the drilling, cursing himself the while for bringing it rather than the more powerful though shorter-range magnum, for none of the three loads in the drilling was designed for anything approaching dragon-slaying. The most he could hope to do with one load of birdshot, one of rabbit-shot and a single round of .22 Magnum was to distract the beast, possibly—with extreme luck—blind it and keep it away from the unconscious Japanese officer long enough to himself get possession of the sword . . . And then what? It was not a familiar weapon to him, he'd just have to do his best. But had he had the foresight to bring the heavy revolver instead, now . . . ?

"And if a bullfrog had wings," he muttered fiercely to himself, "he wouldn't bump his arse so much!"

A blast from the first barrel resulted in a pulpy, bloody mess where the monster's left eye had been and evoked an immediate roar of rage and pain, but Fitz doubted if it accomplished much else, for only a stroke of unimaginable luck could have propelled enough of those tiny pellets into the brain to do any good in permanently downing the long, massive reptile. But if he could somehow get the other eye, as well . . .

Arm-long, blue-black forked tongue flickering in

and out of a mouth that was running bright blood, with a lower jaw that seemed crookedly and incompletely closed, the scaley predator turned its head and still-functioning eye in the direction of the creature its tongue-sensors detected.

As he observed its actions, Fitz wondered if the giant reptile's tongue might be its principal sensory organ. "The driller's other barrel is birdshot-loaded" he thought, "and it has a more open choke than the first one; that tongue has no scales to protect its surface, so the pellets will do a lot more damage to it than they could against its hide. If it doesn't do any good I can always try to put the twenty-two into the other eye, shouldn't be a difficult shot at this range, either."

Waiting until the deeply-forked tongue was again exposed, Fitz snapped off the second barrel. This time, the hissing-roar had to it a fluid, gargling quality. When the tongue was thrust out again, the left lobe of its fork was dangling, attached to the tongue's base only by shreds of bleeding, lacerated flesh. Abruptly, the reptile rose onto its thicker hind legs and took a long step toward its attacker, clawed forefeet extended, long tail suddenly whipping at the legs of its small adversary.

Reflecting that just such a stroke had felled the Japanese officer, Fitz dropped the drilling and willed himself up into the air high enough that the thick, whiplike tail went swishing beneath the soles of his boots. Then he will himself off to the side, partly to escape the monster's charge, partly to secure for himself the young officer's *katanga*, it surely being of more value just now than a single round of .22 Magnum could be. That such intimate proximity to the steel blade would render him irrevocably earthbound so long as he held it was something that he must simply bear with.

"What I need," he thought to himself, "is weapons of some non-ferrous metal—copper, brass, bronze, like that. I recall they used to fabricate guns out of brass and bronze, 'gunmetal' was even the word for bronze, I think. I wonder if it would be strong enough to use for a modern Magnum? I'll have to ask Danna or Pedro to check that out for me, that and run down somebody who'll undertake to make me some edge-weapons of bronze, brass, anything that will hold a decent edge and doesn't contain any iron or steel."

Furious that the two-legged interloper was on the verge of taking possession of its "kill," frustrated in the fact that its fearsome jaws no longer seemed to work and that not even the shrewdest swipes of its muscular tail had connected, maddened by the pain of its many wounds, the reptile again reared up onto its hind legs and lunged to renew the attack, clawed forelegs extended, its hissings projecting a fine spray of blood before it.

Had his perspective been less perilous, Fitz would have pitied the monster. Of necessity, it was canting its head in order to get maximum use of its one remaining eye, it seemed to be having trouble in controlling its long tongue—the once-smooth, once-rapid movement of that sensory organ was now jerky and perceptibly slower—and the nearly-severed muscles at the corners caused the lower jaw to gape quite widely open, so that the beast's movements increased blood-loss and undoubtedly produced grinding agonies as well. But even so, the scaled-down tyrannosaurus rex, with its blocky head and its dangling, blood-dripping dewlaps of scaley skin came on.

Fitz knew that there was great danger, in trying to protect the unconscious young Japanese officer. Yes, he had been a fair swordsman in college, years ago, but with foil and épée—point-weapons, both of them—not with the saber. Therefore, this Japanese *katanga* (at best, a two-handed saber) did not naturally lend itself to his grasp, it felt odd, unwieldy, point-heavy and ill-balanced. Yet the lieutenant's handling of the weapon had looked to Fitz like pure, fluid motion, steel-poetry, and he now sought desperately to recall just how the officer had set about using the antique sword.

The battered but still fearsome beast continued its now-cautious seeming advance. Fitz knew not whether the brain within its blocky head was of sufficient development to really lend it caution or if the lack of former speed and outward ferocity was the result of its succession of grievous injuries, pain and loss of blood, but the slight respite was welcome. At length, when the dragon had come within reach, it swiped at him with one clawed foreleg. Fitz, holding the hilt of his strange weapon with both hands much as he would have held a golf-club, the point almost touching the ground, swung the long, keen blade up and out in a circular slash that met the threatening talon in mid-swing and, to his surprise, severed it at its wrist. He recovered balance and blade-control just in time to wield it against the swiping of the thick, whiplike tail; it he did not completely sever, but the great, gaping, blood-spouting wound that the *katanga* inflicted clearly crippled the member to some extent.

"Now what?" he gasped aloud to himself. "There's just no way for one, lone man with a sword to put down a dragon of that size and bulk—even crippled up like it is—without getting hurt himself. The thing still has one good forepaw, not to mention the two big back ones and even if it can't bite anymore, the teeth, fangs, whatever, in that damned upper jaw could shred me in no time flat if it gets close enough to use them and I can't retreat without exposing this poor bastard here to the same thing. A sword just isn't long enough for this kind of work; what I need is one of those Nip spears."

After briefly applying the vision of its remaining eye and the sense of its mangled tongue to the blood-spurting stump where its right forefoot had so lately been, the remorseless reptile took yet another step toward the two-legged thief that was trying to steal its kill. But, abruptly, it halted and swivelled its gory head about so quickly and forcefully as to send an arc of red blood splattering out around it. A sizable drop caught Fitz full in the eye and he pawed frantically to clear it away, then he too looked toward the stream to see what had distracted the beast.

"If it's another one of these bastards, then my ass is grass, for sure. . . ."

Sergeant Kiyomoto, his muscular legs working like pistons, came along the bank of the stream at a full run. He had heard the gunshots and recognized them for what they were—smoothbore rather than rifle or pistol reports—he had never before heard of gods using shotguns, but he imagined that true gods more or less made up their own rules as they went along. And why should they not so do?

His feet, thick-soled with callouses, spurned dry sand and gravel, splatting in mud and damp clay, and he bore the bronze axe easily in both his hands before him, at high-port, as if it had been a rifle; sharp-honed, blood-smeared blade-edge bearing forward. He had seen the god fly through the empty air, along the stream and around the bend and he ran in just such course, never casting even once glance back at the knot of spearmen, confident that the loyal, disciplined troops would follow wherever he or Lieutenant Kaoru might choose to lead.

As he rounded the bend, he caught sight of the god. Grasping Kaoru's *katanga*, the divine personage stood between the sprawled body of the lieutenant and a sizable dragon; that either the god or the officer had used the ancient blade well was evident from a single glance at the gashed and bleeding dragon.

Without breaking stride, the sergeant raced up to the side of the erect dragon and swung the bronze axe, driving the edge deep into the thick haunch—through scaley hide, through layered muscles—to finally reach and sever the tough tendon. The dragon's tail swept around to thud against the sergeant's legs; but the feet were firmly set down and, in any case, the buffet was a mere shadow of the tail-strength of an uninjured beast of the sort. Then, when the animal collapsed onto its belly and remaining two, sound legs, Fitz leaped forward and drove the point of the *katanga* straight through the snout in a spot he recalled having seen (through Kaorus' eyes, while he was visiting in that young officer's mind) a spearman thrust his spear, thus pinning down the head long enough for Kiyomoto to step up and cleave the spine where it met the head of the dragon.

When he had jerked out the axe blade and stepped clear of the quivering, jerking body, Sergeant Kiyomoto bowed low in indication of his complete submission and awaited the commands of the newcome god. He was not at all surprised when the god spoke in Kiyamoto's own dialect of Japanese, did not even realize that he was not "hearing" the speech, not at first.

"Your officer took a nasty crack on the head, Sergeant," Fitz informed him. "It might be best to just make him comfortable and leave him prone until we can judge how badly he's injured."

When the last of the Norman retainers had fearfully, grudgingly followed the example and firm orders of their liege-lord, Sir Gautier de Montjoie, had bathed their bodies, hair and clothes in deodorant soap and icy water, the march was recommenced, cleaving to the marks hacked into the treetrunks by Fitz the day before. The blue lion took point, moving well out in advance of the van, occasionally within their sight, but usually not. Following as he was the fairly fresh scent of Fitz's passage, rather than advancing from tree-blaze to tree-blaze, Cool Blue moved faster and straighter than the Normans, far outstripping the men over and over again, then perforce having to wait for them to close.

Coming at a fast walk around a bend in the waterway, Sir Gautier suddenly found it necessary to plunge a foot nearly knee-deep in the muddy verge of the onrushing stream to avoid stepping on the blue lion, He swore a cracklingly blasphemous oath in Norman French and demanded, "Sir Lion, must you sprawl your ensorcelled, heathen bulk in the very path of Christian men?"

"If you sadass cats don't like lift up your boots a little faster," replied the lion telepathically, "we gone be like tomorrow catchin' up with ol' Fitz. You dig, man? And you don't want to travel or much less camp out and sleep in this here stretch any longer then you fuckin' got to, neither, man. This here's hostile territory with a like capital fuckin' H."

"What is your meaning, Sir Lion?" demanded the Norman knight. "Save for a seeming dearth of larger game, it appears a goodly and well-watered land."

"And that's all you know, buster," stated the blue lion, giving emphasis to his projected words and thoughts with short, powerful flicks of his tail. "And you stay 'round here too long, you'll find out just what I'm like talkin' the hard way, too. So hard a way that maybe not even you Norman dudes will like live to think about it, neither. You dig?"

CHAPTER XIV

"Is this then the holdings of the noble-born wizard of whom you so often prate, Sir Lion?" demanded Sir Gautier. "This Comte de Saint-Germain, these are his feoff on which we tread?"

"Aw, naw, not really," replied the lion. "Bestest I know, don't nobody own none this here land. Naw, but like we are gettin' damn close to that no-good, fuckin' brownie-king's place too, you know, and that's why we better be lookin' hard to spot his pets 'fore one them fuckers spots us. You dig, man?"

The eleventh-century knight shook his helmeted head. "No, Sir Lion, I do not comprehend your disquietudes and fears. Whilst in this odd land, my retainers and I have fought and slain fearsome beasts and hellish monsters, alike. Although now somewhat worn, our weapons remain keen and deadly, our arms are strong, our resolve is firm. No pack of hounds or coursing-cats yet spawned can ever prevail against Sir Gautier de Montjoie and his sturdy band of retainers."

The lion growled softly, low in his chest, then beamed. "It's just like I told ol' Fitz back at square one: you Norman fuckers is long on guts and damn near lacking brains altogether. Look, man I ain't talking dogs and cats, see? Hell, no, that kinda pets Saint-Germaine is got running around in this part of the country don't never run in bunches lessen Saint-Germaine sets them to, 'cause they don't like each other at all, man . . . 'cept to eat. Wanta see what they looks like?" The blue lion projected from his own memory the appearance of a huge, long, thick-bodied lizard, then added, "And, cat, they big—I mean like humongous!—take three, four your biggest dude and lay 'em out end to end and that's how long some them scaley fuckers gets. They can move fast-er'n you ever would b'lieve, faster'n you even wanta think about; yeah, they can't keep it up for too long at a time, but then they don't gotta, 'cause they lays in wait and picks the time and the place and the critter they're gonna jump, see. And they ain't like snakes and littler lizards and all what ain't worth a shit at nights and on cool days, see; they can see as good at night as a cat can and they don't need the sun to keep them warm, so they can come after you 'round the fuckin' clock."

The knight pinched his stubbled lower lip be-tween two, grubby fingers, then nodded. "I thank you for the warning, Sir Lion. A creature five or six ells in length, empowered of such awesome speed and which hunts both by day and by night is indeed much to be feared. We will from hence move in wariness of such creatures.

"But why are these beasts set here to roam, then, are they the wardens of the marches of the noble Comte, perhap?"

The blue lion arose to his feet and, while stretching fore and aft in typical feline manner, then yawning prodigiously, replied, "Hell, man, like I dunno. I ain't no bunghole buddy of that goddam Saint-Germaine, see, not no way, man. I only know them fuckers and where they stomps on account of that friggin' carrotpuller, he set them to chase me out after he'd done put me in this damn lion-rig, see. And I come right through this damn glen, too; if you and your dudes hadn't of gone up that bluff when you landed here, if you'd of come this way, instead, chances are wouldn't be none of you left un-et, by now, you know.

"If you do have to camp out here, you better plan on climbin' up trees and sleepin' there, see. They can stand up and walk and all on their hind legs, but they can't seem to climb any tree that ain't got lotsa thick branches and limbs low down for them to step up on, they can't none of the fuckers shinny and they all built the wrong way, looks like, to do much jumpin', too.

"Look, you and your dudes could move lots faster if you'd do like me and keep down here where it's flatlike, 'stead of up on the ridge looking for trees been hacked on. Ol' Fitz ain't' dumb . . . mostly, and you can bet your ass he picked the easiest way to go, see. I'd damn sure rather catch up to him and his

guns before we come on one them fuckin' badass
lizards, and that's for damn sure, man."

The group of spearmen who set about butchering
the dragon slain by Fitz and their sergeant did so in
unaccustomed silence; none of their usual jabbering
and joking and horseplay could be seen or heard.
Only Sergeant Kiyamoto had witnessed the white
man soar to the aid of the downed officer, but one
and all had seen him rise unaided from the ground
beside the dead carcass of the dragon and move
swiftly through the empty air to a point high in a
huge tree, then return with a medical kit and certain
other objects. To state that the experience had left
them all abashed would have been to utter the gross-
est of understatements.

Kiyamoto, on the other hand, who had been prepared in advance by his dreams and his earlier priestly
training, rendered the newcome god all due respect
and deference, but otherwise felt and gave the appearance of behaving much as was normal of him.
He sent one party of the spearmen to work on this
dragon and the rest back upstream to finish butchering the first, while fending off any inroads of possible
scavengers drawn by the smell of spilled blood.

With the assigned details underway, the stocky
noncom came back to squat near where the god knelt
by the unconscious form of the lieutenant, his sure,
white hands applying field treatment to the young
man's hurts. When the god had elevated Kaoru's
feet, loosely bandaged his head-wound, sponged blood,
sweat and dirt from his face and covered him from
feet to neck with a sheet of what looked to Kiyamoto

like seamless eelskin, he took a long pull from his canteen, then offered the bottle.

Hesitantly, diffidently, Kiyamoto took the proffered refreshment, thinking, "I, a mere man, to touch my human lips where those of a god have just rested . . . ? How can I essay such sacrilege? It is not right, not at all proper." And so he just squatted there, reverently holding the water bottle as if it were some sacred and irreplaceable relic.

Fitz entered the stocky man's mind, found the reason he refrained from drinking the water his body obviously craved and spoke to him in blunt gentleness. "Sergeant Kiyamoto, despite appearances, I am only a man, no whit different in most ways from you or this young man or any of your soldiers. Yes, since first I set foot into this land that I am told is called Tirnann-n-Og, I have been finding within myself, or developing—and I'm not yet sure just which of those two choices it really is—strange and miraculous powers.

"The first of these talents was this ability to speak or, rather, to communicate mind-to-mind with men and some animals, as I am now communicating with you whose language I do not speak at all. As possibly a part of that previously unsuspected talent, I have found, too that I can secretly enter the minds of men and scan their memories and innermost thoughts without their knowledge. Thus, I know them oftimes betters than they know themselves, and could easily manipulate them if I so chose . . . though I have not done so, to date.

"More recently, I have learned that I possess the abilities, under certain conditions, to move myself, other persons and inanimate objects through the empty air from place to place, to "fly," as it were. Please don't ask me how I can do this, Sergeant, for I have no idea how I do, I just have come to know that I can. However, I do not consider these abilities to be in any way, shape or form god-like. I am no god, just a man."

But even as he spoke the words, he could not but wonder if they were in fact truth. Tom . . . Puss . . . the grey, panther-size cat who came of some nights and communicated with him telepathically (in dreams?), was always assuring him that he was *not* a mere man, never had been, not really, and that the longer he stayed in this land or world or whatever, the less like a mortal man he would be.

"Tir-nann-n-Og . . . ?" questioned Kiyamoto. "What do the words mean? The lieutenant here, despite everything, maintains that we are still in Burma and that the stream, yonder, is a tributary of the Irrawaddy River."

"And you do not agree with him," stated Fitz. "Well, you, not he, are right, Sergeant. You're also right about the passage of time; the mules did, indeed, die of old age." At the noncom's look of astounded surprise, Fitz smiled and beamed. "Remember, I told you that I could enter the minds of others, bide unsuspected therein and sift through their memories? Well, I did just that in the case of Lieutenant Kaoru, here, while my body lay hidden high in a huge tree near where you all killed the first dragon this morning.

"But back to the point: yes, you are correct. When I entered this place, that war had been over for more than thirty years. Italy was the first of the Axis powers to surrender, then Germany and, finally, Japan. I, too, fought in that war, Sergeant, as a younger man, of course. I fought the Japanese Army, but on the Pacific Ocean islands, not in Burma."

"As a younger man?" queried Kiyamoto, slowly. "Just how old are you, now, then?"

"I'll soon be fifty-seven years old. I was in my twenties when I fought in that war, in the United States Marine Corps," answered Fitz, readily.

The noncom stared at him for a long moment, then said, "Your race must age differently than mine, then, for you look to be no more than thirty years old . . . perhaps a little more than that, but not many."

Fitz nodded and said, gently, "I can understand and appreciate your doubts, Sergeant. Believe me, when first I set foot here I did truly look my fifty-odd years, that and more. But before you keep on silently questioning my veracity, go down to a still backwater of the stream and look closely at your reflection, calculate your own age and imagine how you ought to look . . . how you should look and don't. Look at the lieutenant, look at your men. Tirnann-n-Og means, in Old Gaelic, Land of the Young. Humans residing in this place apparently fail to age and in the cases of some, the aging process is even reversed, it would seem."

Kiyamoto looked down at his strong, scarred hands, thinking that yes, assuredly, they were not those of a man of advanced years. Nonetheless . . . He shook his head, "It seems impossible."

"It is!" agreed Fitz. "Yet it happened; it's going on

right now for you, me, all the rest. And we, here, aren't all or even the most extreme cases. Somewhere, roaming around in this place are a Norman knight and his band of armed retainers. He and his men are firmly convinced that they are all somewhere in the countryside of Syria, on their way to free the City of Jerusalem from the Moslems during the First Crusade, which occurred nearly *nine-hundred years ago*, Sergeant. None of *them* has aged, either, in all that time. True, some have died fighting beasts, but none of the survivors of the original band looks a year older than when first they literally fell into this place almost a millenium ago. And, just like the lieutenant averred when you spoke to him on the matter of the mules, that honest young knight is of the firm opinion that he and his have been here in this place for no longer than a year or, perhaps, two.

"Now, true, these men all are unlettered—I doubt that Sir Gautier de Montjoie can write so much as his name—but lack of sophistication does not always mean lack of intelligence, as you know. Sir Gautier is possessed of a fine, intuitive mind, just like Lieutenant Kaoru's and yours, so I suspect that there is something in or about this place that warps a man's sense of elapsed time."

Kiyamoto nodded slowly as he "heard" and absorbed the thoughts of the white man, then said, "Yes, that last well could be. I, too, weighed out a similar thought when first I came to the realization that none of the men and, indeed, not even the lieutenant, himself, seemed to understand just how long a time we had been in this place, that this place was not only not Burma, but not even a part of the

302

ordinary world of mortal men. Although I ended by speaking of all this to the lieutenant, I have said little to the men, in general, for their morale is still mostly good and they continue to talk among themselves of their plans when they return to Japan . . . after our victory and the end of the war. I think that it would adversely affect discipline to detail my suppositions to them."

He paused for a moment, then asked, "Please tell me. You say you took part in, fought as a marine soldier in the war and that my land suffered defeat in the end. Was it an honorable surrender following defeats in the field or . . . or was it a forced capitulation come out of an invasion of the Home Islands?"

"Troops, American troops, did land in Japan and occupy it . . . but only after the surrender agreement had been signed," replied Fitz adding, "though I understand the Russians forcibly siezed Sakhalin and a number of smaller, northerly islands . . . the Kurile Islands, I think they were. It's been a long time to remember clearly . . . for me."

"Yes, the Russians always had wanted all of Karafuto—that which you call Sakhalin—because of the mines it holds, the minerals."

"But," continued Fitz, " the courageous communist bastards chose to wait until *after* a prostrate, defeated Japan had actually signed a surrender before they sent their troops into those islands, Korea and Manchuria."

"When did all those occur?" inquired Kiyamoto.

"Informally, Japan capitulated on the fourteenth day of the eighth month of 1945, but the terms of surrender were not officially signed until the second day of the ninth month of that year."

"Why?" demanded Kiyamoto. "Our armies all were well-armed, well-fed, well-led; we could have fought on for many years past that date. Why would the Emperor and His advisors have countenanced a surrender? I do not understand it."

Fitz sighed. "Sergeant, there in Burma you may not have been fully aware of what was going on in the rest of the world. Starting in 1942, we Americans, plus British, Australian, New Zealand, Dutch and French forces, started island-hopping in the South Pacific, while our navies and aircraft worked on reducing the size and effectiveness of your fleets. The Philippine Archipelago was reconquered in 1944 and by the seventh month of 1945, American planes based on Okinawa and many another island Japan had once and very lately held were tormenting the cities and military installations of the Japanese Islands around the clock with untold tons of high explosive and incendiary bombs, seldom toward the end as much as seeing Japanese aircraft of any kind or description.

"Then the United States developed a new and extremely terrible type of bomb. Two of these were dropped and wrought then-barely believable devastation and death in the target areas. After the second of these, overtures of surrender were made and, shortly thereafter, the war was formally concluded, Germany having been defeated months earlier. Capitulations of the various forces still in the field in the battle-areas took longer, of course, but by the end of 1945, all contingents of any size had been reached and had laid down their arms . . . though in some places, such as Indo-China, it was found necessary to temporarily rearm them and use them to maintain order among the indigenous peoples, always under supervision, of course."

"But . . . ?" began Kiyamoto.

"I think," interrupted Fitz, "that that man there, behind you, is awaiting orders."

Lieutenant Kaoru's unconscious body was raised high enough by Fitz's mental powers to slip beneath it a litter hastily constructed of axed-down saplings, bark-strips and fresh, bloody dragon-hide. A lot of dragon-meat needs must be borne back to the site of the first kill, so Fitz stopped the sergeant when he would have detailed some of the few available bodies to bear the littler and, rather, raised it and the body on it some feet above the ground, then flew along beside it to the confluence of the streams. He was awaiting the sergeant and his party when they arrived, bathing the face of the injured man with a handkercheif soaked in the cool, running water.

"We got trouble, dude!"

The Baby-blue Lion had come back along his own trail at a fast, distance-devouring lope to halt before Sir Gautier and his strung-out band of warrior-retainers. Drooping a little where he sat in classic, feline posture, red-pink tongue hung out and dripping onto his big forefeet and the tail lapped over them, he silently beamed the bad news.

"Fitz is up ahead, but it looks like he's being held. It's like a whole bunch of little short, skinny slope-heads—Chinks, Nips, gooks, I don't know; all them

305

slants looks the same to me—all of them damn near buckass naked, up at a place where another stream joins this one on the other side."

Sir Gautier leaned tiredly on his spear, his face serious. "How many of them, Sir Lion? More than we number, here?"

"Oh, yeah, man," Cool Blue assured him. "Least half again's many as you guys, maybe like twice as many."

The Norman knight frowned. "How are they armed and equipped?"

The blue lion arose from his seat and padded the few steps to begin lapping water from the stream, though still in telepathic communication with the leader of the warband, the while.

"The mosta them gooks ain't got nothing but long old spears, man, though I did glim at least two swords and one or two axes, too. But, Like I said, they're all wearing damn little more'n their fuckin' birthday-suits, man—no armor, no shields. Looks like the bunch of them just finished killin' and butcherin' a big deer or elk and one those humongous lizards I tol' you about, you know. The mosta them has got blood up to the yingyang, like, and they taking turns standing out in the deeper part of the stream and rinsing it off, you know."

"Lord Fitz," demanded Sir Gautier, "does he appear ill-used?"

"I couldn't like see him all that clear, man, you know," said the blue lion. "He's like on his knees with them bunched up 'tween me and him, see. But somethin' I could see was he ain't wearing his pistol-belt anymore and one the gooks is got his three-barrel long gun strung crost of his back. So, like whatcha gonna do, man?"

"Why, what must, in honor, be done," replied the knight. "What else? We will advance and, if needs be, fight; either my lord Fitz be freed of this bondage or we will die in the attempt to free him, of course, Sir Lion."

"Now, hold on there!" the blue lion beamed in alarm. "What you mean *we*,' white man? This cat agreed to *guide* ol' Fitz, teach him the ropes, see, guard his back when won't nobody else to do it around. Won't nothing said 'bout yours truly like going up 'gainst no dozen or more slants with spears and swords and axes, see. You dudes, you gets your rocks off doin' this kinda shit, so you do it; just count the Cool Blue out, you dig, baby?"

Sir Gautier tried not to allow his face to indicate his contempt. He gave a Gallic shrug. "Behave as you will, Master Lion; I and mine will do as we must. I had not truly expected honor in a heathen, ensorcelled, man-eating beast, but neither had I ever expected to encounter a craven lion. King of beasts, no more, now more alike to Prince of poseurs, methinks, Crown-prince of cowards."

With a deep, ferocious growl, the blue lion came up and around from his water-lapping crouch at the stream-side, to come down facing his tormentor, tail lashing furiously, slitted eyes both flashing, fearsome fangs bared. "Who you think you callin' chicken, you muthafucka? Not even your whole fuckin' pack of stinkpots or all your stickers or you steel tee-shirt is gonna stop me from wastin' you, man. I'll like spill your chitlins all over this here place, asshole. I'll . . ."

Thin-lipped, eyes showing cold a river-ice, Sir Gautier stood up straight, pulled up his padded coif, donned his helmet, then took a good, two-handed grip on the shaft of his spear, beaming, "At your pleasure, Master Lion. I regard you with about as much warmth of amity and fraternity as you regard me and only my oaths sworn to our lord Fitz has kept my steel from out your body many's the time, you should know. I slew both a lion and a mountain panther in Syria, whilst afoot, with spear and sword, and I doubt me not but that I can as easily put paid to you.

"But, ere we two lay on, think you not that we should better spend our energies in winning the freedom from odious bondage of my lord Fitz, that generous man who has so often seen your belly filled? Or, if matters of obligation and honor do not, will not move you, then recall that if these captors be slain or driven off, then their fresh kills as well as the freed person of Lord Fitz will be our spoils and that which you earlier described sounds like verily enough bloody flesh to sate even your ever-empty belly."

Taking full advantage of every fold of terrain, every hint of vegetation, Cool Blue, Sir Gautier and the latter's new sergeant, one Wulfhere, crept as close as possible to the bloodsoaked, fly-swarming site of the butchering. But only six men were to be seen there. Fitz was kneeling beside a slender, yellow-brown man lying recumbent on a rough litter, on whose other side squatted an older, stockier man of similiar skintone, Fitz's three-barrel gun across his bare back on its sling. Some yards distant, three other of the near-nude, yellow-brown men squatted filling woven reed-baskets with meat from a dwindling pile. At least a score of buzzards circled at different heights over the scene, carrion-crows watched from every nearby perch and, keen-eyed and experienced hunter that he was, Sir Gautier easily spotted a double handful of small, furry scavengers waiting impatiently in the underbrush around and about the site.

He asked silently of the blue lion's mind, "What of this dozen or more warriors awaiting us here, Lion?"

"The rest has just all gone into that thicket what the littler stream comes from out of," replied the lion. "I can hear the fuckers, see, they like headed north and they all got heavy loads they toting, too . . . prob'ly baskets like that of meat. But what's got your bowels in a uproar, baby? The less slants it is, the quicker you and your hotshots can kill 'em all and take all the meat away from them and free ol' Fitz. Reet? Hell, you 'n Wolfie, there, can prob'ly put them fuckers there down just by your own se'fs."

"Possibly," agreed the Norman. "But then who is to know how many would be drawn from out those thickets by the din of combat, eh? No, caution must be the watchword, herein. Had we only a few good horses, now . . . ?" he sighed mournfully.

"Wulfhere?" he whispered aloud. "Get you back and summon the band to me here. Bid them advance in quietude and unseen, just as we three did, but advance full-armed and all ready to fight."

As the English-Dane crept back in obedience to his lord, said lord bespoke the blue lion again. "Master Lion, you must creep into yon thicket, find the trail taken by the other unclad warriors and warn me

309

immediately if any commence to wend their way back in this direction."

"You want I should try to scare the fuckers from comin' back, man?" asked Cool Blue. "Maybe jump one of them and make him scream enough to make his buddies shit their diapers, huh?"

Cooly, the knight beamed. "I ask not that you do aught which might endanger your over-precious hide, Lion, only that you serve me warning when more foeman approach my position."

"Well, then, fuck you ass, mac!" came the lion's reply. "That's just what you'll get . . . and all you'll friggin' get out of this cat, you stinkin' tin-plated cocksucker!"

The Baby Blue Lion found a spot to lie in such a way that no human could spot him, even from bare-feet distance. Therein, he arranged his big body comfortably, relaxed, closed his eyes and slept . . . but, lightly, feline-lightly, all senses save only sight at full alert. The shadows lengthened, all about him dark and full night descended slowly on Tirnann-n-Og, but still the blue lion kept to his post, ignoring the growling of his empty stomach, lest he do aught which would earn him more of the unbearable contumely of Sir Gautier.

The log-walled longhouse inside the stockade was, this night, more full with humanity than it had been in many a day. After Fitz had rendered airborne and flown the litter bearing Lieutenant Kaoru over the twisting gully full of brush to the very door of the place, he had returned to the streamside to do the same for not only the remaining baskets of meat, but for all the men—Japanese and Norman, alike—and finally, his pack and gear from out the tree. So novel had been the experience that Sir Gautier had clean forgotten the Blue Lion; indeed, he gave not a thought to the miserable beast until well after sunrise of the next morning.

ENTER A NEW WORLD
OF FANTASY . . .

Sometimes an author grows in stature so steadily that it seems as if he has always been a master. Such a one is David Drake, whose rise to fame has been driven equally by his archetypal creation, Colonel Alois Hammer's armored brigade of future mercenaries, and his non-series science fiction novels such as **Ranks of Bronze**, and **Fortress**.

Now Drake commences a new literary Quest, this time in the universe of fantasy. Just as he has become the acknowledged peer of such authors as Jerry Pournelle and Gordon R. Dickson in military and historically oriented science fiction, he will now take his place as a leading proponent of fantasy adventure. So enter now . . .

AUGUST 1988 65424-1 352 PP. $3.95

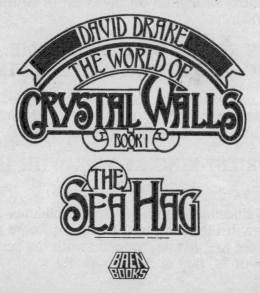

DAVID DRAKE

THE WORLD OF

CRYSTAL WALLS

BOOK I

THE SEA HAG

BAEN BOOKS

THE KING OF YS
POUL AND KAREN ANDERSON

THE KING OF YS—
THE GREATEST
EPIC FANTASY
OF THIS DECADE!

by Poul and Karen Anderson

As many authors that have brought new life and meaning to Camelot and her King, so have Poul and Karen Anderson brought to life a city of legend on the coast of Brittany . . . Ys.

THE ROMAN SOLDIER BECAME A KING, AND HUSBAND TO THE NINE

In *Roma Mater*, the Roman centurion Gratillonius became King of Ys, city of legend—and husband to its nine magical Queens.

A PRIEST-KING AT WAR WITH HIS GODS

In *Gallicenae*, Gratillonius consolidates his power in the name and service of Rome the Mother, and his war worsens with the senile Gods of Ys, that once blessed city.

HE MUST MARRY HIS DAUGHTER— OR WATCH AS HIS KINGDOM IS DESTROYED

In *Dahut* the final demands of the gods were made clear: that Gratillonius wed his own daughter ... and as a result of his defying that divine ultimatum, the consequent destruction of Ys itself.

THE STUNNING CLIMAX

In *The Dog and the Wolf*, the once and future king strives first to save the remnant of the Ysans from utter destruction—then use them to save civilization itself, as the light that once was Rome flickers out, and barbarian night descends upon the world. In the progress, Gratillonius, once a Roman centurion and King of Ys, will become King Grallon of Brittany, and give rise to a legend that will ring down the corridors of time!

Available only through Baen Books, but you can order this four-volume KING OF YS series with this order form. Check your choices below and send the combined cover price/s to: Baen Books, Dept. BA, 260 Fifth Avenue, New York, New York 10001.

ROMA MATER • 65602-3 • 480 pp. • $3.95 _____
GALLICENAE • 65342-3 • 384 pp. • $3.95 _____
DAHUT • 65371-7 • 416 pp. • $3.95 _____
THE DOG AND THE WOLF • 65391-1 • 544 pp. • $4.50 _____